THE BLOOD HEIR CHRONICLES

ORIGINS

A PREQUEL

THE BLOOD HEIR CHRONICLES

ORIGINS

A PREQUEL

GARRETT M.
PEARSON

The Blood Heir Chronicles:
Origins

Garrett M. Pearson

Editing & Proofreading by Bodie D. Dykstra
Cover Art made by Jeff Brown

ISBN (e-book): 978-1-63968-000-9
ISBN (paperback): 978-1-63968-001-6
ISBN (hardback): 978-1-63968-002-3

ACKNOWLEDGMENTS

The creation of this book and the contents within is all thanks to the inspiration of a dear friend and fellow author, Miranda Lynn! Thank you for your insight and knowledge and for showing me the strength I had within me to create some of my all-time favorite content!

PROLOGUE

"Zähd Wüarbaer, your presence has been requested . . ." a hooded man said eloquently as an orc's decapitated head rolled past him.

"What does your *dark lord* want from me, demon?" the hulking warrior barked as he lifted his dual claymore swords onto his shoulders.

Covered from head to toe in both blood and scars, Zähd stared off into the abyss, his thoughts drifting elsewhere. Flinging the blood from his blades, he returned them to their resting place at his waist. Zähd watched as the orc he had decapitated rose to retrieve his head while he reached for his cloak to wipe the blood from his face. The orc healed his wounds as he dropped to one knee, bowing before Zähd.

"Will that be all for today, sir?" he asked politely.

"It will. Be gone from here," Zähd acknowledged, waving for the orc to leave.

Zähd turned his draconian gaze to the monk before him, his disgust permeating the air around them. Though his face carried his age well, the eight centuries of fighting showed themselves across the warrior's body. Cleaning the last of the blood from the scars on his scalp, Zähd rested his hands on his pommels and walked toward the demon. As Zähd circled him, he sniffed in disgust at the messenger's sulfuric stench. He questioned whether or not he should slay the demon where he stood. Zähd held no love for demons, and his contempt for his servitude only strengthened his hate for being disturbed.

"Speak, demon."

"Events are transpiring, and a Blood Heir is soon to be selected—"

"Are you certain?!" Zähd demanded, turning to face the demon.

"Yes, we have finally found them. They are few in number. A member of the bloodline currently holds the power, but it is soon to be passed on. You are to report to the Apostles for further instruction."

It had been over three hundred years since he last had his chance to exact revenge on his ancient adversary. Pondering this new information, he wanted another chance to destroy the bloodline that cursed him to his wretched fate. Even more, he had the opportunity to catch the Blood Heir in transition, to change the course of events and possibly break his binds to Hell. Seeing an opportunity before him, Zähd played the role of servant to his master.

"I will seek an audience with the Apostles. I will do *his* bidding. Now leave me, scum. I have much to do." Zähd commanded as he waved for the demon to leave.

Turning back to the abyss, Zähd stared off and thought of days long past. A fire sparked within his chest as the sounds of war drums rang in his ears. He remembered every encounter with a member of his adversary's bloodline, and he craved a real fight once more. The old berserker blood within him writhed at the prospect of war. He missed it, and it missed him. Feeling the blood run down from the brand on his chest, Zähd smiled as his power swirled inside of him.

.

You can change your surname, run to a different country, but you cannot run from me, Lazarus. I will find you, and I will bring an end to your bloodline.

CHAPTER 1
THE LAST SMILE

"**D**o we really have to do this? Is there no other choice?" Steven begged his brother.

"I told you before, Steve, this is what must happen. I can't fight his battles," John replied while looking to the setting sun to keep track of the time. He then stood and turned to his younger brother.

In a secluded, wooded knoll outside of Washington D.C.'s city limits, Dominic, his father, Steven, and his uncle, John Salvatore, gathered around Dom while he ran and jumped about. Dominic grinned gleefully as his uncle knelt next to him. Meanwhile, Steven leaned back and folded his arms; the disapproval was apparent on his face. Looking toward his brother, then back at his son, he was left conflicted.

"But, John, he's *five!*" Steven protested while looking at John incredulously.

"I know, Steve. I know. But what I've seen, what's to come . . . The most we can do is prepare him for it," John convincingly replied while trying to maintain his uplifting tone and tapping the black worn leather patch over his left eye.

Steven protested as he exhaled and turned around, immediately regretting the choice of training his only child to fight and eventually to kill. After wiping his tears, he turned back to his son; Dominic was laughing with John, who made funny faces in response. In that moment, Steven caved to the idea. He begged and hoped to God that someday he would be forgiven.

Snapping his fingers, John grabbed Dominic's attention. Focused on him, Dominic anxiously waited on John. John reached down toward his thigh and pulled his KA-BAR knife out of its sheath. Holding it defensively as if he were protecting himself, John made sure Dominic witnessed his actions.

"Okay, Dom, now remember the last time I was over? You kept grabbing at this. Well, this is a knife. Do you know what a knife is used for?" John smiled as he presented the knife.

Dominic shook his head and stared up and down the blade's edge.

"Well, there's kitchen knives, and you used those for things like jelly, butter, and cutting your food. And then there's knives like these. They're used to defend yourself from people who want to hurt you," John carefully explained.

"Li-Like your leg and your finger and your eye, Uncle John? Somebody bad took them?" Dominic asked as he pointed at John's left leg, where a metal transfemoral replaced his leg from the knee down.

John chuckled as he rubbed the leather cap over his pinky nub; he was impressed by his nephew's perceptiveness. "Yes . . ." John paused as he chuckled. "*Someone bad* took them because I couldn't hold a knife properly. I don't want that to happen to you, so you had better listen. Learn what your father and I teach you," he continued while he stepped back and took an offensive posture with the knife. "Now, unlike the last position, this is an offensive stance to use if you were going to attack someone. But, Dom, I need you to understand, this is a tool, not a toy. It can be helpful just as much as it can be harmful. It can hurt people if you aren't careful. But most importantly, only act with a clear mind. Do not let your emotions guide your actions with this, okay?" John said while looking sternly into his nephew's eyes.

Taking in his uncle's words, Dominic understood the emotion behind them, even if he didn't understand all that he had said. Nodding, Dominic smiled before picking up a small stick from the ground and mimicking his uncle. John chuckled and watched Dominic swinging the stick and switching between an offensive and defensive pose as if he were fighting people.

"Other than the flailing around, he's practically doing things you showed me already. How?" Steven asked, baffled by what he was seeing.

"I told ya!" John playfully jabbed Steven in the arm as he turned to him. "Our bloodline is full of fighters. I was just like him when I was his age. With time and training, he'll outshine both of us!" John stated, sheathing his knife. Walking toward a nearby tree, he reached out for the oddly rectangular sheathed katana that rested against its trunk.

"Is that your intuition or more of *what you've seen*?" Steven half sarcastically asked while making air quotes with his hands.

"Heh, intuition, my dear little brother. The fact that I *may* have seen that is irrelevant. I trained you and you will be training him, just like Father trained me. We Salvatores are like wine when it comes to fighting: we only get better with age—and in our case, generations!" John replied joyfully with a big smile, still working to convince his brother before reaching for an old black leather shoulder bag that he had sat next to his sword.

Throwing the strap over his shoulder, John adjusted it until it was comfortable. John secured the sword in its sheath and glanced down as it rattled the red chain that wrapped around its grip. Steven looked over at the sword while crossing his arms. He was conflicted about his feelings. Glancing back at his son, he watched while he continued swinging the stick around.

"You taking that with you?" Steven asked while leaning over toward John.

"Yeah, I'm going to need it if I'm going to have any chance at stopping this," John admitted before adjusting his footing so he could lean back while watching Dominic.

"Are you sure he should be learning this early? He *is* only five." Steven whispered again to his brother.

"Father taught me well before I left for Vietnam, and I had more than one Hell to contend with back then. He'll do just fine," John explained while smiling and nodding toward Dominic. "Unfortunately, Father died before he could teach you, and after you were born, I knew your training was going to have to be done differently. That's why I waited till you were older to begin your training. Not by much, but back then, you didn't take to the train-ing like Dominic and I. But you should believe in him. I trained you so that you could train him when I'm gone. You play a much larger part in this, brother, than you realize. Someday this world will need him. I leave it up to you to prepare him for that." John smiled while looking toward Dominic. John, admittedly surprised by his own words, looked off to the horizon. Steven couldn't help but believe his brother; he knew his words were true.

Breathing heavily, Dominic ran up to John and Steven. Catching his breath, he stared at the knife on John's leg. John could feel Dominic's desire to hold the knife as he looked down at the young child. Catching a glance from Dominic, he chuckled as he unbuckled the restraint on his handle and pulled the blade out of its sheath.

"You're not giving him that knife, are you?" Steven protested in disbelief.

"Now how do you present a knife to someone that wants to see it?" John asked Dominic while ignoring Steven.

"Handle first! So you don't hurt them. And always hold the knife by the flat side, not the edge," Dominic confidently replied.

John laughed. "It's called the spine, but yes, you are correct. You may take the knife now." He handed him the knife.

"You're not seriously letting him play with that knife, are you?" Steven protested again. "That damn thing is almost half the size of him!" he continued before attempting to walk toward Dominic, only to be stopped by John's outstretched arm. "But what if he hurts himself?" Steven winced with every swing Dominic made.

"Then it will be a valuable first lesson," John replied as a slight grin crept across his face and he glanced back at his brother.

Dominic had only managed to get five swings in before losing his grip and throwing it into the ground by John's foot.

"Now be careful, Dominic. This is no stick, and it's far from a toy. This is a tool, an instrument for fighting and self-defense. You need to take good care of it." John pulled the knife from the ground and cleaned the dirt off its blade.

Catching a glance at a mysterious engraved brand underneath his uncle's collarbone, Dominic pointed toward the right side of John's chest. "What's that, Uncle John?"

"Uh, it's our family crest. It represents you, me, and your father. Family, above all else. It'll always mean family." John struggled to find words that Dominic would understand. He didn't want to lie to him, but Dominic was far too young for the truth.

Trying hard to maintain his composure, John smiled as he placed the knife back into Dominic's hands and showed him how to grip it tightly. When he watched his nephew grin and hold the knife tightly, his emotions swelled inside of him. Today would be the last time he would get to see him, and it hurt him deeply.

"Dominic?" John struggled to speak as he got down on one knee and held the knife and Dominic's hands in his own. "Take good care of your father, and listen to what he has to say. He's a very smart man and will teach you all that I could. Okay?" John bit down on his lip as he held back the desire to cry.

"I promise I will, Uncle John! But why do you look so upset?" Dominic asked, confused by the pain in his face.

"Someday, when you're older, you'll understand." John moved the knife from his nephew's hands and brought him in for a hug. "Someday, when you're older, it'll all make sense." John held him close, taking in every second of the moment.

"Is it that time, John?" Steven asked as he lent a hand to help John stand back up.

"Unfortunately it is. I have a lot ahead of me . . ." John locked his knife back in place before walking over to give his brother a hug. "I'm proud of you, dear little brother. You're going to be a great father and teacher. I know it's been tough since she left us, but when you find that strength within you, it will carry forward in life. You'll find that strength in you someday, Steven. I promise you!"

"I'm going to miss you, John!" Steven choked up as he held his brother. Despite how much he knew he had to leave, he didn't want him to.

"I'm going to miss you, too, brother, but I'm going to try and stop this all from coming to pass, but if I fail, it will fall on his shoulders to save us someday." John held onto his brother tightly as he spoke into his ear; he had done all he could to comfort his brother.

"I'll train him. I'll teach him all I know. Godspeed, brother. Godspeed." Steven pulled back to look his brother in the eye before hugging him once more.

"I'm proud of you, Steven, and I know Father would be, too." John rested his hand on his brother's shoulder while he spoke to him, confident in his trust of him.

The setting sun blinded Dominic as he watched his uncle leave. John pulled on the sword's grip, and with ease, he broke the chains that held it in place. Looking toward the sunset, he rested the blade at his side. While he struggled to hold back his tears, Dominic couldn't understand why his uncle had to leave.

John felt the blood creep from his brand, and his right eye changed from its vibrant green to a crimson red. His pupil, elongated and narrow, transformed into a vertical slit. Reaching over, John gripped his sword with both hands before raising it above his head. Resolving the conflict within him, John thrust the sword down in front of him, creating a blinding light around him.

In a flash of light, both Dominic's and Steven's vision were completely obscured. As the temporary blindness disappeared, Dominic found it impossible to hold back his tears when he couldn't find his uncle. He couldn't begin to understand why his uncle had left him and his father. With John gone, the two Salvatores comforted each other and grieved over his departure.

CHAPTER 2
SCRAPES AND BRUISES

Two years later

The August sun shined brightly on Steven and the young Dominic, where in their spacious backyard, they trained together. In the past two years, since Dominic's training began, he already had a firm grasp on both Kali and Krav Maga, two forms of martial arts that would help him with the training he was about to undergo.

Landing on his back, Steven let out a surprised grunt. Shaking his head, he rose from the ground while the young boy cautiously caught his breath and maintained his defense.

"That's better, Dom, but you're still not committing to the throws! When you're in a real fight, you can't take half steps or measures," Steven expressed while readying himself to attack again. "If you're not committed in a fight, it can mean the difference between winning a fight and losing a limb or even your life," he continued while sending strike after strike at Dominic with his limbs.

"I know, sir, but it's difficult when it's you, Dad," Dominic explained as he blocked Steven's incoming attacks.

"You have to stop thinking of me like that! When we're train-ing, I am your mentor and opponent, nothing more." Steven pain-fully powered through his stern words before exploiting Dominic's opening. "Keep your guard up!" he shouted as he pushed harder with Dominic.

Dominic focused on his father's movements as his words echoed through his mind, taunting and pushing him further. The two were relentless with each other, neither giving the other any quarter. Dominic studied his father's moves, carefully looking for any open-ing he could take advantage of. Seeing the intent in Dominic's eyes, Steven couldn't help but be impressed by his son for finally taking his training seriously, though shortly after, he was reminded of all he'd withheld. Knowing he couldn't linger on his thoughts, he fo-cused on the fight at hand and pushed Dominic further.

"Finally, you're takin' things serious. And here I thought you were just going to waste my time," Steven taunted before grabbing Dominic's leg.

"Waste your time? I'd never!" Dominic teased as Steven held his leg.

"Then let's see what you can do with this," Steven excitedly re-torted as Dominic jumped and kicked with his other leg.

Able to read the move, Steven remembered back to John doing the same to him once before parrying Dominic's roundhouse kick. The tight grip and sudden stop were jarring as Dominic looked down to his father's hands wrapped around his ankles. With both feet off the ground, Dominic quickly realized he had made a mis-take as the trees began to spin around him. Holding himself back as he released his son, Steven threw Dominic across the yard. With a little aim, he shot for a soft patch of ground next to their picnic table.

Dominic bounced and shouted in pain as he slid across the ground. Each hit forced him to bury his pain deep down. Digging his nails into the dirt, Dominic brought himself to a stop. Enraged, Dominic glared up at Steven. Using the table end for leverage, Dominic stood and looked to his father, then to the training batons next to his hands.

Tossing one into his right hand, Dominic grabbed both batons before advancing on his father. Surprised but happy that Dominic had begun to utilize his training, Steven readied himself for Dominic's attack.

"Adapting and constantly finding a new way to win is key in a fight. Finding a way to get the upper hand and overpowering your enemies is an essential part of your training, Dominic. It's good to see you're finally applying it!" Steven explained as he dodged as many strikes as he could from his son, surprised by the ferocity he was displaying. "Now we begin the next step of your training: facing an enemy with a weapon!" Steven added before he swept Dominic's feet out from under him and took one of his batons before he hit the ground.

Realizing his position had been compromised, Dominic quickly tried to roll away from Steven as he bore down on him. Steven attacked with precision, hitting him in the arms, the legs, or, even worse, the torso when he couldn't escape fast enough. Bouncing his baton off of Steven's, Dominic struggled to quickly get back on his feet. Clutching his arm and baton tightly, Dominic stared down his father, angered by his attack on him. Not willing to give up and refusing to back down, Dominic brushed the dirt off his uniform and stood, ready to end his fight.

The fiery passion burned brightly in both their eyes. Unequivocally, they respected each other as they slowly walked toward the other. Neither broke eye contact as they leaped forward. Rapidly they struck at one another with their batons, throwing in a punch or kick when the opportunity arrived. Steven was shocked by how much his son had changed since they had begun their training two years ago. So much so that he couldn't help but wonder if this was how he was when John was training him. Lingering too long on his thoughts, Steven allowed his performance to slip just before his arm took the brunt of Dominic's barrage. Mentally smacking himself in the face, Steven returned his focus to the fight. Knowing he couldn't fail his son, Steven pushed the pain to the back of his mind as he fought to give his son a fair fight.

The sun slowly set as the two, covered in sweat and bruises, knelt and heaved heavily as they tried to catch their breath. It was clear that Steven wasn't going to give in and that Dominic wasn't going to give up. Steven pondered deeply on how to end their fight. He had put so much energy into the fight and was surprised by how exhausted he had become. Knowing that it was time to call it a day, Steven rolled his head around to pop his neck before loosening up his arms and legs. Walking toward Dominic, he refused to give his son a moment's rest.

Dominic knew the look in his father's eyes as Steven drew near. Pushing himself up, Dominic prepared for the assault. With no plan of attack and exhaustion already taking hold, Dominic struggled to avoid his father's attacks, finding no end to them. With no choice but to fight through his exhaustion, Dominic reached down within him and pulled out the strength he needed. Deflecting one of Steven's hits, Dominic found time to put some distance between them. Finding his second wind, Dominic roared at his father with frustration and excitement.

The two swung at each other, bruises accumulating as the

pain radiated throughout their bodies. Dropping his baton, Dominic clenched his side as he fell over, his painful cries signaling the end of the bout. Steven tossed his baton aside, hating what he had done. Quickly rushing to his aid, he comforted his injured child.

"Hey, hey, hey, you're okay, Dom. Come here! I got you!" Steven embraced his son, helping him to his feet. "Hey, come here. I'm so proud of you!" Steven hugged him while gently trying to check where his last strike had hit Dominic. "You gave it your all, son. I saw that today, and I'm so proud of you for that," Steven added as he wiped away his son's tears and fixed his long hair.

"You mean that?" Dominic asked as he sniffled and tried to stop crying.

"I do. You surpassed any expectations I could have had for you!" Steven gave his son a high-five before picking up their batons.

"Thank you, Daddy! I promise you, next time, I'll win!" Dominic grinned up at his father, determined to keep his promise.

"Ha, alright, son! I'll hold you to that. The day you best me in a fight will be the day your training will have reached its end," Steven proudly stated. "For that'll be the day I have taught you all I know!"

"I'll still come to you for help when I need it, Dad. Just 'cause my training ends doesn't mean I can't still learn from you!" Dominic said as he turned and hugged his father.

"Well, that's good to hear, son." Steven remarked as his emotions swelled within him and he held his son.

The father and son walked back toward their gray bungalow-style house, ready to make dinner and nurse their wounds. Before leaving the backyard, Steven motioned for Dominic to grab their training tools while he continued indoors. Walking into the kitchen from the back door, Steven grabbed a hand towel off the table and wiped the sweat from his brow. Wincing from the bruises he had received, he grabbed an ice pack from the freezer and wrapped it in the hand towel, then slowly moved it from one bruise to another.

After washing his hands in the sink, he prepped his planned dinner for the night. Looking back and forth between his son bringing in their training tools and the food in his hands, Steven tried his best to be positive and not let his negative thoughts linger in his mind. The past two years had been difficult for him. Training his son was easy, but thoughts of the dangers he could face later in life scared him. Would he be strong enough? Would he train his son enough, or would all his training be for naught?

"Hey, Dad, I brought all the tools in! Y-You okay, Dad?" Dominic cautiously stood at the entrance of the kitchen, looking on at his visibly upset father.

"Huh? Oh, yeah . . . Yeah, I'm fine, son!" Steven pulled himself away from his thoughts as he turned and smiled at Dominic. "Hey, why don't you come over here and let me teach you something just as important as your training?" Steven smiled and motioned for Dominic to come toward him.

"Sure, what's that?" Dominic ran over to his father, examining the food laid out on the counter.

"How to feed yourself. More important than many things in life is the ability to feed yourself. Tonight, in an effort to teach you, I'm going to show you how to cook this!" Steven paused to reveal the food. "Smoked salmon, mashed potatoes, and asparagus. It was your uncle John's favorite!" Steven smiled down at his son before moving over to the stove.

"I miss Uncle John," Dominic sullenly said as he followed his father around the kitchen.

"I do, too, son. I do, too," Steven said quietly to himself. Exhaling deeply, he pushed his thoughts away and began to teach his son more of what he knew.

The night passed on as the two of them bonded over the proper way to smoke a salmon. With a little assistance from Dominic, who stirred the mashed potatoes, the two of them were soon enjoying their well-earned dinner. After compliments on the flavor of the food and remarks about how great it turned out, the topic of conversation changed to Dominic's schooling, with him talking to no end about his classes. From science to history, arts and gym, Dominic found something fun about each one of them. As the night carried on, Steven sat back and listened to his son talk about his day, finding true joy in his genuine happiness. Steven trailed off in his own thoughts for a moment until his attention was brought back to his son by the wave of a hand.

"Hey, Dad, what was Mom's favorite food?" Dominic cautiously asked a second time.

Stunned by his son's interest in his mother, a subject they hadn't spoken of in almost two years, Steven paused drinking from his cup. Taking a moment to acknowledge his sudden surprise, Steven thought back to collect his thoughts. Remembering a significant day in his youth, he had the answer for him.

"There was this drive-in diner me and your mother used to go to when we were younger, and this is before we ever got together, but there was this diner we went to, and she'd always get the classic burger they had there. Wasn't anything too fancy, just their own take on a bacon cheeseburger, but she loved it." Steven paused for a moment as he stared off, biting his upper lip as a mix of emotions churned within him. "But yeah, she'd get the classic burger with a fry and vanilla malt. Now, let me tell you, their malts would always give you brain freeze, but boy, they were worth it!" Steven chuckled briefly before Dominic joined in. "But well after we moved across town to this house, she always wanted to go eat there whenever the opportunity came about, no matter the drive." Steven ended his speech, thinking back fondly on the memory.

"Is that the same diner you took me to last summer?!" Dominic asked excitedly.

"Ding ding ding, that it is!" Steven happily replied. "After your mother passed, I couldn't go back there for a long time, but when you started asking about her, which is good that you did, but after you started asking, I had to deal with my feelings about going there because it was my favorite spot to eat, too." Steven grinned as he looked away guiltily and snickered. "I didn't want to deprive you of enjoying something she loved. I wanted to give you something to connect to her, a means of someday understanding the woman she was and how much she loved you." Steven inhaled sharply before speaking, but as he carried on, he held the slightest of smiles as the words left his mouth. "She was a wonderful woman. The best, really." Steven looked away and held that tiny smile. He missed her, but he knew she was in a better place.

"Will you tell me more about Mom, Dad?" Dominic anxiously asked. He both wanted to know more but knew it was still difficult for his father to talk about her.

"Well, of course I will. What would you like to know?" Steven spoke lightly as his heart swelled. He was happier than ever before that his son wanted to know more.

Dominic and his father carried on talking about his mother well past dinner. Finally breaking through the awkwardness of the conversation, Steven leaned back in his chair as he started telling a story from a time long past. Pointing out objects around the kitchen, Steven walked over to a little prize teddy bear on a shelf, recounting how he tried to win it at a fair for Dominic's mother one year but she ended up winning it for him instead. Happy and a little embarrassed that *she* won the bear for him, he gently held and massaged its tiny brown paw and smiled.

Together, they talked for hours until it neared midnight. Surprised by how much time had passed, Steven wrapped up their conversation with the promise to tell Dominic more tomorrow after practice. Happy with all his father had told him, Dominic wasted no time cleaning off his plate and setting it in the sink. With everything finished, he ran over and tightly hugged his father, excited for the next day to come.

"Thank you for dinner, Dad!" Dominic held him tightly. "And thank you for telling me more about Mom. I want to go eat at that diner again sometime!" He finished as he held onto Steven.

"You're welcome, son!" Steven chuckled as he held his son. "And sure, we'll have to make a trip out of it someday. I'll take you to see your grandpa while we're out there," he added as he leaned back to look down at Dominic. Memories of a secluded graves site flashed though his mind as he thought of their resting place.

"Where's my grandpa at?" Dominic asked curiously.

"He's with your mother. Well, to be accurate, your mother is with him, but I don't think it really matters in this case." Steven briefly pondered his statement before pulling Dominic in to hug him again.

"Oh, okay." Dominic, while initially confused, realized what his father meant shortly after.

Ending their hug, Steven sent Dominic off to bed before he carried his plate over to the trash can. The warm water stung to the touch of his battered hands, but Steven powered through the pain as he washed the dishes. After setting down the last dish to dry, Steven exhaled as he looked up at the clock on the wall. It was nearly three.

Steven turned the kitchen lights out before stepping into the living room. Around the room he searched, making sure he had cleaned everything before going to bed. Finding one of Dominic's toys lying around, he picked it up before catching a glance of his family shield above their mantle.

The polished and battle-worn steel shined in the dim light, a proud heater shield from a time long past. Steven was left with contempt for it. Tracing the blood-red cryptic symbol painted on its face with his eyes, he scowled. It was one of the few things he had left of both his brother and father, but after everything he had learned, he found it difficult to appreciate his *family crest*. Still, he missed his family.

Inhaling, he walked closer to it and stared at his reflection. Steven noticed that Dominic had gone out of his way to clean the mantle and the shield before training. He was happy that his son's growing enthusiasm extended to his chores. The ceiling lights reflected back at him as he looked at the symmetrical symbol once again. Like a ball of snakes under water, his emotions swirled around in his mind while he traced every line of the red paint. He never forgot all that it meant to him and all that it stood for. Exhaling deeply, he looked to the corner of the shield, where the teddy bear could be seen faintly in its reflection. Steven had sacrificed so much already, but still, he trusted his brother's words and their promise.

After Steven checked on Dominic, his eyes shifted to the gun safe across his room. Quietly, he turned the dial on its face until the clanking of metal signaled the safe had been unlocked. A shrine dedicated to his brother and father adorned the bottom of the safe.

Lighting incense, he held the stick between his hands as he sat and prayed for his brother, his prostration an expression of gratitude for his brother's well-being.

Finished with his prayer, Steven opened a weathered wooden box. Retrieving a battered and reforged machete, Steven rested his grip in the worn handle. The alder wood and its hand-carved family crest left Steven wondering about all the adventures it had seen with John. The blade had been reforged in the trenches of the French countryside in World War Two when his father carried the blade. Almost no blade held a candle's flame to the history carved on its steel.

"Ow!" Steven reacted as he accidentally cut his finger while returning the machete.

Though it had not seen service in many years, its edge held true. Grabbing a picture frame out from the safe, he sat back on his bed. John hadn't smiled that much ever in his life, and the two of them couldn't have been happier as they celebrated the pregnancy of Steven's soon-to-be child. Steven's gut turned cold as his heart ached.

"You're going to be a great father and teacher. Someday you'll find the strength, I promise!"

John's words rang in his head as he traced the wrinkles in his cheeks. Tears ran from his eyes as he held the picture close. Setting the frame out on his nightstand, Steven began to reconcile his misery. He had a responsibility, both to his brother and his child. He was left in charge of the task before him because they believed in him. It was time to believe in himself as well.

CHAPTER 3
THE NEXT LEVEL

Steven laid out the day's training weapons across his outdoor table while Dominic arrived home from school. Going over the lesson once more in his head, he pointed out the transition and progression of weapons, from knives to batons, then lastly touching on short swords. Should the lesson go well, Steven was ready to begin his son's *real* training.

Dominic quickly looked out the back window through the kitchen to confirm his father was waiting for him before running off to his room. Dropping his bag, Dominic quickly changed into his training gear and grabbed a hair tie before rushing back out toward the back door. Closing the door, Dominic then quickly ran up and stood at attention for Steven. Noticing that he had forgotten to pull his hair back up, he quickly grabbed his hair and fixed it before Steven turned around to face him.

Steven watched Dominic's shadow as he finished his preparations. "I've told you that you need to cut that. I'll take advantage of that hair every chance you give me," he monotoned while grabbing the training knives.

"Then I'll just not give you the opportunity." Dominic smirked as he stood at attention.

"Alrighty, let's see how that works for you today," Steven acknowledged, impressed by his son's spunky attitude today. "So I'm guessing you had a good day today, huh?" Steven added curiously.

"Yeah, it was great! History class was fun, and for lunch, I had chicken and mashed potatoes," Dominic excitedly told him.

"Make any friends yet?" Steven asked as he stood at attention before him.

"No, not yet, but it's only been two weeks since school started, so I'm not too worried about it," Dominic stated confidently.

"Well, that's good that you're keeping a positive attitude toward it." Steven remarked, feeling conflicted.

"But I'm getting along with almost everybody, so that's something!" Dominic quickly added.

Steven nodded, impressed by his son's resolve. With no further questions, Steven carried on with today's training.

"Okay, so today, we begin weapons training. While I didn't expect to start you so soon on it, after yesterday, where you finally applied your training and grabbed the batons to try and win the fight, I figured you were ready to advance. That's key in your training, Dominic, and for doing so, we begin hand-to-hand combat with training knives. They don't have edges, but you will treat them like they do. But don't think they can't still hurt you. When your uncle trained me, he once busted my nose for letting my guard down," Steven began explaining as he walked toward Dominic. "Now, can you tell me the proper way to hand somebody a knife?" Steven asked inquisitively while holding back one of the knives.

"Handle first. You hold the flat of the blade so you don't cut him.

By presenting him the handle, you ensure neither person is hurt." Dominic responded confidently.

"Good. That's what I like to hear." Steven applauded him as he extended the knife's handle.

Dominic accepted the knife before resting the blade in front of him, one hand in the other. Excited and anxious, Dominic adjusted his footing in the event Steven would attack him while he walked away. Watching every motion, Dominic remained vigilant and waited as every instinct told him Steven was about to attack. Dominic froze in fear at Steven's incredible speed as he leaned forward with an attack. Seeing the anxiety in Dominic's eyes, Steven held nothing back as he pushed on his son's defense.

Forced back, Dominic rolled away to break free from Steven's attacks. Shocked by the speed with which his father struck at him, Dominic wracked his head for a plan of attack. With a moment to breathe, Dominic stood up from the ground, determined to best him.

"To advance in today's lesson, you must strike me five times with each weapon. If you manage to hit me but I strike you back, your number will reset. If you fail to advance through all three before today is over, you will be continuing this lesson until you pass it. Do I make myself clear?" Steven instructed.

"Yes, sir!" Dominic exclaimed as he began charging at Steven.

Despite the fear he had for getting stuck by the training knife, every bone in Dominic's body propelled him forward as he sought out his victory. Matching each other block for block, the two danced back and forth with one another. Dominic pushed himself; for he found that fighting with a knife came almost effortlessly. Dominic jumped around both the yard and Steven while utilizing all he had been taught. Pleased to see his son applying his training, Steven pushed him harder, testing his resolve and reflexes. The two locked into one another with no holds barred. Thrusting toward one another in the same moment, together they immediately parried, disarmed, and flung the other in the opposite direction.

Sweat rolled off their brows as they caught their breath. Realizing they both had been disarmed and then, immediately after, realizing their knives were lying side by side, the two ran toward their weapons. Ready to fight for their tools, they quickly turned their training into a fistfight. As they fought for the knives, fists and feet flew.

Despite his young age, Dominic's fists still felt like a hammer. After a few jabs to the ribs, Dominic grabbed hold of his stunned father. Leaning his weight into it, Dominic lifted and flung his father over his shoulder and away from the knives. He had made some space to breath. Scooping them both up, Dominic watched as Steven struggled to lift himself up.

Dominic squinted at the sun in his face as Steven slowly rose from the dirt. A surge of confidence rode through his veins like lightning in a cloud as he could see the surprise painted on his father's face. He was shocked and hurting from the attack. Unwilling to lose so easily, Steven brushed the dirt off his gi before changing his stance. He was prepared for Dominic.

Vicious the young boy was as he attempted to strike his mentor. Batting away each of his strikes with open palms, Steven carefully backpedaled around the yard. Determined to make contact, Dominic pushed himself as hard as he could while sweat poured from his brow. Dominic was getting sloppy and Steven could see it. With Dominic worn down, Steven took this opportunity to retrieve his knife again. Disarming Dominic with one hand, Steven palmed his son with the other.

The force from his palm left Dominic breathless as he winced and fell back onto the ground, gripping at the pain in his chest. This fight was different from their last; his father had never quite struck him like that before. Looking down and realizing the knives were no longer in his hand, Dominic woefully looked up to the terrifying vision of Steven with both knives in his hands. Dominic swallowed his anxiety as he rose to his feet and readied himself for Steven's next attack. Pleased to see his son not backing down from a superior threat, Steven held back his grin as he slowly advanced toward him.

Picking up his pace, Steven raised his knives, ready to test Dominic even further. Dominic, falling back on his training, backpedaled as he dodged as many attacks as he could. One after another, Steven slashed out at Dominic, inches from his skin. Each attack so precise, Steven carefully applied the needed pressure on him. Nearly free from the barrage of attacks, Dominic tripped over a rut he had previously made in the dirt.

To the ground, Dominic tumbled away as Steven stabbed down at him, purposefully missing his hits. Finally able to stand, Dominic buckled over and heaved heavily as his sweat muddied the dirt and dust on his face. With no choice, Dominic held his ground as Steven gave him no quarter. Blocking and swatting away every strike he could, Dominic fought to find a weakness in his father's new strength.

"What're you going to do, Dominic? Are you going to stay on the defensive all night or are you going to get your knife back?" Steven taunted as they circled one another.

"I thought I'd ask nicely first!" Dominic sarcastically remarked as he found his moment to grab Steven's wrist.

Repeating the move his father had performed on him earlier,

Dominic retrieved his knife. With a golden moment, Dominic grazed his father twice before jumping away. Rejuvenated with a boost of confidence, Dominic found proof he could beat his father. Hiding his pain from his son, Steven could tell he was going to need more than an ice pack tonight. Rolling his shoulder around, Steven brushed the dirt off his beard and scalp, impressed even further by his son. Slowly, he walked forward, carefully examining his son's impeccable defense. He stood resistant to Steven's intimidating stare, patiently awaiting the next strike.

"Good job, that's twice! Now let's see you keep it." Steven smirked before rushing toward him.

The two were ruthless with each other as Dominic held off Steven's attacks. Avoiding Steven's knife became almost entertaining as he quickly found more flexibility within himself. Now that his son had a grasp on making contact with another blade, it was time to mix things up. Smacking Dominic's knife, Steven attempted to knock it out of his hand.

Quickly, Steven's charades grew annoying for Dominic. Returning the smacks between hits and kicks, he fought even harder, striving to succeed. Harder and harder they hit each other's blades as they fought to disarm one another. Angered, Dominic struck out, managing to both knock Steven's hand away and strike him once more in the arm.

Both father and son tested one another for hours as they fought vigorously throughout the evening. Repeatedly, Dominic would work up his count, only to have it reset. While the sun slowly set on the afternoon, Dominic pushed himself to his limit once more as he neared his fifth strike on Steven. Meanwhile, Steven ignored the sweat that dripped from his brow, focusing instead on keeping up with Dominic's attacks and parries.

The fatigue was apparent in his father's eyes, and Dominic knew it. Faster and harder Dominic pushed him until he finally broke through his father's guard. Landing his final strike, Dominic jumped with joy, relieved he had finally passed the first stage. Steven buckled over as the welts blistered across his skin, waving his hand to acknowledge Dominic's achievement. He never did like the training knives. Ready to move forward, he signaled for Dominic to toss him his knife as he backpedaled toward the table and their weapons.

Grabbing the batons, Steven inhaled deeply and turned back toward his son. Reminded of the days he and his brother trained, Steven was excited to be at it again, even if he still held it all with contempt. Dominic reached out and grabbed the thrown baton from the air as he walked forward. Battered and bruised, he twirled his baton in his hand as he continued toward Steven. To see the same look in his child's eye that he saw in his brother's years ago, Steven knew he couldn't fail either of them.

Relentless were the two as their batons bounced off one another. Dominic's body reverberated every one of Steven's powerful attacks. The two winced back and forth as their attacks broke through the other's defense, for with each successful hit, they felt the pain mirrored in their own wounds. Between the batons and the knives, a slashing welt from a dull blade hurt far less than the club's blunt bruising. Still, they fought on through the setting sun.

Crawling to his feet, Dominic hastily wiped the dirt from his face, then pulled at his hair and hair tie until it dropped to his shoulders. Smirking at him, Steven watched as Dominic made his first *real* mistake. Deflecting his intimidation tactics, Dominic rushed at him. Stepping backward, Steven guided Dominic move for move as they danced around their backyard. Feeling the anger in his strikes, Steven played into Dominic's rage as it built inside of him.

Steven continued his dance around Dominic. Thanks to his height and size, Steven utilized his extended reach with his baton as he prepared for his next move. Finding a break in his son's attacks, Steven held true to his word as he reached out and grabbed a full head of Dominic's hair. Quickly, Dominic felt the rush of pain from his mistake of lowering his guard, followed swiftly by the helplessness of flying through the air. Mercilessly tossing Dominic aside, Steven let him slowly rise from the ground.

Steven bounced his baton around in his hand as he paced back and forth. "If you insist on keeping your hair long, then be prepared for shit like that to happen. I told you I'd take advantage of that hair every chance you gave me!"

"And I told you that I wouldn't let you have one!" Dominic replied before spitting dirt from his mouth. Running back toward Steven, Dominic threw his baton at him.

Caught off guard from his attack, Steven blocked the flying baton before barely seeing Dominic's sneak attack. Using his hands and feet, Dominic gained the offensive as he simultaneously blocked Steven's baton and attacked him in turn. Forcing his hand, Steven began to take their bout more seriously as he saw the fire in Dominic's eyes. With another attempt at his hair, Steven was left dumbfounded as Dominic matched his reaction time and avoided the attack. With a strike at his wrist, Dominic snatched Steven's baton as he slid away.

"What will you do now, *Father*? Looks like the ball is in my court!" Dominic taunted with both batons now in *his* hands.

"Well, son, I'll just have to take the ball back." Steven cracked his knuckles as he ran toward Dominic.

The six-foot-four man barreled across the yard, purposely landing his punches against the batons as they made contact. Dominic held his ground as Steven's immense strength warped and bent the batons. Feeling the earth move beneath his feet, Dominic held strong to his defense despite Steven's strength. With no end in sight, Dominic panicked, wondering how he was going to break away.

Rolling away, Dominic attempted to place some distance between him and Steven, but to no avail. Every time he managed to get some distance, it wasn't long before Steven crossed it and was attacking him again. Sweat covered his face as he realized his father had been holding back the entire time. Hysteria and confusion seeped into the back of Dominic's mind as he found Steven's attacks too quick to follow. Finally seeing the opportune moment, Steven swiftly struck at Dominic's hand and chest, retrieving his baton and knocking Dominic back down to the ground.

"You're pretty good, son, but it's going to take a lot more than that if you want to best me someday!" Steven rolled his head around, loosening up his joints while waiting for Dominic to stand back up.

Dominic gripped the dirt beneath him as he slowly lifted himself off the ground. His arms shook from exhaustion as he pushed himself past his limits. Quietly, he once again knocked the dirt off his face and uniform. Feeling a bite mark inside his cheek, Dominic spat out blood. Wiping away the blood that remained on his lip, Dominic pushed his hair from his face and began walking toward Steven once more. Looking to the setting sun, Dominic knew that the day's training was about to end and he wanted to win one more time.

Five hits. Just five hits and he would advance twice in one day. A new feat to accomplish. One hit after another, Dominic struck back

at Steven's baton. Hit for hit, they violently bounced off of one another. The two were in perfect harmony.

A fire he had never noticed before burned inside of Dominic,
fueling every inch of his body. Fatigue and pain left his body as
each move felt effortless. The moment left him craving more.
Seeing the fatigue in Steven's face, Dominic held nothing back as
he high-kicked him in the chest, knocking him backward.

It didn't take long for Dominic's assault to bear fruit. One hit
after another, Dominic struck Steven. When Dominic reached the
fourth strike against him, Steven hastily changed his stance to
avoid a final strike. Struggling on his feet, Steven became aware
of how much their fighting had worn him out. Fatigue weighed on
both men as their scrapes and bruises slowly beat them down.

Nightfall came sooner than either expected. The faint crescent
moon was their only light as they fought farther away from the
house. Neither gave in as they swung their batons at one another.
Grabbing a nearby tree, Dominic paused to catch his breath. He
was at his limit's reach. Steven didn't deny the reprieve as he too
paused to catch his breath.

Steam rolled from their bodies as the night air cooled them.
Though no words were shared, they both agreed the next attack
would decide the battle's end.

Dominic's muscles led him as he focused on his composure and
stance. Never had his heart raced so rapidly before. Something in
him sought victory. Steadying his breathing, he knew he was close.
Steven fought to maintain face as his son once again reminded him
of his brother; he had the same calm composure, piercing gaze, and
fighting stance.

*"We Salvatores are like wine when it comes to fighting: we
only get better with age—and in our case, generations!"*

The scene only helped to prove his brother's words as they echoed in his mind. Though *fairly* beaten and weathered from their fight, Steven knew the match had to end. Dominic had surpassed all of his expectations, and he couldn't have been more pleased.

"The night's almost over, Dom. You haven't passed all three trials tonight, but you have impressed me! You've shown your dedication to your training, and for that, I commend you. I will give you five more minutes to try and land two more strikes on me. If you succeed, we'll continue tomorrow with the short swords."

Dominic listened carefully as his labored breathing calmed him down. "And if I don't?"

"You'll start over tomorrow. This is just the first lesson of many when it comes to wielding a weapon. So prepare yourself, give no quarter, and hold nothing back!" Steven bellowed as he reset his grip on his baton.

Running toward him, Dominic held onto Steven's words; he wanted to succeed. More so, he needed to. Refusing to make a single mistake, Dominic left his doubt in the dust as he matched his father hit for hit. Steven felt the desire within his son and he refused to give him anything less than his best. He was proud of him, and he knew it was his duty to not fail him.

With nightfall around them, their attacks became more and more varied, but with only the crescent moon's light to illuminate their battlefield, the two struggled to maintain their fight. Nevertheless, they carried on, slowly inching their way to the house while maintaining their fight. Together, they pushed one another as the seconds ran down.

Finally getting his fifth hit on his father, Dominic celebrated early before breaking away to a safe distance. With a split second to react, Steven seized the opportunity to strike. Going straight for the breach in Dominic's defense, Steven firmly struck his right arm, ending the match.

"That's match!" Steven exclaimed as the shock set in on Dominic's face. "You fought well, Dominic. Had this not been your first day of training with a baton, you may have bested me and moved on to the next stage. But tonight is not that night," Steven added as he lowered his weapon and relaxed his stance.

Bitter but accepting the results of the battle, Dominic shook his head in confirmation. "Thank you, sir. I gave my all today!" Dominic looked up, seeking Steven's approval.

"That you did. You did damn good today. Now let's see you do that tomorrow when all those bruises have had time to set in." Steven laughed lightheartedly before he gently slugged Dominic in the arm.

Dominic caught up to his laughter after rubbing his bruised arm. "I know you'll have fun with that tomorrow yourself. I got you plenty of times myself."

"Yeah, but I'm used to them. Those bruises are going to be whipping your ass more than I will be tomorrow. Just you wait and see." Steven chuckled more before sliding his baton up under his arm. "Will you grab the tools while I start dinner? I'll get some aspirin and ice packs ready for us both as well."

"Sure thing, Dad. I'm probably going to shower before dinner. That okay?" Dominic asked while he ran toward the backyard table.

"Sure thing, son. I'll probably do the same," Steven replied as he opened the back door. "Oh! Before I forget, did you have any homework tonight?"

"Finished it on the bus," Dominic happily replied.

"Got any tests coming up?" Steven questioned him again.

"Already studied for them today, but I was going to study again before bed," Dominic replied as he snapped his fingers and made a finger gun at his father.

"Good." Steven returned the finger gun before opening the door the rest of the way. "Carry on!" he added as the door closed behind him.

Dominic rested his baton on the table as he watched his father go inside. He could feel the pain from the day pulsating across his body and in places he had never hurt before. Despite the pain, he was happy. In his body, he could feel that his training had reached a new level. He had grown so much since his training began two years ago.

Soon after, his thoughts turned to the memory of his uncle. The day he left was still fresh in his mind, and so was the pain. All he ever wanted to know was what happened to him, but he knew that his father would never tell him. Holding back his tears, Dominic wiped his face and grabbed the weapons that lay before him. Walking to the back door, Dominic did his best to keep his head held high. Catching a glimpse of moonlight, Dominic turned around. Looking up to the moon as it crept through the night sky, he wondered if his uncle was out there or if he was truly gone.

CHAPTER 4

ACT I: FEAR

Year: 1999
Location: Fourth Layer of Hell

After successfully teleporting himself to Hell, John found himself in a rundown alleyway in one of the few centralized cities created by the denizens and damned souls of Hell. Seeing the busy streets filled with the souls of the damned, he quickly ducked out of sight and searched for something to hide his appearance. Quickly finding a cloak, he set out, searching for answers.

Vaguely familiar with the section of the dilapidated burrow he had landed in, John hugged the shadows of the alley wall. Glaring up at the tarnished gold megacity that surrounded him, John kept his head low to avoid being seen, for being a human in Hell brought its own dangers. But that wasn't the worst of them. To avoid the migraine that came from bearing the sight of the constant dull red glow the fourth layer had, John kept his eye toward the ground. The combination of the heat, the dim red glow, and the nearly silent, mind-numbing melodic hum pulled on the Greed in one's heart and mind. The trapped and damned souls were locked in a constant struggle with their quest of Greed.

Absolved of his Greed, he had already begun feeling the distinct slow chill of misery there within. Hearing the familiar demonic screeches of the corrupted Popobawas flying above, John kept to the shadowy spots on his path. Well aware of the flying cycloptic imps and their sensory skills as scouts for the demonic guard of Hell, John sought out a stranger carrying a strong odor, looking up from the shadows as the Popobawas screeched to one another. Second only to hellhounds, the twisted imps' sense of smell made them a nuisance to any human unlucky enough to find themselves in Hell. Still, John made no mistake as he slipped through the crowds and escaped their patrols.

As the roads opened up, so did the city. The various burrows carried their own style, a perfect mockery and reflection of the areas where the damned souls once lived. The rolling landscape spiraled in such a fashion that the center of the megacities towered over the outlying burrows. Yet throughout the entire city, the dirty glow of the golden buildings enthralled those around them. The widespread influence of Greed was palpable enough to be felt in the air as it left a physical affect on the body. Exasperated, John rolled his eye before casting a glance in the direction he needed to go.

Sticking to side streets, John knew well enough to not look up as he passed by the dead and demons alike. Gliding through the crowds and down the twists and turns of the streets, John made sure that anyone would lose track of him. Upon arriving to a residential area of town, John plugged his ears with cotton. Quickly, he passed building after decaying building where the wailing screams of dead infants called out. The cotton blocked out all but the loudest cries.

As he passed by window after window, the babies' cries would grow and dissipate one after another. John hated using this shortcut to get across town, but with little time and no other choice, he forced himself through the maze of buildings. John gritted his teeth while picking up his pace, the double vision was setting in as he drew closer to his release from the screams. John struggled to maintain his balance. The nausea had set in, and almost like the light at the end of a tunnel, John separated himself from the howling cries as they dissipated behind him.

Rubbing his eye as he regained his footing, John quickly glanced around, searching for what he had come such a long way to find. The familiar deep red glow of the neon sign above a door caught his eye. He had found the spot. Quickly, he snaked his way through the crowd of passersby. *Xaljō Vinariam*, the sign above read. With no time to waste, John quickly walked inside and closed the door behind him.

The dusky lobby was empty. Squinting through the heavy dust in the air, he looked around the old familiar thrift shop. The eclectic store never did any business, but it never stopped people from perusing its dusty shelves. Many of the same items had sat on the shelves for decades. John noticed only a few new items scattered around them.

Bits and bobbles and broken artifacts lined the shelves, though not all of the items bore an origin from Hell. Whether it was a pencil, a single shoe, or drinking glass, anything that arrived from Earth meant something to somebody. But thirty years of dust did nothing to help it sell. Seeing a dust-covered doll nearly emptied of its stuffing near the end of one of the shelves, John found himself missing his nephew. Gently picking up the tattered little doll, John carefully held it in his hand.

"You don't have the money to buy that, skipper. I hope you know that," a old voice called out from behind John.

"Yeah, you're right. But I'm sure we can work out a trade," John cheekily replied. Continuing to hold the doll, John turned around, happy to see an old friend. "Hello, Abraham. It's been too long." John greeted the equally eclectic old soul, hugging him and holding him close. Feeling safe now, John removed his hood.

"And even longer down here, my old friend." Abraham halfheartedly smiled as he pulled away.

Hobbling around John with his cane, the one-legged man moved to his counter. Looking to his wooden peg of a leg, John noticed how splintered and old the wood had become since he last visited. Suddenly reminded of what he had brought, John began shuffling through his leather pack as he walked toward the counter. Finally finding what he was searching for, John pulled out a brand-new hand-carved peg leg.

"I swear, forgetfulness will kill me 'fore anything else. I almost forgot, I made you a new leg. I remember the last time I was here. It was looking pretty rough. I knew the next time I saw you I wanted to replace it. So I made this for you." John struggled with his words as he presented the gift to the old soul, unsure if he'd appreciate it.

Looking back and forth between his peg and the one John was offering him, Abraham was taken aback by the act of kindness. "It's so rare to find anything of quality in Hell that isn't controlled and maintained by the demons or confiscated by them. When you're stuck living through this shitty eternity, you just eventually give in to it and accept your lot in all. Everyone becomes so jaded and self-centered you forget kindness and compassion are a thing. But it's those two things that always make me want to work with you again." Abraham leaned forward, accepting the wooden prosthetic. "I thank you, John. This is the first gift I've received since, well, before I died." Inspecting the craftsmanship further, Abraham could see the care that had gone into it.

"I should be the one thanking you. I reached out to you because I knew no one else could find out the information I need like you could. No one has connections like you do on this level of Hell or lower!" John expressed gratefully.

"I wouldn't say that now," Abraham replied, rolling his eyes. "But regardless, I appreciate this gift," he continued as he worked on removing his old leg.

"I made sure the finish on it was strong. I don't know if it's strong enough for Hell, but I made it with the best materials I could find. Simple, elegant, and light enough to where you won't be dragging it as much." A smile slowly crept onto John's face as he assisted by holding Abraham's cane.

Adjusting the peg, Abraham rose from his seat, quickly finding his balance. "It's perfect." Abraham stood happily in shock as he looked down at his new peg. "Thank you, John. Truly, thank you!"

"It's the little things that can make any Hell bearable to endure. That's something I learned a long time ago." John pursed his lips as he shook his head up and down.

"That they do, that they do." Abraham inhaled quickly as he caught up to John's nodding. "So I guess we should get down to brass tacks, shall we?" Abraham added before signaling for John to follow him to the back room.

Quietly, they walked to the back door, their feet knocking against the hardwood floor. John followed Abraham down through many twists and turns. The route had been ingrained in his mind, so they quickly reached their destination. After one short walk through a dimly lit corridor, they came upon a stone door with no handle. Looking back at John, Abraham signaled for him to open the door.

"Can't you do it?" John claimed as he walked past him.

"Can't you?" Abe joked in return.

John rolled his eye before waving a few hand signs, one after another, channeling his powers through his hands. With the proper mudras cast, John reached his hand out to the stone slab. Sending energy into it, he pushed the door open. Met with a singular room, Abraham stepped around John as the door slab resealed behind them. Waving a few signs himself, Abraham lit the scones around the room as the two sat at an empty wooden table.

"I can, but I *need* to know you aren't slacking." Abraham's abrasive tone caught John's attention, and his head snapped toward him.

"So things must be serious?" John asked while taking a seat facing the door.

"They are." Abraham's tone shifted as he sat down with him. "I couldn't find out much, but let me tell you, everyone's on high alert!" Abraham began. "This time I came really close to getting burned by everybody from your run-of-the-mill enforcer all the way to the governors. They've all been cracking down and rolling out extra punishments. I came to find out, it's across the whole realm. Both the layers above and below. Everyone's getting the beating stick and no one seems to know why."

"But were you able to track him down?" John asked, needing an answer.

"I'm getting to that part." Abraham's irritated sarcasm spoke volumes. "So all this starts happening before I can even begin looking for him, right? Next thing I know, I get a tip on an officer's meeting in an off-the-grid location. I dig a little deeper, come to find out the governor's making an appearance. So I sneak in and learn a lot, but nothing helpful or even related to your request, although on my way out, I did find something. Sneaking by where the governor's office was, I overheard him on a conference call with the higher-ups down below. Well, one of them was thanking him for allowing *Zähd* to come through and conduct his investigation."

"Did they say where he was headed after that?" John asked as he leaned forward.

"Thankfully, they did," he replied. "The governor added how he made sure he had a speedy send-off through the checkpoint to the next layer. One guy sounded off, saying something similar, so if I had to guess, he's at least another two layers in, and if he's that far down, then he really could only be meeting with a handful of people." Abraham threw his hands back, baffled by the information himself.

"I wouldn't call them 'people,'" John commented as he rolled his eye and exhaled heavily. "So what you're telling me is he's meeting with *the* Apostles?" John regrettably asked as he leaned forward in his seat.

"I'm not saying he is or he did, but a while later, I found something else out. His last known whereabouts after all that was Earth. For what, I do not know! It's extremely rare when someone leaves for Earth these days, but they kept that information redacted to Oblivion and back."

"You couldn't find anything out?" John pressed.

"I didn't say that. I did find a location. Cost me a lot to get that information, and I lost a few good men getting it, but it's somewhere near the eastern border of Kazakhstan. Supposedly an underground military base. He was only there for a short time before coming back, so whatever he was there for was reconnaissance.

That or a snatch and grab. Either way, he's gone to ground and hasn't been seen in a minute." Abraham exhaled as he leaned back again, winded from retelling all his information.

Back on the city streets up above, enforcers combed the buildings around Abraham's shop, searching off a tip of a *living being* walking around Hell. Grabbing people by their throats, they openly interrogated those around them while others tore apart and sifted through storefronts. The brutish ghouls carried their authority with pompous pride as they moved down the road, closer and closer to Abraham's shop. Back down in their safe room, John began to feel their presence.

"—and don't make me lecture you again about the price on your head alone! You can't be making trips down here thinking that you—"

"We need to get going!" John interrupted Abraham abruptly as his eye fixated on the door. Feeling out around him, Abraham sensed the danger himself, then shook his head in agreement.

"Stay behind me. They're going to be close when we get back up there," Abraham ordered as the two of them quickly rose and began to leave the room.

Sealing the room back off, John signed even more mudras. Combining his power and the energy around him, he manipulated the rock walls to cover the stone door as they began their ascent to the shop above. John kept up with a steady pace as he stuck to the shadows the entire time. Abraham held a strong stride as he and John felt the demons draw near. With his hood up, John fell behind Abraham as he opened the back door to the shop.

"Are you the proprietor of this business?" the first enforcer asked.

"I am. How may I help you two today?" Abraham begrudgingly replied.

"We had a report of a *living being* running around the area. We're conducting a search of the area. As long as you comply with our search, no harm or punishments will be handed out. Do you choose to comply with this?" The first enforcer held his authority in the room as he looked around at the goods on the shelves. Peering out from the shadows, John watched the two demons from a crack in the door.

"I do. I just ask that your boys not tear my shop apart." Abraham bowed his head before shutting the door behind him completely.

Walking over to the counter, Abraham followed the second enforcer with his eyes. Stepping outside, he signaled for the others to come inside. Aisle after aisle, the four of them searched for hidden compartments, false doors, and any sign of a living human being. After a quick search of the small lobby, the captain noticed the removal of a single item from one of the shelves. Its outline, left from the dust around it, made the shape of a doll. The shelves showed that no other item had been moved in many years. Taking a sniff of the air around him, the demon could tell something was off.

After looking over at Abraham, he turned back to the spot where the missing item had lain. "All the dust on these shelves and only one item missing from the lot. I'd wager to say you haven't sold a single item in over two to three decades, so tell me, what was right here, and who purchased it?" he asked, looking to Abraham out of the corner of his eye. While lightly gripping the doll he had picked up previously, John remained absolutely silent as he listened to their conversation.

Faking slight surprise, Abraham walked over to the shelf, examining the spot in question. "Ah, of course, I had a little doll there. I recently moved it behind the counter. I planned to try and repair it before I tried to sell it again. It was old and dry-rotting." Reaching under the counter and sliding his hand over a knife, Abe reached further into the open cupboard. "I'm sure you guys understand. Leave something lying around forever and you come back and find it all dried out and ruined." Abraham chuckled lightly as he continued his tall tale, pulling out the tattered remains of a similarly sized doll.

Ripping the doll from his hand, another of the enforcers examined the cloth figure before tossing it to his superior. Suspicious of his claim, the captain examined the doll before reexamining the shelf. "Hm, okay. Well, I suppose we've seen all that we need to see here," the captain announced before tossing back the doll. "Move out," he ordered as he and his men began to walk to the door.

Gripping the doll, Abe watched carefully as, one after another, the enforcers left his shop. With the last ring of the hanging bell above the door, John slowly cracked open the door. Looking to Abraham, he could see the rage behind his eyes. Closing the door behind him, John slowly walked over to Abraham and rested his hand on his shoulder.

"You got this, man?" John asked as he checked on his old friend.

Running his fingers over his eyes, he shook his head before setting the tattered doll on the counter. "Yeah . . . Yeah, I'm fine. I just really hate them. They're so full of themselves just 'cause someone else gave them a little power." Abraham inhaled deeply as he looked out the window to see the destruction they had caused along the way. "Motherfuckers . . ."

"Look, Abe, I'm sorry about the doll. I just saw it—" John tried to apologize while holding out the doll he'd grabbed earlier.

"Don't worry about it. Just be lucky they came as a set. The other was destroyed when I got them, so I only tried to sell the other,"

Abraham explained as he looked back. "Keep it. You wanted it, so it's yours," he added as he walked past John.

"I'm sorry I cause you so much trouble sometimes, Abraham," John sullenly apologized.

"Don't be. I help you *because* of the trouble you cause. I can't fight them like you can. I can't cause the damage to those that matter, but you can! That's why! You're the only person in the last five and a half millennia who's caused any trouble here in Hell." Abraham chuckled briefly. "At least any trouble that's mattered," he finished as he slumped back in his chair.

John sympathized with him. Looking out the window, he watched as those wrought with despair and misery from the searches picked up the pieces of their demolished businesses. He could feel their pain, everyone's pain. Looking back to Abraham, he could see the despair affecting him, too. Gathering all the pain within him and the hate that came with it, he applied it to his mindset, sealing his commitment to his mission even more.

Walking over to Abraham again, he looked to him while he looked to the tattered doll in his hands. "Someday, I'll find a way to free you, my friend. Someday." John comforted Abraham as he pulled him in and hugged him.

"I know you will," Abraham replied, smiling, almost believing the words himself. "You're going to have to use the back door to get out of here. It winds around to the street out front, but it'll get you back out there to escape," he added, sending John on his way.

"Thank you, friend. I am eternally grateful for you!" John smiled before turning to leave the shop.

"Promise me," Abraham said before John left the room. "Promise me when the time comes, you'll give it your all!" Abraham's voice trembled as his hands shook.

"I promise," John stated firmly, looking back at him.

"All the way, John," Abraham propositioned. "Push it all the way to *Sha'are Mavet*."

"All the way!" John cracked a smile as his change in tone confirmed what Abraham needed to know.

Opening the back door, John made his way through the building and out into the alleyway. With only one path to follow, he hugged the wall as he watched his corners. John pulled at his hood as he carefully integrated into the crowd around him. Hearing the enforcers demolishing another shop ahead of him, John couldn't help but intervene.

Walking up behind one of the enforcers guarding the rest, he quickly grappled and snapped the demon's neck. Hearing the shrieks from those around them, the other enforcers quickly turned around and watched as their comrade's body dropped from John's hand. Quickly rushing outside the building, the remaining enforcers began chasing after John.

Through one alleyway after another, John led the enforcers on a wild goose chase. Across the megacity, he searched for a place to teleport back to Earth. Taking the time to think on all Abraham had told him, John knew his journey was just beginning. He wasn't going to let Zähd succeed in his mission, and John refused to allow his vision to come to pass. But before he could stop him, John needed to retrace Zähd's steps.

Finding an opening in the city limits, John booked it as he outran the demons without the assistance of his powers. With the screeching of a nearby patrol of Popobawas, John knew that they would soon catch his scent. Still, he pushed himself further. Leaving the final buildings behind him, John ditched his cloak as he pulled its pin.

The time was near, and with one mudra, John released the chains that held his sword in place and quickly pulled it from its sheath as the screeching howls echoed from behind him.

Both aerial and ground forces had joined in the chase of the intruder. With no more time to spare, John began focusing his energy within him, activating his curse powers. Feeling the blood run down from the brand on his chest, John easily broke the sound barrier as he entered the first stage of his powers. The dry ground and dirt crumbled beneath his feet with every step, violently shooting out in his wake.

Quickly losing his pursuers, John continued running until he was too far away to follow or track. With nothing around him in the rust-colored wasteland, he raised his sword and swung it down in front of him. Immediately, John jumped through as he created a portal back to Earth. Looking back, he sealed the portal behind him. Unsure of where he had landed, John sheathed his sword and began to explore the grounds around him. His heart raced as he stomped over to an abandoned cottage in a European valley. His mind raced as he looked down at his family sword. The race had begun, the clock was ticking, and John knew his time was short.

CHAPTER 5
BLUES EYES AND GOOD GUYS

Three years had passed since that night of Dominic's training. Since the young boy turned ten, almost monthly he and his father visited the diner that Steven and his late wife used to share together. Staring out the window, Dominic watched the autumn leaves blow in the wind. With his chin resting in his hands, Dominic was excited to arrive at the diner. While the food was lovely, Dominic was more excited to hear the stories his father would share about his mother and him.

Changing the radio station, Steven exclaimed happily as one of his favorite songs came on. Dominic cheered as the baseline came in, playing along with his air drums. It was funny to Steven to see the childlike wonder and energy in a boy that could kill a full-grown adult if pushed. With each passing year, Dominic grew stronger, and each year, he wondered if his brother had succeeded. Regardless, seeing his son's smile brought Steven a sense of joy he never quite got tired of. Together, the two sang the AC/DC song as they traveled to their destination.

Arriving shortly after lunch, they quickly grabbed a seat at one of the outdoor tables and waited for a waitress to arrive.

"Hey!" Steven whispered as he playfully tapped Dominic on the arm.

"Yeah? What's up, Dad?" Dominic asked curiously, looking up from his menu.

"See that spot over there on the pavement? Where it's not level?" Steven asked while pointing toward the concrete slates near the front counter of the diner. "Now, let me start by saying I had known about the spot for quite a while before this happened. But one time, when me and your mom were out here, for some reason that day I had just completely forgotten it was there and I tripped over it while walking back with my ice cream!" He laughed heartily as he retold the story. "Now, we had already ate our food and we were just going for dessert, and your mom already had hers and was back at our table, but boy, she saw it all!" Steven continued laughing while Dominic caught up to his laughter. "What was worse, she made fun of me for it for the rest of the night!" Steven finished as the two laughed together.

"Oh, you two having a good day today?" the waitress eagerly asked the father and son as she stepped up to their table.

"Oh, we're having a great day, hon. How about you?" Steven replied as he lowered his menu.

"It's going pretty good. Can't complain about this nice weather today! So what can I get for y'all today?" she replied with a smile while clicking the top of her pen.

Watching Dominic frantically look through his menu, Steven chuckled slightly before responding. "Two classic burgers, please, and waters for the both of us," Steven replied with a smile.

Surprised, Dominic quickly shot his head up. "How'd you know I was going to pick that?"

"Fatherly intuition," Steven teased with a smirk.

"Alrighty, I'll have that out for you two here in just a minute!" The young server smiled before stepping away.

Returning to his story, Steven carried on the conversation for the both of them while they waited for their food to arrive. Interjecting his own questions periodically, Dominic asked his father more about his mother, yearning to know who she was. Finishing one story and starting another, Steven smiled while he recounted his memories. Feeling the swelling emotions in his heart, Steven couldn't help but feel at peace with the loss of his wife. He missed her, but he knew she was in a better place.

It wasn't long before their food arrived and their attention turned to the delicious meal before them. Even though the majority of their attention was on their food, they still held small conversations between bites. Looking around at all the colorful autumn leaves falling from the trees and the old townhouse buildings around them, Dominic loved the location and how beautiful it was. When he looked back toward the diner though, something caught his eye.

Noticing the rosy-haired young girl standing in line with her parents, Dominic couldn't help but gaze at her beauty. She was about his age, and her soft ivory skin glistened in his eyes. The gentle altruism in her voice complimented her compassion as she offered to allow another young child to cut in front of her so he could refill his drink. Feeling a pat on the shoulder, she turned back to her father, smiling. Her father approved of her kindness. Giving her father a hug, Dominic watched on as they returned to their spot in line. As the girl stood waiting for her chance to order food, the feeling of an enthralled gaze upon her grabbed her attention. Glancing over, she was met with the wide-eyed Dominic.

His olive eyes shined as he sat in awe of her, unaware of how obvious it was that he was staring at her. Giggling at his agape mouth, she waved at him playfully, then turned and locked eyes with him. The striking gaze of her baby-blue eyes and the sweet sounds of her laughter left Dominic flustered as he dropped his head back into his menu. Hearing her giggle and laugh some more, Dominic returned to his food, too embarrassed to look back up at her.

Hoping to see her once more before he left, Dominic looked around the patio as he finished his food. Saddened that the girl was nowhere to be found, Dominic returned to his conversation with his father. Time had flown by for them, and before Dominic knew it, it was time to leave. After throwing his trash away, he looked around once again for the girl he saw earlier, wishing to see her once more.

Dominic found himself encapsulated in his thoughts of the girl he had seen. He had never seen someone who captured his attention as much as she had. As time passed on, Steven's curiosity grew too much. He wondered what had kept Dominic so distracted all day. When he thought back to when his mood had changed earlier, all he could remember was the distinctive giggle and laughter from a little girl. Steven felt a surprised grin spread across his face as he put the pieces together from the look on Dominic's face.

"So . . ." Steven began. "You have a good day?" he asked with a smirk.

Pulled from his thoughts, Dominic shook his head rapidly. "Yeah, the food was amazing."

"Yeah? What about that girl, though?" Steven eagerly searched Dominic's face to gauge his reaction.

"She was amazing—" Shock and embarrassment gripped him. "I . . . uh . . . what girl?" he asked, trying to act casual.

Steven bellowed out a laughing cry, amused by his son's embarrassment. "No need to be embarrassed! You saw a cute girl today. There's nothing wrong with that. You probably shouldn't stare so hard next time, but it's your first time, so you're still learning." Steven carried on his laughter while patting Dominic on the back.

Somewhat relieved of his embarrassment, Dominic chuckled with him. "Yeah, she was really pretty!" Dominic looked away shyly. "I looked for her when I threw my trash away, but I couldn't find her."

"So that's why you had that really lost look on your face when you turned around." Steven's laughter turned to a light chuckle. "I was beginning to think you forgot where you were."

"No, but I really wanted to see her again." Dominic sighed helplessly.

Rubbing his shoulder, Steven comforted him. "Hey, it's okay, son. You never know, you might see her again someday."

Dominic thought long on his father's words. Somehow, he found comfort in them as the night carried on. Dominic lay back in his seat while thinking of the girl. Her eyes stayed in his mind, the image locked in and clear. As he fell asleep, his last thoughts were of the girl's eyes, those glistening baby-blue eyes. He could feel the pull in them and knew she wanted to see him again, too.

The next day flew by for Dominic. Before he knew it, he was packing up his bag and making his way to the school buses. Shuffling through the bus door and up the stairs, Dominic scanned for a seat. Noticing that all his usual spots were taken, he moved further down until a strange voice with a chipper Southern accent spoke to him.

"Wanna sit next to me?"

Curiously looking over to the smiling blue-eyed boy with short black hair, Dominic spoke up. "Sure, it's as good a seat as any."

"Hiya, how's it going?" The boy extended his hand. "My name's Justin. What about you?"

"My name's Dominic, Dominic Salvatore." Dominic happily shook his hand.

"Nice to meet you, Dominic Salvatore. May I ask you a question? What's better, an AR or an AK?" Justin propositioned.

Slightly confused but not without an answer, Dominic fired back, "AK. They're so much cooler than an AR! Besides, you can get an AK dirty and it'll still fire." Dominic's tone and voice did nothing to hide his smugness.

"That may be true, but you can customize an AR far more than an AK," Justin retorted. "But I'm glad you at least answered me. I tried asking those guys up there, and they just looked at me weird," he continued, chuckling.

"I don't think it's weird. It's like ninjas or pirates. Ninjas always win!" Dominic acknowledged proudly.

"Now them's fightin' words, sir!" Justin joked with him before bursting into laughter.

"I'll take your pirates on anytime," Dominic teased before reaching out to shake his hand again.

The two carried on the entire trip to their homes. The boys quickly bonded as they shared their mutual love of metal, rock and roll, action movies, and video games. Before either of them knew it, they were already planning to hang out, eager to see the other's weapons collection. Dominic was eager to learn how to shoot firearms, and Justin was equally eager to learn how to wield a sword. A friendship had begun.

Not even a full day into their weekend, Dominic was at Justin's house, learning firearm safety and shooting targets. With his only prior experience with a firearm being his father's shotgun and rifle, Dominic found an appreciation for Justin, who showed him the finer details of proper firearms safety. The two boys had a blast as their evening carried on. But as fun as the day had been, Dominic had one question he wanted to ask.

Gently setting his rifle down on the table in front of him, Dominic pulled off his hearing protection. "Justin, can I ask you something?"

"Sure, man, what's up?" Justin replied, pulling his hearing protection away.

"Shouldn't your dad be out here with us? I mean, don't get me wrong, I'm having a blast, but shouldn't we have an adult with us?" Dominic asked, raising his concern.

"Oh, we totally should, but . . . my *dad* doesn't really pay any mind to me or to what I do . . ." Justin lowered his head as his voice fell.

"What do you mean?" Dominic carefully asked Justin as he reloaded a magazine.

"You remember me telling you about how my parents are divorced and my mom lives back in Kentucky with my sister?" Justin began, looking to Dominic out of the corner of his eye. "Well, my dad wasn't too happy about gaining sole custody of me. He always said I was too much to take care of on his own." Justin paused, taking a moment to compose himself. "After a while, he just stopped doing things a father should do, and shortly after that, he stopped staying around the house. He didn't care what I did as long as I didn't bother him. Unless there was a medical emergency, he didn't pay me any mind." Justin bit down on his lip, holding back his tears.

"My god . . . I'm so sorry, Justin! No kid should have to live like that," Dominic protested as he pulled Justin in for a hug.

Resisting at first, Justin gave into his friend's care and affection. "Don't feel sorry for me. I take care of myself and he at least keeps food in the house. I have to cook my own meals, but I've survived on my own up to this point, and I'll continue to do so!" Justin confidently replied, patting Dominic on the shoulder before pulling away. "But back to your original question, yes, he should be out here with us, but he's out getting drunk somewhere, so fuck him. Plus, I've shot these guns more times in the past four years than he has in the last seven. They're mine in my eyes." Justin chuckled as he reloaded his gun and put on his hearing protection. "But if the neighbors or someone pulls up, we definitely need to hide these!" Justin jestingly added on as he and Dominic bursted out in laughter.

As the night came to a close, Dominic and Justin waited out on Justin's front porch. The two sat back and looked up to the night sky, waiting for Steven to arrive. Looking around, Dominic couldn't help but notice how little traffic Justin's rural road had. More than that, Justin's father hadn't come home yet. Looking to his phone, Dominic cleared his throat before speaking up.

"So about the next time we can hang out . . ." Dominic began.

"I was actually about to ask if we could hang out at your place next time," Justin chimed in.

"Ah, I don't know about that . . ." Dominic sullenly turned away. "It's not that I don't want to. I think it'd be awesome as hell for us to hang out at my house, but I don't think my dad would allow it. He's really strict about me bringing friends over, and I don't know if he'd be open to the idea so soon."

"I understand, and as you see, my dad is hardly here. So until you can convince your dad I'm cool with us hanging out here . . ." Justin replied, nudging Dominic's arm with his elbow.

"Really?" Dominic asked excitedly.

"Yeah! It's no big deal, man! But when I can finally come over, you gotta show me your sword collection!" Justin laughed as Steven pulled into the driveway.

Looking to his father, Dominic smirked, certain he could convince him. "Deal! I gotta go. I'll see you at school Monday!"

Grabbing each other's hands, they pulled in and hugged it out before parting ways. Steven waved at the young boy as Dominic ran up to the car. Hopping in, Dominic quickly buckled up as Steven began to pull out of the driveway. Dominic careful approach the topic. Unfortunately with one word, the brief conversation was over. Though with an idea in mind, Dominic began his plan to bring Justin over.

Unable to convince his father it wasn't a bad idea to bring a friend over, Dominic knew a change had to come. For months he worked to balance school, hanging out with Justin, and his training. Not willing to miss a day of his training, Dominic worked twice as hard to try and cram all three into his days. Month after month, Dominic pushed himself to do better, all the way to his birthday.

It wasn't long before March arrived, and with it came Dominic's eleventh birthday. For the past few months, Steven had noticed not only his son's attempts to bring a friend over but also the newfound effort he put into his training and schoolwork. Apprehensive about the idea of bringing anyone into their home and well aware that Dominic would undoubtedly try to bring Justin into his training, Steven cautiously looked to find some compromise.

After taking the time to learn about Justin and his parents' marital status, he began to understand and sympathize with the young boy. He knew that Justin was just like Dominic and looking for a friend. It didn't take much for Steven to understand why his son wanted to bring him over. Believing it wouldn't be a terrible idea for Dominic to have a friend his age whom he could connect with in his training, Steven devised a plan. Surprising Dominic on his eleventh birthday, Steven allowed Justin to come over.

Anxious for Justin's arrival, Dominic looked out his window once more, waiting for Justin and his father to arrive. Seeing their worn, deep green '98 Tahoe pull up into the driveway, Dominic excitedly leaped from his bed and ran barefoot down the hardwood hallway. Rushing out the door, Dominic easily ran across the gravel that separated the front porch from the driveway.

"Does that not hurt you?!" Justin yelled out as he hopped out of the Tahoe.

Catching his breath, Dominic bent over for a moment. "Huh? Wha . . . Oh, that? No, that stopped hurting a while ago." Dominic brushed off his concern before reaching out to greet Justin with their personal handshake.

Grabbing a wrapped box from his seat, Justin closed the passenger door. "I got you something, by the way. It was pretty hard to find what *I* woulda thought would've been better, so I just thought, what would Dominic get?" Justin anxiously explained as he handed Dominic his gift.

"Hey, boy," Justin's father sternly called out to him.

"Yeah . . . Dad?" Justin's happy face sank as he heard his father's familiar call.

"Just call me whenever you're done here. Otherwise, don't pester me. Got it?" he ordered.

"Okay." Justin looked away as he listened to the rev of the engine before the vehicle pulled away.

"Hey, you wanna—"

"No, you have no idea how great it is to come over here and not be at home." Justin quickly answered before Dominic could ask his question.

"I'm happy too, man, and after today, you'll be welcome over anytime, man!" Dominic reached out and hugged Justin, showing his friend that he was safe here.

"Not a very friendly guy, is he?" Steven's candor was clear and almost comical as Justin held back a smile. "No, no, it's okay. You're fine to smile here. My name's Steven Salvatore. I'm Dominic's father," he continued as he reached out to shake his hand.

"It's nice to meet you, Steven. My name's Justin." he confidently replied, shaking his hand.

"You know, when I was planning his birthday out, I asked Dominic, 'Who all do you want to invite to your birthday party?' And all he could say was you. Realizing that you two were really becoming close friends, I couldn't help but accept that and make it easier for you two to hang out," he explained.

"And I want to thank you, Mr. Salvatore, for that!" Justin interjected.

"As well, I'd like to apologize for me not allowing you before. As I'm sure you know from Dominic at some point telling you, me and my son have a very strange home life. His training is a private matter and was intended to stay that way . . ." Steven briefly paused as he jetted his eyes to Dominic. "But I can see that you're not one to judge, and I believe that you coming over here and hanging out with him would be a lot more fun. At the same time, I'm sure you'll want to join in with Dominic at some point and spar with him. All boys do!" Steven teased Dominic while subtly encouraging Justin.

"Actually, I have been wanting to. Ever since he told me about it, I've been wanting a go at him. He said you guys recently finished your new training field?" Justin admitted as he playfully punched at Dominic.

"Did he now?" Steven commented as he turned to Dominic, who was pretending to remain innocent. As he thought of a way to entertain the boys, an idea came to mind. "Hey, Dominic, why don't you take Justin inside and let him borrow one of your training uniforms?"

"Sure! I'll meet you at the field out back." Dominic's eyes lit up as he started running across the gravel again and into the house.

Retching from the sight of him stepping on gravel barefoot, Justin followed him inside. "That's not human, bro!" Justin's unintentional humor sparked a quick outburst from Dominic while he grabbed two uniforms from his room.

"You'll get used to it, too." Dominic winked as he tossed him his uniform and boots.

Opening the back door for Justin, he patted him on the shoulder before jumping ahead of him. Excitedly, he jumped up and down as he started running toward the tree line at the edge of their backyard. Justin's curiosity grew as they ran through the small opening in the tree line. After a near quarter-mile jog away from Dominic's house, a break in the forest trees emerged. In an enclosed plot of land sat a recently refurbished khaki barn as well as an obstacle course and a large open arena, the ground of which was covered with smooth gravel.

At the entrance of the arena, Steven stood at attention. Bowing to his father, Dominic walked over to their old wooden table and picked up the edgeless steel sword that was laid out for him. Walking back over to his father, he stood next to him and awaited his father's next words.

"Welcome, Justin, to our training grounds! Every day, Dominic and I train out here. Here, I've trained him in hand-to-hand combat, including Kali, Krav Maga, Karate, as well as various forms of combat that involve the use of a weapon. This can include blunt objects and bladed weapons. If you wish to join in, these will all be things you will learn. As well, you'll be learning alongside Dominic, who has been training now for over five years. But I must warn you, he is already at an instructor level in his Kali training and is a brown belt in both Karate and Krav Maga. The learning curve will be steep. I'd ask your parents for permission, but I can see that—"

"That he doesn't give a shit?" Justin bluntly interjected.

Holding back his laughter, Steven composed himself. "Yes. Here, I will test your mettle, your resolve, your retention skills, and your strength. Should you choose to accept this responsibility, know full and well that you will get cuts and bumps, bruises and aches. But know we will always work together and recover together." Revealing a sword from behind his back, he stepped forward and held it out. "So my first question is this: how do you present a bladed weapon to someone you trust?"

"Handle first, never the blade," Justin replied, looking into his eyes.

"My next question is this: do you accept all that I have told you and with a clear conscience accept the information I have given you and understand the potential consequences of it as well?"

"I made my decision a long time ago that I wanted to do this with you guys. Dom has been the first person that's truly been nice to me since I moved up here. He's my best friend and I want to do this with him. So yes, I accept. Besides, it gets me away from my dad, and that's just the icing on the cake!" Justin's blue eyes shined in the gentle sunlight.

Seeing the same look in his eyes just as Dominic had, Steven knew that he was making the right decision. "Then my final question for you would be, why aren't you dressed yet?" Steven smirked as he extended the sword, allowing Justin to take it from him. "I trust you around my son. He trusts you enough to tell you about this. He understands the importance of its secrecy. I now entrust that with you as well. Is that an issue?" Steven added as he stepped back.

"No, by no means. My mom's back home in Kentucky, and you see how much my dad pays attention to me. I want to be here. I wouldn't want to ruin that or my friendship. This stays with me," Justin reaffirmed to him.

"Good. Go ahead and run into the building and change clothes. There are some lockers just right of the front door. When you come out, stand at attention and watch and learn," Steven ordered him before turning and signaling for Dominic to enter the circle.

After quickly changing into his uniform, Justin held his sword close to his hip as he ran out the door to the sound of steel clashing. Seeing an entirely new side of Dominic, Justin watched in amazement as the two gracefully clashed against each other. Surprised by his friend's speed and mobility, he exclaimed excitedly as Dominic leaned back to avoid a horizontal strike at his face. In the years since Dominic had begun his weapons training, he had become ruthlessly keen at following his father's attacks. Feeding off of Justin's shock and amazement, Dominic felt his pride begin to take the reins.

Quickly rolling about, Dominic swung at Steven's legs before feeling the swift kick from the underside of his boot. Reeling from the sight, Justin winced at the thought of receiving that blow. Sliding across the stones, Dominic forced himself to stop just before falling out of the circle. Grunting and spitting the dust out of his mouth, Dominic rose and wiped the spit from his lips. Standing at the edge of the circle, Justin felt the intensity burning from the father and son.

"Don't step in the circle unless you're ready to fight," Steven announced as he caught Justin's movements out of the corner of his eye while maintaining eye contact with Dominic.

Looking down to see that his feet were at the edge, he quickly took one step back, waiting for what was to come. Staring each other down, Dominic and his father adjusted their stance and grip before running back at one another. Their years of training together was apparent as they smoothly danced around one another. Flinching to the dull blades and their sting, the two broke away from one another to pause. The dull pain they both felt was sufficient enough to cause for a break.

Lowering his sword, Steven signaled for a pause in the combat. "So, Justin, let me ask you, do you want to step into the ring?" he asked as he sheathed his sword.

Seeing the grin on Dominic's face as he winked at him, Justin couldn't resist the temptation. "Aw, hell, somebody's gotta knock that ugly mug around some. Might as well be me!" Justin exclaimed as he stepped forward.

Laughing heartily, Steven clapped his hands to his response. "I like you more already!" Stepping over to where Justin was, Steven cleared his throat. "Alrighty, Justin, being this is your first time and Dominic has been at this for a minute, I'm going to give you the rundown and see how you do for yourself. Sound good?"

Nodding in confidence, Justin unsheathed his sword and held it tightly in both hands. Noticing his hand placement, Dominic silently adjusted his own accordingly. Seeing the mistakes that were already arising, Steven knew he needed to speak up.

"Alrighty, before we go any further, Justin, there's a few fundamentals you need to know. Not all bladed weapons are held the same. Some are one-handed. Some two. Some are staffed and can be held in a variety of ways. There are long handles and short handles. You get where I'm going with this. Now, what you have there is what's commonly referred to as a hand-and-a-half-arming sword. Decent enough to start you off strong and long enough to where you can reach out and touch somebody. Now, holding your hands so closely together like that, that's a quick way to get it knocked away and out of your hand. Having your grip too far forward or too far back can also get it knocked away and out of your hands. You want to have your hands evenly placed between the front of the grip and pommel," Steven explained as he demonstrated. "At the same time, your grip is too tight. If I can see your blade shaking from here, it means you're too tense or your grip is too tight. Care to guess what too tight or too loose of a grip can do?"

"Disarm you?" Justin replied, looking over at him.

"Ding ding ding! Winner winner, chicken dinner! You want to have a comfortable grip on your sword. Or any blade, for that matter. It's an extension of your body. Where it goes, you go. Treat your sword well, and it will do the same. Now then, Dom, show him how it's done," Steven hollered out while signaling with his hand for the children to continue with their bout.

Dominic slowly advanced on Justin as Steven continued speaking. "Now then, in a real fight, your opponent will most likely *not* give you any quarter." Dominic pushed against Justin's defense, barely giving him room to dodge. "Such is the case it should be treated in training. So from this point on, you will fight with the intent to stop your opponent." Steven walked around the circle as Dominic swept at Justin's feet, nearly knocking him to the ground.

"Your opponent will be doing the same." Finding his first opening, Justin struck at Dominic, nearly hitting him.

"Now, of course, in this training, you will be taught how to do that swiftly and efficiently without killing your opponent." Knocking Justin's sword to the ground, Dominic held his to Justin's throat. Meeting Dominic's eyes, Justin found himself momentarily frozen by his friend's intimidating gaze. "We'll leave that for if a real fight should ever occur," Steven finished as Dominic pulled his sword away and stepped back.

Hearing the drumming heartbeat in his chest, Justin pulled himself back, accepting the realization of everything. Looking down at the sword in his hands, then back at his best friend, who happily waited for him to attack, Justin felt wanted for the first time in his life. Feeling the weight in his hands, Justin found a comfortable grip, and from that, a stance. Stepping forward lightly, Justin made one strike after another, meeting Dominic's defense every time.

The two friends tested one another as they circled the ground. Finding plenty of challenge from the experienced fighter, Justin pushed himself despite not having the mobility that Dominic possessed. Happy to finally spar with his best friend, Dominic reveled in the moment. Steven, meanwhile, cherished it as well as he held his serious demeanor with the slightest of smiles.

Satisfied after seeing the two spar, Steven was ready to continue the lesson. "Now, of course, you won't always be fighting with just a sword or a knife. Sometimes it's a firefight. Pray you're never in one of those, but more likely, you'll be in your current situation: hand to hand." Steven paused to signal for Dominic to act.

Swiftly repelling Justin's attack, Dominic brought his elbow across Justin's cheek. Catching himself at the ring's edge, Justin leaned forward and propelled himself back into the fight. Bringing his sword around to distract Dominic, Justin returned the punch to his friend, lifting him off the ground. Surprise struck all three as Dominic tried to catch himself without falling.

Grabbing his cheek, Dominic felt a swelling in his chest he had never felt before. Overwhelmed with a sensation to win their bout, Dominic rose back up and faced his best friend. In that moment, the boys knew they were ready for more. With their blade's in the air, they charged at one another.

No words were spoken as the two let their actions speak for nearly two hours. Drenched in sweat and bruised from their heads to their toes, the two boys knelt over, aggressively staring each other down. Dominic's ability to fight for so long was matched by Justin's desire to beat him. Their ears rang to the sound of their racing hearts as they tried to catch their breath. They had pushed themselves that evening, their bond and friendship sealed in their pain and sweat.

"And that's game!" Steven announced as he stepped between the two boys.

Shocked by the draw, they both protested aloud. "What?! No way. Come on!" Dominic angrily shouted.

"Come on, Mr. Salvatore. I almost had him!" Justin cried.

"No, it's a draw. You boys both showed your true selves today! You both have shown me that you wanted to win and that you, Justin, have what it takes to do this with us." Steven paused briefly before looking to Justin. "You didn't waver once at the chance to win against him. That was a joy to see!" Steven paused once more to look to his son. "Dominic, today's your birthday, and damn did it look like you enjoyed it! You've done an amazing job finding a way to balance all that you have going on in your life now. Truly, I'm impressed, but today, we call this a draw." Steven stepped back as the boys stood up and continued staring each other down.

Turning around, Steven walked back to the circle's edge just as the two boys dropped their swords and ran at one another, quickly blocking every strike they could. Before Steven could turn around, both Dominic and Justin struck each other in the face. Witnessing Justin's face bounce off the ground once, Steven disgustedly looked to Dominic, who stood there in guilt. Groaning at the lack of surprise in their actions, Steven rubbed his eyes. Reaching out for Justin's hand, Dominic helped him up from the ground.

"You good, man?" Dominic chuckled as he brushed off Justin's uniform.

"Yeah, but I'm gettin' ya next time, ya hear?" Justin glared at him while teasing Dominic with a finger in his face.

Grabbing his hand, Dominic agreed to the challenge. The two laughed together while helping each other walk back, satisfied with the outcome of the fight. Justin felt loved and wanted by someone other than his mother for the first time in years, and Dominic had made a best friend that day. Their bond flourished in the sunset of that March afternoon.

Signaling for the boys' attention, Steven motioned for them to come over to him. "You two did great today, especially for your first day, Justin. You really impressed me! You have a lot of potential with this if you stick to it. And, Dominic, your display of discipline was superb. I'm going to be expecting that from you from this point on. Do I make myself clear?" Steven inquired.

"Yes, sir!" he replied happily.

"Good. Now then, who wants some cake?" Steven asked, clapping his hands together.

Hearing a resounding "yes" from both of them, Steven ordered

Dominic to grab Justin's things while they both began walking back toward the house. After running and grabbing Justin's clothes, Dominic rushed back out to the training circle and grabbed both of their swords. Catching up with Justin and his father, Dominic wrapped one arm over his friend as they carried on to enjoy the rest of their night.

CHAPTER 6

ACT II: ANGER

Year: 2001
Location: The forest mountains outside
of Kurchatov, Kazakhstan

Two years, three continents, and five countries later, the now sixty-one-year-old man hiked up the overgrown hidden trail toward the black site he had searched for tirelessly. Dressed in his old camouflage fatigues and climbing gear, John kept his weight down and only brought the essentials. With his climbing stick in one hand and a machete in the other, he trekked through the thick brush. Sweat poured down his face as the morning mist helped slowly soak his clothes.

He reached the discrete markers on the ground. They showed him that he was nearing the entrance to the base. Stopping at a flattened patch of grass, John surveyed the area. Following the clues he had obtained, John pieced together the rest of the path up the mountain. Finding himself in a small clearing, he found the entrance he was searching for. The featureless, rusty steel door was almost completely masked by overgrowth and moss; were the sun's faint but direct cone of light through the treetops not hitting it just right, John would've missed it initially.

Upon closer examination, John found the door was left slightly open. Peering through the crack in the door, he searched for any traps or dangers. Finding nothing of concern, he gripped at the side of the door. With a light tug, John only managed to rock himself back and forth while the door remained still. Chuckling at his belief that the door would move so easily, John reset his grip on the door's frame.

Feeling the surging strength and power course through his body, John entered the first stage of his powers and gripped the door once more. Then, with ease, the screeching squeal of rusted steel against stone echoed through the forest as the door broke free from its anchored position. Peering into the darkness, John stepped into the facility and began searching around. Keeping his powers active, he used his improved sight to his advantage. Reading the remains of the Russian signs on the walls, John carefully began to piece together what Zähd would have been looking for.

Coming to an office in ruins, John found a journal that had been tossed aside. Checking the room again, he remained skeptical of the easily seen book. Was it there purposely or aimlessly tossed aside? Despite his initial trepidations, he knelt and picked it up. John found it difficult to read the scratchy Russian handwriting, yet even with the decayed state of the pages, he began to piece together some of the puzzle. Sifting through the writings, John discovered that this facility was once a warehouse for stolen supernatural items, texts, and occult-related objects that the Russians had hidden for conducting research.

After further investigating the notes, John learned how all their efforts throughout the Cold War were unsuccessful, both in activating any of the artifacts they had recovered and revealing any of the secrets in the texts. Like a child unknowingly playing with his father's gun, they knew not what they were doing. At the end of the Cold War, the Russians were unable to determine if anything they had collected was real or fake. But with the fall of the Wall and the Communist party, the facility was locked up and abandoned. Reading the final scribblings of the disgruntled author and their opinionated distaste for so much wasted time, John pocketed the notebook and carried on with his mission.

As he followed the hallways and moved further into the mountainside, John's hair stood on end, and a cold, dead air slowly surrounded him with each step. When he turned down the hallway toward the records room, John's intuitions served him well. A blast of powerful energy had completely liquefied the walls and doors around him. John knew he was on the right path. Feeling the melted concrete and metal around him, he walked forward and felt the residual power within the liquefied mess. Sharpening his gaze, John proceeded ahead, steadfast. Ducking through a hole in what used to be the door, John found that the records in the room had been trashed. Folders, loose papers, and manuscripts half devoured by rodents were strung about the room.

Finding an oddly arrayed trail of discarded files, John followed the paperwork to a manifest partially hidden among the pile atop it. Adjusting his weight to his right leg, John knelt as he reached for the book. His eyebrows stretched wide as he struggled to read some of the damaged writings. Despite the struggle to translate the text, John found nothing substantial on the list as he turned the pages.

Skimming through the last page, he quickly traced back to a different page when an idea came to mind. "Let's see here." John sighed while squinting at the text.

After initial reviews by Lt. Ogiyevich about the retrieval from Squad 3 revealed a series of grimoire on the binding of the Buddhist demons known as Māras to a physical body . . .

Finding the passage interesting, John sat back on his right foot and pondered, *Hmmm, now how could something like this be useful to me?*

While the idea of body possession, to John, seemed useless for Zähd, he still found it to be the most notable item in the entire manifest. Looking around, John realized he needed more information. Standing back up, he carried the manifest with him as he continued through the facility. While he examined the extent of the damage in the hallway once more as he left the room, John's brand pulsated on his chest. He had never felt such a resonance of power before in his life. The chilling emptiness left from Zähd's singular display of power left John short of breath. If he were to succeed at stopping Zähd, he would have to pour every ounce of his strength into it. Swallowing his feelings, John exhaled, then returned his sight back to the path ahead of him.

The echoing sounds of his footsteps resonated through his ears as he searched room by room. The stakes had never felt higher for John; he knew that the risks and dangers hadn't prepared him for the reality of the threat before him. The nightmarish warrior from Hell was quickly beginning to live up to his reputation. Feeling a cold stream of liquid run down his stomach, John was momentarily pulled from his thoughts.

Reaching into his pocket, John pulled out his trusty weathered and blood-stained rag. Taking a moment, he stopped, and shifted his leather shoulder strap before he opened up his top. Revealing the streams of blood from the engraved brand on his chest, he quickly wiped from his waist up. With precision, he cleaned away the blood, making sure not to leave a drop behind. For him, the act was second nature by this point in his life. He folded the thick rag into a square, then pressed the rag against his brand. John held it in place as he closed his shirt back up before readjusting his straps. After a final check of himself, he carried on down the hallway.

Finding a dilapidated wall map, John retraced his steps to where he had already visited. Plotting a path to the storage rooms, John quietly talked to himself as he reaffirmed the path he would need to take. Picking up his pace, he followed the hallway down. Reaching a partially caved-in section of the hallway, John was met by a surprise: a fresh footprint, dried within the dirt and roots of the overgrowth from the mountain above him. John traced the footsteps as they continued through the hallway. With no other footprints to compare the age of this one to, John knew it was Zähd's. Finding a shocking lack of destruction along the path before him, John walked carefully beside Zähd's steps as he weaved through the vines and overgrown roots. Taking the time to move aside the small amount of debris on his path, John began to piece together a more physical profile of the warrior he chased.

With only rumors and whispers to fuel the fame of the ancient supernatural entity, John trod carefully, checking for any traps along his cleared path.

Does Zähd know he's being followed? Is he leading me down a specific trail? Or have I stayed under his radar so far?

John pondered these questions as he drew closer and closer to the storage rooms. Step by step, he inched toward the nearly halfway opened door before him. Prompted by the sound of metal clanging against the floor, John quickly drew his faithful 1911 handgun and locked his sight on the door's opening. John's crimson cat-like eye dilated as he fixated on the opening. Hearing no other sounds, he cautiously stepped forward.

Reaching the door's edge, he peered into the dimly lit room. A tiny hole in the ceiling provided the only light source. He found nothing in sight. Careful not to make a noise, John inched further into the room. Hearing claws on concrete and unsure of what awaited him, John, with a steady inhale, entered the room.

Like he had done a thousand times before, John efficiently scanned and cleared the room. From corner to corner, John found nothing that could have made the noise. Stepping further in, he examined the rest of the room. Catching the scent of a wild animal, John swiftly locked his eyes onto the source of the sounds. Turning a corner, he found himself facing a pack of mutated wolves. Finally aware of John's presence, the pack attempted to ward off the stranger, only to be intimidated by the gaze of his crimson, glowing eye. Cowering down to the menacing figure, the pack quickly turned to a hole in the wall and ran away.

Relaxing at the sight of the wolves running away, John released his powers while holstering his gun. Curious of where the wolves had run to, he followed them through the eroded hole in the wall and into an adjacent room. Greeted with more sunlight, John stepped forward, into the partially caved-in room. Moving some of the overgrowth out of his way, John realized he had reached the other side of the mountain. Resting on a steep edge, he peered out, impressed by the elevation he was at. Accidentally knocking loose a piece of the floor, he quickly pulled away from the hole while ensuring his pack was safe.

Returning to the previous room, John looked over all the cataloged and boxed supernatural items, from scrolls and manuscripts to tomes and ritualistic tools. John pulled out the manifest and began his search for some answers. Needing more light, he reached into his pack and grabbed a small handful of glow sticks. Breaking them in, he sat them about on the shelves while he walked back and forth, cross-referencing items from the manifest. Finding more than what was initially on the list after the first few pages, John quickly realized he would have to search every single box. Setting the list down, John began checking each box one by one.

Finding amusement, surprise, shock, and disgust in some of the stolen artifacts, John pocketed the occasional useful item he came across. Periodically referring back to the manifest, John slowly worked through the pages as he finished searching half the room. The items came from all across the globe, but not many of them held any actual power. After John found mostly fakes or nonmagical items, his face grew long. With a long, groaning sigh, John rubbed his eye, underwhelmed by what he had found.

As he neared the end of his list, something began to itch at the back of his mind. Looking around at the pile of boxes around him, John began to wonder what he had forgotten. Checking the list again and again, John couldn't grasp what it was. Looking back to the last page, John stared at it until it clicked in his mind.

"The grimoires!" John exclaimed, jumping up from the floor.

Knocking over boxes on his way to their location, John slid across the floor before stopping at it. Quickly sifting through the various items in the box, he could not find the books. Frantically, John checked the box again and again before throwing it aside.

"Fuck!" he shouted before grabbing the box next to it.

One after another, John flung the boxes aside as questions of what Zähd could use the grimoires for returned to him. While he cleared the shelf, all the pieces started to fall into place. Paying no mind to it before, John questioned why Zähd would want a book on what was, essentially, demonic possession. John knew little of the Buddhists methods and ways of binding techniques, but John knew if it was important for Zähd, then it couldn't have been good.

Leaning against the metal rack, John sighed while trying to search for answers. John glanced over at a torn scrap of paper. It was a box label, torn in half. Upon closer examination, John found that it held the partial titles of the grimoires. Resting his back against the rack, John examined the manifest and label. Dropping his hands, John came to the realization that all the books were missing. Feeling hopeless and without direction, John bargained with the idea of using the one way he knew to get the answers he needed. Remembering Abraham's words, John closed his eye and dropped his head.

Ever since his last vision, John swore he would never peer into the future again. The images he had been fighting for so long to change were still burned into his mind more than a decade later. Reaching a trance-like state, John reneged on his promise. Focusing his accumulated energy within him, John centered it into his left eye. Within moments, a faint glow of blue light shined out from the cracks in John's eyepatch. Feeling a sense of clairvoyance come over him, John peered out with his left eye, searching for answers. The same images of unfolding future events showed themselves to him as John pushed further into the future. Tirelessly, he searched for the answers he needed to learn Zähd's plans.

Finding a tread of events, John followed it down into darkness. Further and further down into a dark abyss, he searched until an image came to him. Piles of bodies lined shipping crates around him, each branded with one of the two sibling curse marks that John had. Their tortured corpses gave John more information than he could've asked for. Like a boiling pot, a theory began bubbling within him. Trembling, John needed to know more. He needed the truth.

Deeper into the abyss, John descended as the images of the rotting, misfortunate souls lingered. He had heard of ancient stories of mass sacrifices, but never in his lifetime did he imagine he would see it. He had been through the trials and withstood the torment that had taken all those innocent lives. The power he wielded came at a heavy price and an even heavier loss. Such a powerful curse was never meant for your average human.

Deeper and deeper, he searched until the answers finally revealed themselves. In a flash of blinding light, John witnessed two figures before him, and in that moment, he understood what Zähd needed the grimoires for. He couldn't believe what he was witnessing. The unholy joining of two powerful supernatural beings. A demon possessing the body of a curse-wielder. A proven impossible feat appeared before his eye, and with it, the future became clear to him. Fear quickly boiled into a feverous rage as he soaked in every detail. Seeing Zähd beside the abomination, John realized his time was short. Even though the events unfolding to him were only years away from happening, to John, it felt like days. Pulling away from the images, John shut his left eye. Wiping the sweat from his brow, he found a reinvigorated drive within him. In all of his whirlwind of emotions, only a singular thing was clear: save his nephew from the life he led. A normal life was all he wanted for the child, and a normal life he was going to give him. The cycle had to be broken.

As if the sun had burned it into his eye, John stared at the images in his mind. He examined every detail in them, searching for clues to change the course of events. With the information he needed, John knew where his mission would lead him next. Setting the scrap note in the manifest, he returned them to his pocket before standing up.

Grabbing a few more scrolls, books, and trinkets on his way out of the room, John kept his vision in his mind. The constant image of the abomination fueled his rage, like kindling to a fire. Pushing the door off its hinges, John stopped just outside of the room. Grabbing a ball-like trinket made of glass and metal from his pack, he looked down at the old archaic grenade. Familiar with the object's abilities, John shook the liquids within before injecting his energy into it. With the aid of Natural Energy,[1] the dark liquid within the ball began glowing bright orange, activating its explosive power. Throwing the grenade into the room behind him, John maintained a single hand sign as he walked away.

Following his path back through the facility, John soon reached the entrance. Looking back, John released the hand sign before snapping his fingers. Feeling a deep fissure beneath his feet, he watched as the fires rushed up from out of the ground and out the front door. Destroying the facility in one explosion, John returned to the path in front of him.

Reaching the forest's edge, John could hear as the mountainside behind him crumbled to pieces. The cracking and breaking of stones giving in to the force they had just received echoed throughout the valley around him. At his motorcycle, he removed the branches he had laid over it. Rolling the bike onto a rural gravel

---

1 Natural Energy: the all-encompassing force in the cosmos that supernatural beings, magical beings, and celestial bodies can manipulate. The usage of Natural Energy is something one is either born with or learns to use. Natural Energy can be found in all parts of the cosmos, but it flourishes and thrives on planets like Earth, where biological life can grow. Otherworldly planes like Hell are the exception to this rule in that it is composed of Natural Energy.

road, he kicked the foot pedal out before going back for his pack. Rummaging through his pack, he searched for his satellite phone.

He remembered the number by heart. Still, John anxiously listened to the ringing tone. "King? Antoine King? It's John Salvatore."

"Oh hell no! I done told you last time, John, I ain't working with you again!" John chuckled as King shouted over the phone.

"It's good to hear from you, too!" John continued. "So, old friend, are you busy these days? I have a job that *needs* your help." John held back his trepidation about involving his old friend in his mess, but he needed the help.

"What kind of job are we talking about here?" King replied.

"A pretty big one."

"Oh! Don't give me that shit," King quickly replied. "We talking a *job* job or a *John* job?"

Resisting the urge to chuckle, John pulled the phone away from his ear. "It's a John job."

"Yeah, I thought it was. You wouldn't have called me otherwise. You know we're getting too old to be fighting monsters and shit, right?"

Remaining cautiously optimistic over the phone, John rubbed the leather cap over his right pinky nub while remembering a different time. "Yeah, we are, but this one is important. Really important."

"What's wrong, man. You okay?" King asked, noticing the sullen tone of his friend's voice.

"I am, for now, but I need a team. We need to rebuild the old squad." John swallowed the lump in his throat. He couldn't let his fears control him.

"The team's gone, man. Those of them that haven't died yet have gone off the grind."

"Dammit, you serious? They're all gone?"

"Yeah, man. It's pretty hard to readjust to civilian life after what we followed you through. But, man, make your way back stateside and let's catch up! You can fill me in on this *job* of yours and we'll get a team together."

"Alright, man. I'll reach out to you when I touch down." John's smile quickly faded as he hung up.

Learning of the passing of many former team members came as little surprise to the old war vet. Still, he mourned their passing. Shaking his keys, John straddled his bike as he looked to the road ahead of him. With the key in the ignition, John cranked the engine until it roared to life. Envisioning the images of the abomination and his nephew in his mind, John set off, ready to change the course of the future.

CHAPTER 7

BROTHERHOOD, BONDS, AND BLOOD
ON THE SNOW

"Again!" Steven shouted as he watched Dominic and Justin sparring.

In the three years since Justin joined Dominic in his training, together the two of them had become the best of training partners. No bruise, scrape, or broken bone could change their minds or diminish the thrill that training brought them. For the two fourteen-year-olds, their last summer before entering high school would be considered one of their best.

With the new year upon them, the boys found their own challenges in balancing their public and private lives. Unlike in middle school, where they shared most of their classes together, the two found themselves meeting and hanging out in the hallways more than in the classroom. Still, it didn't stop the boys from reaching out to make new friends.

Just like the many past years in school, Dominic found it easy to get along with the other students around him, yet still, he found it nearly impossible to make new friends. Justin was no different in this regard. From the constant bullying for his Southern accent to

him just being a strange human few could understand, the school
year had been harsh from the start, but at least the two boys had
one another. Quickly, the two grew to regard each other as brothers, and in that, they formed a family. With winter break in sight,
the two eagerly awaited their snowy vacation.

Walking home from a trip to the mall, Dominic and Justin stayed
close to one another, blocking the incoming wind and snow. The
winter snows had been particularly rough that year, but it wouldn't
deter the boys from going to the mall on the weekends to window
shop. Passing a nearby alley next to the mall, Dominic couldn't
help but notice a crowd of people. Glancing over, he witnessed a
crowd of adults surrounding a young boy, pushing him around.
Watching as the boy fell to the ground, Dominic quickly stopped
and stretched his arm out in front of Justin, stopping him as well.

"What're you stopping for, man? I'm freezing out here," Justin
asked while holding himself.

As he pointed to the crowd, the emotion was clear on his face.
"That fucker just pushed that kid to the ground," he replied. "Follow
me. I'm going to get some answers."

"No— wait! Damnit Dom!" Justin exclaimed as Dominic escaped his grasp before he could stop him.

"Bobby, grab that kid's wallet!" the ringleader ordered as he
punched the thirteen-year-old in the gut. "Japhcimell? What kind
of name is that?" he added as he looked at the boy's ID.

"The kind your mom screams out at night!" he replied, sitting
up before spitting in the ringleader's face.

Angered, the ringleader swung back again and knocked him
to the ground. "Well! *Cole Japhcimell*, I hope you're ready to regret those words!" Readying another punch, he felt his fist being
grabbed from behind.

"Why don't you pick on somebody your own size!" Dominic tightly gripped the bully's fist before overextending his arm until he fell to his knees.

"Arrrghhh! What the fuck are you guys doing?! Get these assholes!" the leader called out.

Hearing those words, Justin jumped into action. Immediately to Dominic's defense, Justin barreled into the alleyway, raising his fist to the man's face. Down to the ground the man fell as Justin quickly found himself on the defensive while two others ganged up on him. Dazed and confused by the events unfolding before him, Cole leaned away as a man flew over him.

With only one free hand, the ringleader aimlessly swung above his head, catching Dominic in the cheek. Kicking the ringleader away, Dominic rushed over to Cole as he tried standing up. Catching another attacker out of the corner of his eye, Dominic quickly leaned back before delivering a devastating punch. Sending him to the ground, Dominic quickly turned back to check on Justin. A grin widened across his face as Dominic watched Justin hold off two full grown men. Returning his attention to Cole, Dominic extended his hand.

"Hey, whaddya say we beat up these assholes together?" Dominic smirked as Cole wipes blood from his nose.

Confused, Cole looked up to a smiling Dominic. Interrupted by Justin being throw against the wall next to them, Cole quickly grabbed Dominic's hand, lifting him off the ground. Dominic and Cole stood with Justin as the gang began to surround them. Together the three fought off the onslaught of punches and kicks. All the training Dominic and Justin had at their disposal turned out to be their only saving grace as they fought for their survival.

"Name's Dominic," he began while dodging punches and kicks.

"Cole, Cole Japhcimell!"

"And I'm Justin!" he shouted out as he tackled another assailant who was grabbing at Cole.

"So do you guys normally go around beating up assholes and saving people?" Cole sarcastically asked as he laid into the man he sat on top of.

"Not really! But it just seemed like a good, fun time," Dominic remarked back while fighting the leader of the group.

"And who doesn't like a little help beating up some pricks every now and then?" Justin added before taking a heel to the chin.

"Justin!" Dominic shouted as he watched his friend fall to the ground.

Feeling anger surge within him, Dominic finished his opponent before tackling the man who'd kicked Justin. Bringing his elbow straight down on the man's face, Dominic didn't flinch as he broke the man's nose. Slamming his elbow down one more time, Dominic found himself physically removed from atop the man as one of the last two fighters pulled him away.

Getting on top of the young fighter, the man laid into Dominic's face. Quickly, Dominic covered his face, letting the man pound his forearms. Though the punches might have hurt, this was not the first time Dominic had found himself on the ground with an opponent above him, and he refused for this to be the last. Finding the man not nearly as heavy as his father, Dominic swung his legs up and wrapped them around the man's neck. Seizing the momentum, Dominic returned to being on top before knocking the man out in one punch.

Looking up, Dominic watched as Justin and Cole fought against the leader together. Quickly rising to his feet, Dominic sprung into the fight, catching the man off guard and knocking him out cold. Soaked from the sweat under their clothes, steam rolled off their skin as they finally caught their breath. Looking around, the three laughed as they found that they had won. Battered and bruised, they all released a sigh of relief. Remembering that the leader had taken Cole's wallet, Dominic turned his attention back to the unconscious man at his feet. Rolling the man over, Dominic patted him down until he found Cole's wallet. Pulling it from the jacket pocket, he presented it to Cole.

"You didn't have to do that, you know? It's not my first time dealing with bullies," Cole said, accepting the wallet.

"I know, but I wasn't about to let them beat you up."

Dominic's sympathy spoke to the jaded Cole. "Yeah, well, I had it handled," he replied, trying to dismiss Dominic.

"Man, you had handled just about as well as a car missin' two wheels: not at all," Justin chimed in, lightly slugging him in the arm.

"I only had 'em thinking they had the upper hand. I was about to handle them!" Cole smirked as he faked out Justin with a punch.

"I'm sure you did, man, but all the same, I wasn't about to let you handle all of them on your own. They each had a good five inches on you in height, and that's a recipe for disaster," Dominic intervened before extending his fist for a bump.

"Yeah, well, you really didn't have to do that for me. But I've never had anybody stand up for me like that before so . . . th-thank you." For the first time, Cole stomached his pride and thanked the strangers in front of him.

"Hey, it's no biggie, man. Besides, this ogre-looking motherfucker punches harder than any of these limp-wrist dicks!" Justin sounded off before playfully punching Dominic in the arm.

Imitating his laugh, Dominic punched him back before

returning his attention to Cole. "You going to be okay getting home, man? What about that bloody nose? Need one of us to reset it?" Dominic's heartfelt smile never left his face as he offered his help to Cole once more.

"Oh, this? Nah, it's not my first one. All he did was bust it up a little. He didn't break it all the way. But thank you again, guys. It's nice to know there's good people still in this world." Cole reached out to shake their hands. "What're you, guys? Brothers or something?" he added as he shook Justin's hand.

"I'd hope not!" Justin laughed heartily as he released his hand.

"We're best friends, but we might as well be brothers. He's the closest thing I have to one!" Dominic added, tacking onto Justin's comment before grabbing Cole's hand and pulling him in. "I know we just met, but you kicked ass, man. I'm glad I had the chance to be here today!" he added before patting Cole on the back.

Surprised by the hug, but not against it, Cole patted him back. "Well, thank you guys again!" he said before pulling away.

"Hey, you be safe getting home, man!" Dominic called out as Cole hurried away, trying to get away from the cold.

Cole waved back at the two once more before rounding the corner and disappearing. "You don't think your dad will be mad at us for fighting these guys, do you?" Justin asked as Dominic turned around to face him.

"Nah, besides, it would've been pretty shitty if we hadn't stepped in," Dominic replied as he pulled his beanie from his pocket.

Turning around, the two returned to their long trek home. As they reached the edge of the alleyway, only the sound of snow crunching behind him and a blade locking in place gave Dominic any warning of danger. Dominic pushed Justin aside as the ringleader charged at the two boys, knife in hand. When the cold steel tore through Dominic's left arm, his training instantaneously took over. Disarming the man and grabbing the knife from his hand, Dominic slammed him to the ground. With one hand around the assailant's throat, Dominic jumped onto the man's chest before slamming the knife down into the ground beside the man's head.

The boy's eyes were cold and terrifying. Never had green eyes brought such fear or had death felt so near. His breath was slow and steady. The air grew foul as the snow below the man turned yellow. With no air to grasp at, he helplessly squirmed and begged for Dominic to let him live as the hand tightened more. The world disappeared around Dominic as his ears fell deaf, and with it, the whispers of only one idea crept into his mind. The rage inside of him strengthened his conviction as he slowly brought the knife to the man's throat. Feeling a forceful pull on his shoulder, Dominic slowly regained his senses.

"Dom! Dom! Come on, man. Don't kill him, man!" Justin pleaded as he pulled on Dominic's jacket with all his might.

Like a distant echo, Dominic heard the pleas from his friend and fought the urges inside of him. All Dominic craved was to sink the blade in, to have the man feel his pain, but in that moment, he paused. Looking to the knife in his hands, he remembered his uncle's words.

"Dom, I need you to understand, this is a tool, not a toy. It can hurt people if you aren't careful. But most importantly, only act with a clear mind. Do not let your emotions guide your actions with this."

He remembered what he had taught him and how his emotions had taken hold. Slowly relaxing his grip, Dominic pulled away from his attacker. He felt the man's throat slip from his fingers, but the urge remained, still yelling for him to plunge the knife into the man. Refusing to let the transgression against him go unpunished, Dominic quickly grabbed the man's arm and snapped it over his knee before throwing the knife away.

Standing, Dominic allowed the sniveling coward to rise to his feet. "Let today be a lesson to you. Don't be a piece of shit!" Dominic wore his disgust on his face as Justin pulled him away from the man.

Checking Dominic's arm, Justin could see that the wound ran deep. "Jesus Christ, man. That's pretty deep! We need to get home! Now!" Justin persisted as he applied pressure to the wound.

"You're right, man. Let's get going." He paused while shifting his weight onto Justin's shoulder. "I have some bad news, though . . ." Dominic dropped his head as they rushed away.

"What? What's wrong?" Justin shouted as they stopped in place.

"*Now* Dad's probably gonna be mad," Dominic joked lightheartedly.

"You motherfucker!" Justin tried to stop himself from laughing before smacking Dominic on the side of the head.

The rest of their winter felt almost boring compared to their one night in a real fight. Still, they never wasted a day of training as their winter break passed by. Day after day, the boys vigorously fought one another, using their first fight as a template to improve their skills. Even though they surmised that they'd never find themselves in such a fight for their lives again, they still trained as if they would.

Like the majority of their break, the remainder of their freshman year and the next seven months flew by without incident. With so much time devoted to their training, the two boys quickly learned to master the skills they had developed. Earning his first black belt in Karate and his second in Krav Maga, Dominic had really grown both physically and mentally. Justin as well had grown much in this time, earning himself a brown belt in both martial arts they trained in. With their sophomore year underway, they found themselves prepared for whatever was to come.

Bobbing his head back and forth, Dominic glanced around periodically between lines of homework. He had been waiting half of his lunch break for Justin to arrive. Despite normally arriving to lunch ten minutes after him, Justin was nearly twenty minutes late. Looking at all the other crowded tables around him, Dominic slowly noticed that fewer and fewer of his classmates were sitting near him as the school year went on. Hearing another crowd of students enter from behind him, Dominic paid no mind to someone calling out his name.

"Hey, ya big ugly!" Justin hollered out, smacking Dominic on his back.

Looking back, Dominic was shocked to see Cole standing beside Justin. "Cole! What's up, man! Justin, where'd you find him?" Dominic excitedly jumped up from his seat and greeted the two.

Accompanying the two boys was another student dressed in his ROTC uniform. The young man's sandy hair and high and tight haircut seemed almost translucent as he stood silently and observed the conversation. "Hey, man. How's it going? Name's Dominic, it's nice to meet ya!" Dominic smiled as he reached out and shook hands with him.

"Mine's Richard. We've actually met before. It was a long time ago though, back in elementary school." Richard smiled as he greeted his old classmate.

"Really? How come I don't remember you?" Dominic was embarrassed that he had forgotten.

"I changed schools for a while. I only came back this year. I met Cole here on the first day."

"And I bumped into the two of them in the hallway on the way here, so you know I had to bring them over here!" Justin interjected. "And I was thinking, since Cole here has a little experience with, ya know, fighting, I was thinking maybe we could invite them over after school today," Justin added as he tried to persuade Dominic.

"Mm, maybe. Cole I could vouch for, but—and I don't mean this to offend you at all, Richard—but I don't know if he could come over. I don't know you yet, and that would be an issue for my father," Dominic pondered as he sat back down, facing the three of them.

"I know that. That's why I brought him here. So you can," Justin exclaimed.

"Well, I can't fight that logic. Pull up and take a seat, guys." Dominic chuckled as he offered seats to Cole and Richard. "So has Cole told you anything about me or how we met?" he added as they all sat around Dominic.

"He told me how you saved him from a mugging one time," Richard replied.

"Well, me and Justin did, but yeah, that's how we met." Pausing for a moment to reflect on it, he was quickly reminded of his injury. "Cole, that motherfucker in charge actually got the drop on me after you left and we were walking away!" Dominic excitedly blurted out before showing off the scar.

"Damn! Dude, how'd y'all get out of that one?"

"Dom fuckin' went all ninja on him, disarmed him and then took the knife from 'em!" Justin said.

"Goddamn . . ." Richard said softly, amazed by what he had heard.

"Goddamn right! It was fucking insane!" Justin hyped up the boys.

"Yeah, I got the knife from him." Dominic lightly chuckled as he looked down at the scar, remembering the emotions he felt in that moment. "I'm just glad we got out of that situation afterward without any extra bloodshed." Dominic composed himself as he held his smile in place.

Moving their conversation from topic to topic, the group learned that they all shared similar interests, from music to movies and more. The four had found new friends in one another. Like matching puzzle pieces, they all fit together. Agreeing to meet up after each class, the remainder of the school day flew by. By the end of the day, the boys had missed their bus rides home because they were busy learning so much about each other. After calling for his father to pick him up, Dominic felt confident enough to try bringing both of his new friends over.

Pulling up to the four boys horse-playing around a gazebo, Steven already had an idea of what Dominic was about to ask. Making eye contact for a second, Dominic straightened himself up and quickly walked over to meet his father. The two locked eyes as Steven pulled up to the curb. Steven could read the question on his son's face as he stepped closer. Peering into the car, Dominic caught his breath before speaking.

"Son." Steven nodded as he looked to his son, then to Justin and the two new faces behind him.

"Hey, Dad. Remember last winter? That guy me and Justin helped out?" Dominic asked.

"Yeah?" Steven replied as he looked to the two new faces.

"Well, this is him. Cole, this is my dad, Steven." Dominic introduced the two as Steven stepped out from the car.

"Nice to meet you, Mr. Salvatore. You raised a damn good son," Cole complimented the man as he reached out to shake his hand.

"Well, thank you, Cole. I appreciate that!" Steven lightly chuckled as he shook his hand. "And you are?" Steven asked while he stepped out of the car before looking to the well-dressed cadet.

"Richard, sir. Richard Klingemann. It's nice to meet you. I've heard good things about you, Mr. Salvatore," Richard replied as he shook the man's hand, surprised to find someone taller than him.

"Klingemann? Now that's some German if I've ever heard any! Your family move here recently?" Steven asked curiously.

"I'm third generation. My grandfather moved here to America shortly after the Nazi occupation of his hometown. He enlisted here shortly after."

"My brother was in the service. He was in Vietnam."

"Really? I wonder if he served with my grandfather when he reenlisted."

"I don't know. He never talked about those times." Steven held a smile as his thoughts drifted back to his brother.

Taking control of the conversation, Dominic expressed his wishes to his father and taking the time to hear out his son's request, Steven debated the idea of bringing two more into the fold. Even though Dominic hadn't mentioned the idea of training and only wanted to invite them over, he could see his son's intentions. Justin's added comments to the notion only furthered what the boys had cooked up. Leaning against the car after being asked for the third time, Steven contemplated the notion.

"Now, Dom, you know what it means if I say yes?"

"I do. I wouldn't bring someone over if I didn't trust them. I fought alongside Cole once before, and Richard, I don't know what it is, but something tells me I can trust him. Call it a gut feeling, but I wouldn't bring the question to you otherwise." Dominic laid his thoughts out for his father, his confidence shining through his voice.

Hearing his son out, Steven contemplated the idea until he found the confidence in his son's words. "Alright, fine, but you're introducing them this time. It's time you start taking over some of the responsibilities," Steven told him before unlocking the back doors.

Excitedly, Dominic and Justin jumped in the car before Cole and Richard. Throughout the whole ride home, Dominic, Justin, and occasionally Steven explained the nature of Dominic's and Justin's fighting skills and the daily training they underwent. Though the news came as a surprise, the more the two boys sat and listened the more excited they became to join in. Steven smirked as he listened to the boys carry on. While he had made a career out of teaching martial arts to others, there was something special watching his son bond over the training he once loathed. With the boys arriving at Dominic's home before they knew it, Dominic quickly jumped out of the car to grab some extra training gear while Steven guided them around to the back of the house. Stopping in the kitchen, Dominic watched as his father led the group through the backyard. Dominic hadn't been this excited since Justin came over for the first time. Grabbing a set of uniforms, Dominic ran out the back door attempting to catch up to his friends.

"Here ya go. They should fit you guys. They're a little old, but they'll do until we can get you some new ones!" Dominic shouted as he caught up and handed Cole and Richard a gi. "Hey, man. Here ya go!" he added, nudging Justin before handing him two hair ties and putting up his own hair.

With the new improvements made by Dominic and Justin, the others were amazed at the advanced obstacle course and large combat circle they used for training. Giving the full tour, Dominic showed them the inside of the recently remodeled building. It had a new climbing wall, salmon ladder, and workout equipment, and the boys found themselves amazed by all they were seeing.

"Bro, this is going to be fun as hell! We're going to actually get some real training from professional martial artists!" Cole said as he quickly changed his clothes.

"Tell me about it! I never would've known that Dominic was a black belt in Karate," Richard replied as he gently laid his uniform down.

"And Krav Maga? I mean, I saw the man fight, but I had no idea! This is going to be dope!"

Tightening their belts, the two teens left the changing room together. Met with the sounds of stones hitting the outside wall of the building, they quickly ran outside to investigate. Greeted by the sight of Dominic and Justin trading kicks in the arena, Cole and Richard ran toward the ring. The boys were amazed by the speed and grace with which Dominic and Justin blocked each other's attacks.

The two had grown much since their training started almost four years ago. They had nearly mastered each other's moves as they deflected hit after hit. But still, Dominic held a little more experience than his best friend. Hopping away from a swing, Dominic teased him as he moved around the circle. Though Dominic might have been bigger than Justin, he was still more mobile as he juked around an attack. Planting his foot into the ground, Dominic charged at him and subdued him on the ground.

"That's match!" Steven announced as he extended his arm.

"Goddammit, Dominic! You tripped my ass up! That's the only reason you won!" Justin halfheartedly protested as Dominic released his hold.

"You said no groin or face shots. You said nothing about you tripping over my foot! I'm just playing by your rules," Dominic teased as he helped him off the ground.

"Yeah, yeah, I got you next time!"

"We'll see, brother. We'll see." Dominic smirked as he patted him on the shoulder. "Well, I guess there's a great example of how we do things around here! You guys still interested?" Dominic chuckled as he turned to Cole and Richard.

The boys could hardly contain themselves as they shook their heads in unison. They had found a place, just like Justin, that they could call home. Demonstrating to his new friends the proper stances for the beginning of their training, Dominic naturally took to leading them. Steven smiled as he took a step back, watching his son take the reins. It was nice to see such a huge smile on his son's face.

The rest of the day flew by for the boys, and before they knew it, nightfall came. All the boys had cemented new friendships in the arena, both in their collective scrapes and bruises and the sweat they shared. Cole and Richard had a hard road ahead of them if they wanted to catch up to Dominic and Justin, but the pair were ready. Cole had quickly found a purpose in training to beat Dominic, while Richard sought to learn more from Justin and the techniques he deployed. Satisfied with the day's work, the four retired to the building to change clothes before returning to the house.

Following their tradition of recovery after training, the four boys gathered around the dinner table as they nursed their injuries. "That was a great first day, guys. Seriously!" Dominic started. "Cole, you got the flexibility and dexterity for this kind of training, and, Richie, bro, that power in your toss! You guys are going to do great!"

"Thank you, Dom. I think I need to throw my weight into it

more next time. I really stretched my back out on that last one," Richard replied.

"Most definitely, man. Tomorrow we'll get a proper day of training and can get our stretches in." Dominic replied.

"It's super awkward at first, man, but the more you do your stretches, the smoother your movements will be!" Justin chimed in. "Now, that monkey shit you pulled, Cole! Now that was some bullshit!" he added, pointing at Cole.

The boys all burst into laughter as Steven laid dinner out on the table. Sharing a warm meal meant the night was complete for the boys. Together, all of them shared stories and tales from their pasts as the food slowly disappeared. Steven was surprised by his son's actions. Being able to bring people together and watching them form friendships so quickly gave him hope. Hope that he could still live a normal life despite his training. With the night drawing to a close, one by one the boys left for the night, eager to return tomorrow.

Waving goodbye to his friends as their rides came and left, Dominic returned inside to his father, who was sitting in the living room. "You did really well today leading those boys," Steven began as he leaned back.

"Thank you. I learned from the best!" Dominic replied as he stood nearby.

"Your uncle was the best . . ." he replied, looking away.

The words broke the sweet moment they shared as they both realized what Steven had said. Remembering his only memory of John, Dominic desperately wanted to know what happened to him, but after years of persistently asking, he knew better than that. Steven could read his son's emotions with ease. He knew that pain in his eyes. Refusing to stay in the moment, he pressed on.

"But when I started your training, I never thought I'd ever

bring someone else into it, let alone three other people. We practically have a school now!" Steven paused to chuckle. "But I want you to know, if you're going to keep them here and you're going to place your trust in them, then you will start to lead them and teach them all *you* know. I will continue training you, and they will follow along where you're at now, but it will be your responsibility to catch them up to your level," he finished as he stood up and walked to the fireplace mantel.

"I'm fine with that. I can teach them," Dominic stated confidently as he stood at attention.

"Good. You will have to learn to rebalance yourself once more, tackling another responsibility like this," he said, looking to the shield before him.

"I'm capable of it. I won't let you or them down!"

"Good, I believe in you."

"Thank you, Dad." Dominic's smile dropped with his head as thoughts of his uncle returned. "Hey, Dad . . ."

"No, son." Steven sighed. He could tell where Dominic's thoughts had taken him. "I've told you before, I don't want to talk about what happened. I understand that you want answers, and someday you will get them, but not this day."

"But why do I have to wait? Am I not old enough to know now? It's been ten years, Dad! I'm almost sixteen. I'm old enough to know the truth!"

"No, you aren't, son, and we aren't going to fight about this anymore! If you sincerely want to train those boys, you won't bring this topic up anymore. I know I brought it up to begin with, and that was an accident, but you should know at this point that we aren't going to talk about this! Do I make myself clear?" Steven finished, wishing his son would understand.

Dominic was angry at his father, but just as quickly as the anger came, he let it go. He knew his father denied him knowledge of his uncle for a reason, even if he couldn't understand why. "Okay, I'll drop it. I'm sorry, Dad." Dominic's head dropped when he saw how upset his father had become when thinking about John.

"It's nothing to be sorry about, Dom. It just still hurts some days. I miss him just as much as you, if not more." Steven pushed himself away from the mantle as he turned to hug his son. "I was proud of you today. You showed me that you're growing into a fine young man. You know how to pick good friends, and I couldn't ask for anything more. Both of those boys come from military families, too. Richard more than Cole, with his high and tight and all, but you can see it in Cole's eyes." Steven offered his son a seat as they returned to the couch.

"Yeah, Cole told me earlier today how his dad was a drill sergeant back in the army," Dominic explained as he sat back.

"Oooh, you know he gets it bad some days," Steven remarked as he turned on the TV.

"Yeah, he mentioned that." Dominic sighed.

"That Richard guy, though. He normally that quiet?" Steven asked as he searched for a show to watch.

"I would say he's more of the observant type, though I will say he knows how to take direction! He took to my directions far better than Cole." Dominic smiled. "But I will say this: he *loves* guns! He and Justin carried on for like two hours about them without interruption." Dominic chuckled as he thought back to some of the day's events.

Carrying their conversation on through midnight, Steven listened as his son retold stories about Cole and Richard. Despite their strange home life, Steven could finally see that his son was adjusting well to high school and was finally making more friends. The two slowly let their conversation die off as they began to fall asleep. Excited for the training days to come, Dominic thought on how he would continue his friends' training as he drifted to sleep.

CHAPTER 8
BAD BLOOD

"Hey, man, how's it going? I heard you're a new student here. My name's Dominic!" he injected into a group's conversation with an extended hand.

Looking over to him, the new guy ignored him as disgust spread across his face. Seeing his friends turn the corner, he waved briefly before pursuing his previous conversation once more. Moving in closer, Dominic tapped the teen on the shoulder.

"Hey, man. Do you have an issue with me?" Dominic asked as he stepped into the teen's friend circle.

Glaring back at him, the teen inhaled sharply before turning his attention to him. "Yeah, I do, kid. You broke my brother's arm! I've been searching for your punk ass for a minute now."

Confused by the initial statement, Dominic quickly realized who the teen was talking about. The memory flashed like lightning through his mind as the scar on his arm burned. Dominic remembered the man he had nearly killed out of anger, and now, his brother stood before him, seeking revenge. Taking one step back, Dominic realized that he was standing in a bad position to get ambushed.

"Listen, you need—"

"No, you listen! I don't care what you have to say. You ruined his life, and you're going to get what's coming to you," the teen began, slowly walking closer to Dominic. "But don't worry, I'm not going to fight you here. It took a lot of work to get transferred to this school, and I'm not going to ruin that just to beat your ass here in the hallway," he whispered to Dominic as he broke his personal space. "My brother warned me of those ninja skills you got, so don't worry, me and my boys are going to get ours."

The man's threats didn't faze Dominic as he smiled and nodded. Curious, Dominic looked around and saw that both his friends and all the students around him had heard what had just been said. Taking a moment to compose himself, Dominic watched as the group of aggressors began to surround him.

"Your brother was nothing but a bully and a scumbag!"

"Watch your mouth, motherfucker, before I pop you in it!"

"He was. He's a bully and a piece of shit, too, for trying to steal from a kid! That broken arm and ass-whooping was the least he deserved!"

"Keep going, motherfucker, and we can dance!" he replied, getting into Dominic's face.

"What're you thinking? Tango or salsa?" Dominic teased, smiling at the teen.

"Jackson! What do you think you're doing?" the principal called out as he worked to separate the two students. "Now, I done told you when you got here, no fighting! Do you want to get kicked out like the last two schools?!" he added as he pushed the two boys away. "And you, Salvatore, I've never had an issue with you before, so explain what's going on here."

"Oh, well, I just came up to welcome Mr. Jackson here to the school, and apparently he didn't take too kindly to that," Dominic explained as he looked around at the crowd. He was surprised by the crowd of students that had surrounded them. Catching a glimpse of a particular set of eyes staring at him from the crowd, Dominic immediately tried to find them again. They were looking right at him, nobody else. Half listening to the principal as he scolded them, Dominic looked away after hearing a faint giggle. The soft voice felt so familiar to him, like a voice from the past. As quickly as he saw the eyes, they were gone, swallowed by the sea of students around them. Agreeing to never aggravate each other again in school, the two tightly shook hands. Shoulder-bumping Dominic on their way out, Jackson and his group walked away from the scene.

Moving over to Dominic, Justin asked, "Bro, you okay?"

"Yeah, man. You good? That was crazy how you stood up to them," Richard added.

"Man, I can't believe that asshole had a brother and sent him after you!" Cole tacked on as Dominic looked around for the eyes he had caught a glimpse of before.

"Uh, yeah, it wasn't anything too crazy . . ." Dominic looked again and again as the crowd dispersed.

"What's wrong, man?" Richard asked, seeing the confusion in his eyes.

"I'm, uh . . . I'm okay, man. I just thought I saw something. Or somebody." Dominic exhaled deeply when he realized whoever he had seen was gone. "But yeah, man, I wasn't too worried about him. I've dealt with worse fighting the three of you at once," Dominic added as he looked back to his group.

"Yeah, but now you got a target on your back. You worried at all?" Justin remarked as he watched their surroundings.

"It just means we need to change up our training methods. I'm thinking from this day forward, we start doing more group exercises. Three on one, like we did last week." Dominic looked around once more before accepting that he wasn't going to find the person with those piercing eyes. "Let's get going." He signaled for his friends to follow him as they walked to class.

"What, like, each of us taking on the other three?" Cole asked as he came up beside Dominic.

"Exactly. More specifically, you three verses me. But I want all of you to eventually do it as well," Dominic replied as he spun around to face all three of his friends. "Should be fun!" he added, firing finger guns at each of them.

"Oh really now?" Justin egged Dominic on and he started lightly throwing punches at him while he walked backward.

Laughing at their shenanigans, Cole and Richard gave their goodbyes to one another as they approached their next classroom. Following him down the hall, Justin and Dominic played back and forth until they reached their next class. Performing their own personal handshake, the two bid each other farewell as they entered their class. Despite nearly getting into a fight, Dominic couldn't help but think of those eyes.

Dominic struggled to remember the details of their face. He found himself haunted by his inability to recall the details from before. They brought such a sensation out in him, and he couldn't ignore it. Before Dominic knew what time it was, the final bell rang, and school had let out. No matter how hard he tried, Dominic couldn't shake the image of those eyes that stared at him from the crowd. The vaguely familiar glint, the intent behind them, and the intoxicating desire within—they encapsulated his thoughts. From his training to dinner and bed, they pulled at him. Sinking into his sleep, Dominic slowly found peace from the thoughts, and as his conscience slipped into his dreams, he remembered those eyes.

CHAPTER 9

ACT III: HATE

Year: 2004

Location: Orange County, entering Los Angeles

Riding down an empty highway, John, King, and their driver, Gabriella Espinoza, drove in a two-vehicle caravan into the outskirts of Los Angeles. John, dressed in all black, hung his family sword across his back. He rode on his recently acquired blacked-out 1942 WLA Harley. Riding behind in a nondescript black van, King directed Gabriella on their path while working on the radio connection for the team.

Hearing the familiar clicks of the radio signal connecting, John reached over and adjusted the settings for his earpiece while he sped down the road. Navigating the twists and turns, John sharpened his mind and thought of Zähd and Dominic. Reaching into his coat pocket, John retrieved a small photograph. Looking to the recent photo of Dominic, John reaffirmed his resolve.

I'll push this all the way for you, Dom. All the way to . . . Sha'are Mavet . . .

Feeling a tear fly from his eye, John put the picture back into his pocket. Scratching at his mustache, he worked to compose himself before reaching for his receiver. "Hey, King, I want to thank you again for the bike. She drives real smooth!" John called out into his mic as the sound of his Harley roared out.

"Well, don't fuck it up! I may not be able to ride no more, but I know where you're going. You'll need it. Hey, looks like you're just a few miles away from the warehouse now," King replied over the radio.

"Hey, boss, when we arrive, we're going to stay about a block away, but we'll be in complete radio contact unless you say otherwise," Gabriella called out over the radio after King.

"Sounds good, Gabby. Michael, give me a sitrep. Whaddya see?" John replied as he revved the motorcycle's engine.

"Birdhouse is empty, sir. Papa Bird hasn't come home yet," he responded, observing the warehouse from a hidden vantage point in the shadows of a neighboring building.

"Good, if at any point this mission goes tits up, all of you need to run. I'm not joking, either. Zähd is very dangerous and should not be taken lightly." John's grip on the handlebars tightened as he warned his team.

"Oh, believe me, boss, I'm not sticking around here if they see me. You need to see the hardware these guys are packing and moving. This is some serious operation they got going on," Michael responded, looking through his binoculars at the mercenaries loading guns, ammunition, and supplies into shipping crates.

"Any sight of the missing people?"

"No, but there's shipping containers all over the yard here. They could be in any one of them. But if this guy's as bad as you say he is, then you need to know that he has some serious shit here."

"What kind of serious shit are we talking about?"

"I'm talking tanks, anti-aircraft guns, artillery, the works. The guy looks like he's stockpiling for war!" Michael listed off while scanning around further. "Wa . . . Wait, this Zähd guy, what does he look like?" Michael queried as he observed a mysterious figure.

"I've never seen him before. No one has in years," John sullenly replied.

"Well, I'm looking at this really scarred-up, bald-headed, old-looking character!" he replied. "Oh yeah, that's gotta be him. Fuck . . . I wouldn't want to mess with him . . ." Michael felt his resolve tested at the sight of the menacing figure.

"Well, stay out of sight and report back when you see anything new. But keep an eye on him. Let me know if it looks like he's about to leave," John replied, calming his teammate. "If you can see him, then you can understand why I warned you all before signing on. This is something you could not come back from if things go south. So please, use caution and be smart." John ended communications as he pushed the motorcycle to its limits.

Back in the van, King adjusted himself in his wheelchair as he looked over the information they had gathered over the past three years. Scouring through all the files in front of him and on his laptop, he revised his backup plans for the team. King felt sympathy for the new recruits. It had been many years since King had any dealings with the supernatural, and he had planned to keep it that way.

Glancing over to Gabby, King truly felt for her. "Hey, Gabby, I got to ask, have you ever seen combat before?"

"Once or twice, but not in the way you may think. Growing up, you see a lot of bad shit when you live the shit. But I guess when you finally make something of yourself boosting cars and being a driver, you don't get to run away from the violence. It just comes to you in a new way."

"I know that. I guess what I'm saying is, do you know how to defend yourself if things get ugly?"

"Of course I do! What else is a girl supposed to do when she's raised up with nothing but older brothers?" She looked back, chuckling at King.

"Good." King chuckled with her before looking back to his paperwork.

Glancing back at the files out of the corner of her eye, then back to King, Gabby could see the concern on his face. "You're really worried about this mission, aren't you?" she asked while maintaining distance with John.

"Like you wouldn't believe." King was exhausted from all his work. "You'd think after all the missions he and I have done without proper intel that we would've learned to take more time for recon. Or at least I'd learn to say no to the motherfucker," King finished, throwing his hands in the air.

"You've known John for a long time?"

"Oh yeah! You didn't know . . . I forgot you haven't known him all that long. I've known that crazy son of a bitch since I joined the army back in '59. He was crazier back then when he was younger, but still, when he gets his mind set on something, you can't stop him. Trust me, I've seen it," King regaled as he sat back in his chair.

"Is this mission really *that* dangerous?" Gabby asked.

"If John Salvatore is on the mission, then *it's* a dangerous mission," he replied, unfazed by the notion.

"Like, how dangerous?" she pressed.

"Want me to be blunt?" King asked, looking to Gabby, who nodded. "He's trying to save the world. Literally. This guy we're going after, Zähd, is supposed to be some kind of crazy-powerful warrior from Hell. Motherfucker's reputation follows him so much that it has *John* hellbent on stopping him. No pun intended," King explained as he looked to John ahead of them.

"So, actual Hell? Like, fire and brimstone Hell?" she asked, finding his words difficult to believe. "I thought all that supernatural talk was a little crazy to believe when John mentioned it before, but I didn't know what to think of it all."

"Oh, it's real! It's all real! I don't know about the brimstone, though. I never asked John what Hell looked like when I found out, but I've seen some crazy shit fighting alongside that man, and I guess . . . all that *crazy shit* we've been through together is why I'm still here, helping his crazy ass out right now. He'd do it all alone if he could, and I can't have him doing that." King's voice sank as he rubbed the scars on his legs. "But trust John when he tells you to do something. He'll help keep you alive." King cleared his throat before returning to his paperwork.

Gabriella felt the truth in his words. Looking to John in front of her, she could only begin to wonder how much he had seen.

Seeing his destination, John pulled off to the side of the road about a block from the gated warehouse. With no time to infiltrate at night, John refused to give Zähd any further lead. Hugging the shadows of the abandoned buildings around him, he advanced further. Through the use of clicks over the radio, Michael periodically gave John signals that he was safe to move while looking toward his position. The high walls of the warehouse were too steep to rappel. Still, John scanned tirelessly for a way to get in. At a corner's edge, John caught the voices of two armed guards posted outside of a door. Nearly avoiding detection, John retreated and listened as one of the guards remarked on his movement.

With two knives drawn, John hugged the shadows and stared at the clueless guards as they scanned their surroundings. Holding his breath, John remained still as the guards stepped inches from him, unaware of the dangers around them. As the guards turned and walked away, John silently stepped out from the shadows and quickly dispatched the two men as he ran up behind them.

Dragging their bodies away from the scene, he searched them for any useful information. Throwing one of their rifles over his shoulder, John shoved his spare mags in his pockets while continuing his search. John's ears caught the sound of rustling and found a folded up sheet hidden under one of the guards' vests. It was a copy of the warehouse and its layout. Memorizing the layout of the facility, John charted his way to the main office, hoping to find the missing people. With nothing of value left on the guards, John signaled with his radio for a response from Michael.

Receiving an all-clear from Michael, John slipped through the door and into the warehouse. Michael hadn't exaggerated the amount of firepower Zähd had amassed. Shipping crates filled and labeled with ammunition, small arms, and the works. John knew he couldn't let Zähd take any more than he already had. Making his first stop at a munitions shed, John avoided detection as he stole plastic explosives and a detonator from a crate, shoving them into a pouch hanging from his leg. While leaving the shed, he cautiously waited as two guards walked by, unaware of his presence. Taking note of the heavy support weapons many of the soldiers were carrying, John knew if a firefight broke out, things could get very ugly.

Following his way around the base, John found himself eliminating three more soldiers as he crept closer to the main office. Peering through the window, he checked for any guards. With the coast clear, John quietly opened a back window to the main office and climbed inside. He remained on guard as weariness set in. There was a shocking lack of personnel inside the facility, and everything was beginning to feel like a setup. Pushing away his thoughts, John forced himself to remain focused as he began scouring through the paperwork for a manifest. Attempting to leave the room untouched as he searched around, John found it increasingly difficult the further he sifted through all the paperwork. Believing he had found the manifest in question, John quickly ducked behind a file cabinet at the sound of the doorknob turning.

John held his breath as he listened to two guards discussing the differences between their chosen rifles. "You don't get it, man. They fixed those issues with the newest models. That jamming issue is a thing of the past!"

"Yeah, man, I don't know. I'm just not convinced, ya know?" the other guard replied.

"I feel ya, but let's grab that report—" The first guard paused as he looked to the cracked-open window.

Fuck!

John could tell by the sudden pause in the man's voice that something was wrong. Despite his best efforts, John had left a breadcrumb trail to follow. Hearing the charging handles loading a round into their rifles, John quietly hunkered down as he attempted to remain hidden.

Looking to the tall file cabinets at the back of the room, he signaled for his partner to raise his rifle.

"We know you're in here! You can come out with your hands up and we won't shoot you. If you don't comply, we will fire upon you!" the first guard called out as he rattled his weapon.

Sighing and frustrated that he'd been caught, John stepped out with his hands raised, ready to play the guards. "Yeah . . . I'm sorry, boys. I didn't mean for you to find me." John's apathy took the guards aback as they saw the heavily armed old man.

"Stay right there, old man! Don't move a muscle!" the second guard shakily barked out.

Happily agreeing, John took a step back. "My bad. Didn't mean to scare you. Oh hey, son, you left your safety on." John pointed while keeping his hands up.

Distracting the guards long enough to look down, John, in the smoothest of motions, pulled his knives out and flung them into the eyes of both soldiers. "I'll never get to do *that* again," John remarked while chuckling to himself.

Walking past the bodies to grab the knives, John wiped them clean of blood before grabbing the manifest. Quickly, he searched through it, looking for any mention of human cargo. Alas, no answers. John shook his head as he ran through the list again and again. With an exasperated sigh, he was determined to find answers.

C'mon, I know they got to be here.

Finding a repeated pattern of some particularly heavy cargo that would be too light for weaponry or military hardware, John searched for the location of the crates.

Looking over the cooling bodies on the ground, John knew his body trail was going to catch up to him soon. It hadn't been his first time, but the point of no return had come and passed. His cover would soon be blown. Tearing the room apart in search of answers, John found their location as another guard entered the room.

"What the fuc—" the guard began before John pivoted and threw his knife once more, into the mouth of the guard.

John watched in amazement as the body fell to the floor. "Okay, maybe it can happen again," John surprisingly remarked as he walked over and started dragging the body to the others.

Pulling the knife out, John memorized the crate numbers as he ran back to lock the door to the room. Back through the window he had entered from, John crept out and continued along his path. Cautiously, he moved around the base, planting his explosives on vehicles and mounted weapons. Feeling a cold chill emanating from his brand, John knew Zähd was close by.

Closer and closer, John inched further as he felt the presence of his adversary around him. Feeling the icy chills run down his spine, John knew he was in the dragon's lair. Even though he could not pinpoint his exact location, John snaked around the tight corners as the sounds of a group phone call could be heard.

"Ah, well, I expect your full cooperation like the rest, Senator. Am I clear?" a commanding voice called out. "Good, make sure your subordinates don't fail you. Your colleagues listen well to their orders. Thus far, you are the only one I've had to reprimand. This won't become a habit," he continued while his heels knocked against the hardwood floor. "Sounds good. I like that kind of enthusiasm! Having an attitude like that is how you'll have a good place for yourself in the New Kingdom. Say hello to the missus for me! Oh, and remember, Senator, do not fail me again," he concluded before ending the call.

Shit! He has senators under his control?! How far does his power reach?

Hanging the phone up, Zähd looked to the wall beside him as a presence revealed itself to him. Slowly he cocked his head as he listened carefully. As he stroked his gray goatee, his vertically slit eyes widened to the presence of energy. He could feel real power behind the wall. He hadn't felt such an immense power in so long. It teased him. The sounds of war drums echoed in his ears as he pivoted toward it. Nostalgia painted itself across his grin. Taking a step toward the wall, Zähd found himself distracted by the sound of the door opening.

"What?" Zähd barked at the soldier as he turned his glowing gaze to him.

"Sir! The cargo is ready for final transport." The soldier shook while he stood at attention.

Realizing that this wouldn't be his last opportunity to find out who had snuck into his base, Zähd signaled for the soldier to lead the way. Leaving the building, Zähd remained looking forward, aware his intruder was watching him. The time would come again for him to finally see the face of his adversary.

John released his breath after hearing the door close. Never had he been in the presence of someone so powerful. The closer Zähd drew to him, the more his energy reverberated in response to John's. With his heart racing, John continued to search for the missing people, checking each shipping crate around the base. The distinctive cracking of lightning followed by the rushing vacuum of air caught John's attention. His ears had perked up to the familiar sound of a portal opening. Quickly running toward the sound, John witnessed Zähd directing soldiers and workers as they wheeled crates into a portal to Hell.

John forced himself not to move. This had been enough to break cover for him, but he still needed to find the missing people first. Making a split-second decision, John allowed their actions to continue briefly while he redoubled his efforts to find the crates he was looking for. Catching glances of the various things they shuffled off into the portal, John felt the constant pressure of Zähd's presence. Ignoring the irritating itch that his presence caused, John pressed on.

Carrying two sheathed claymores and body straps in hand, a soldier ran up to Zähd as he directed the caravan of supplies. "Your gear, sir!"

"Thank you, soldier. Please prepare our guests for transport." Zähd thanked the soldier while he held the rig up and wrapped it around his waist.

Resting his swords on either side of his hips, Zähd smiled as he patiently waited. The game of cat and mouse had begun, and as the two men played, the tension lingered in the air. Realizing he had searched every crate, John frantically looked to the portal to see the people he was searching for.

Chained at their ankles, wrists, and necks, the various prisoners shuffled in a line toward the vortex before them. Pushing anyone who hesitated through the portal, Zähd wasted no time as he continued with his plans. Inching closer without being spotted, John panicked as he tried to come up with a plan. With his explosives too close to cause harm to the hostages, John pulled his sword out and resigned himself to the fact that he was about to make a really bad decision. Gripping the stolen rifle in his armpit, John readied himself to run out, gun in one hand, sword in the other.

John opened fire on a crowd of soldiers as he jumped from cover. Grabbing all the attention of the surrounding area, the other guards scrambled to retaliate. Activating his powers to the first stage, John sped around the open perimeter, firing at the guards around the hostages. Watching patiently as his assailant laid waste to his guards, Zähd allowed his smile to slowly grow as the bodies piled up.

Quickly dropping bodies, John turned his attention to Zähd. Rounding a corner, John leaped into the air and rained lead down on him. Avoiding the gunfire, Zähd observed each move his opponent made, learning the best tactic to end their fight. Seeing the shimmering edge of a sword barreling toward him, Zähd gracefully leaned his head back, avoiding the attack. Taking in the energy his opponent emitted, Zähd knew he was in the presence of the royal bloodline. Zähd's eyes widened upon that realization. He had waited so long for another chance to end the bloodline, and now it was in front of him. Hearing the drumming of approaching footsteps, Zähd turned to find that his reinforcements had arrived.

"Capture that man alive! He's mine!" Zähd commanded as he turned to his soldiers.

Jumping from cover to cover while he avoided gunfire, John realized he was wasting time while Zähd ferried the prisoners along.

"Boss, what do you want us to do? There's a lot of fighting going on down there!" Michael shouted over the comms as he watched from afar.

"Stand down. I got this! I don't want you guys getting hurt out here!"

"John, don't be bullshitting us!" King chimed in.

"Tony . . . I got this," John said as he threw the gun aside.

Calling upon the energy within him, John swung his sword down, creating a portal he could jump through. Reemerging through another portal, John flew up from the ground and landed next to the prisoners. Slashing through their chains, John warned the prisoners to run. Turning to break another person free, he barely found the space to move as the glint of a blade crossed in front of him. Feeling the skin on his cheek open, John jumped away and into another portal. Feeling the blood run down his face, John realized that no blade had touched him. Instead, the wound was caused by the wind from Zähd's attack. Moving a small amount of his energy to the wound, John healed himself.

Fuck! If he can cut with just the wind, then he's even more pow-erful than I thought!

Catching his breath, John peered around a corner, realizing his element of surprise was gone. Wiping the leftover blood from his face, he stepped out from behind cover to face his enemy. Looking to the demon he had chased for six years, John realized that the legends surrounding Zähd were true.

He stood open and confident. Zähd knew where he stood among everyone around him, and he looked down at them all and smiled. Dressed in business casual with only his leather rig to carry his claymores, Zähd stepped between the prisoners to meet his ad-versary. Rolling up his sleeves with one hand, Zähd twirled the massive sword with ease while sizing up his opponent. Signaling for a soldier, Zähd mouthed orders into his ear before having him run away.

"I'm afraid I can't let you take those prisoners, Zähd!" John called out.

"Why hello! I don't think we've been properly acquainted? You seem to know who I am, and while I know *what* you are, I'm afraid I don't know *who* you are," Zähd replied.

"I'm the man here to stop you!" John sinisterly said before jet-ting toward Zähd, swinging at his head.

Missing his mark, John grabbed a prisoner before creating a portal and teleporting her away. Irritated by the intruder's actions, Zähd met his speed as he kicked John in the side, sending him away. Slamming into a crate, John vomited blood as he felt the damage to his body. Focusing his energy once more, he healed his broken ribs and arm before stumbling to his feet. Groaning at that all-too-familiar pain of being thrown against something, John pre-pared to strike once more.

"Now, all I'm asking for is a name. I'm certain a gentleman such as yourself is not above such pleasantries!" Zähd called out as another prisoner was forced through the portal.

"Salvatore, John Salvatore. I'll be your opponent today!" John stood his ground, showing his blade to Zähd.

Zähd's eyes lit up at the sight of its angled steel. Though the steel had been reforged into its current shape since he last saw it, the power emanating from it was palpable. A once lost chance to seize its power returned itself to him. Both his desires and the violence had escalated. "The last names can change, but the story stays the same. Alright, *John Salvatore*, I'll see your wager! Show me what you're made of!" Zähd bellowed out, awaiting John's next move.

Manipulating the wind around him, John propelled himself forward, sword at the ready. Crossing their blades, the two danced around each other, neither even nicking the other's skin. Pointing to a guard to finish transporting the prisoners, Zähd guided the two away from his quarry. Each swordsman was enthralled by the other's skills and ability at handling a sword. John, taken aback by his opponent's skill, evaded the violent gusts of wind that followed each of Zähd's strikes. The precision with which he controlled the air around them was masterful. Never had he faced someone so well-versed in elemental manipulation. Despite the difficulties he was faced with, John held the charging warrior at bay while also teleporting prisoners away.

Back at the van, King impatiently waited for word back from John. Hearing the echoes of gunfire and crates being thrown about, King grew more and more worried. Reminded of how he had lost his legs, King rubbed his scars repeatedly while looking in the direction of the gunfire. Startled by the sound of a portal opening near their van, King and Gabriella grabbed their guns, ready to meet what had just arrived. Jumping out, gun at the ready, Gabriella was met with Michael and a prisoner being thrown from a portal.

"John's out there fighting Zähd. King, what the hell are we going to do?" Michael called out while helping the prisoner stand to her feet.

Rolling out the back of his van, King grabbed his combat vest. "You and Gabriella stay here and help any of the prisoners that John teleports back!" King ordered as two more portals opened, one after another.

"What about you, King? What the hell do you think you're doing?" Michael questioned as he helped another of the prisoners out.

"I'm going to help save my friend!" he replied, grabbing an AR-15 with an under-barrel shotgun attached.

"King, you can't. Look at you, man. You don't have any legs!" Michael protested as Gabriella helped the prisoners John had transported.

"That's not stopping John," King replied, charging the rifle and wheeling himself toward the fighting.

"King! You're going to get yourself killed!"

Adjusting his chest plate, King rested his rifle in his lap before grabbing his backpack off the back of his wheelchair. Pulling out a custom collapsible ceramic shield, King attached it to the front of his wheelchair. With his lower half covered, King wheeled himself to the hilltop overlooking the warehouse John was in. Using his momentum, King propelled himself downhill and toward the base.

Down the hill he raced. With a rifle in one hand, King controlled his speed with the other. As he reached the bottom of the hill, King slammed on his brakes and sent himself into a drift as he made contact. Hearing the screeching wheels, four soldiers turned to see an armored wheelchair barreling toward them. Confused, the soldiers found themselves outgunned as a bloodcurdling war cry echoed out from the rolling death chair. The soldiers scrambled as their squad-mates fell to the raining lead. Cutting the wheels, King turned to face the few who had hidden behind a concrete barrier. Blasting them with his Masterkey shotgun, King wheeled himself forward. Shocked by the deadly speed of the old man, the last of the running soldiers looked back in horror before being gunned down.

Pushing himself, King refused to let his old friend throw himself in harm's way again. "Grrr! I'm coming, John!" King yelled out as he turned another corner.

While the two fought, many prisoners sought shelter from the insane fight as John managed to break their chains. Though as quickly as they found shelter, John would warp them out of the area to safety. Wearing himself down from so many jumps, John spaced them out as he held off attacks from both Zähd and his remaining forces. Saving nearly every prisoner, John found himself out-flanked as Zähd, in a flash, appeared beside a prisoner. Impressed by the seasoned fighter, Zähd knocked John away by lifting and physically hitting him with the prisoner.

Flying away from them both, John refused to allow himself to be slapped around. Turning around, he grabbed hold of the concrete as he bounced off the ground. His fingers tore through the concrete as he buckled down. Glaring up at Zähd, John bared his teeth, hungry for blood.

Dropping the dead prisoner, Zähd stepped forward just as John propelled himself forward. Zähd matched his speed before John reached him, and the two ricocheted off each other's punches, sending them in opposite directions. Tearing through the side of a shipping crate, John terrified a cowering prisoner as he landed right next to her.

A deep, dull pain tortured John as he groaned out to the mangled shrapnel lodged in his guts. Shrieking out in horror at the disturbing sight, the woman immediately became more fearful as she locked eyes with John's glowing eye. "Hey, hey, hey, calm down! I—" John paused as he coughed up blood. "I'm on your side. I'm here to save you!" he finished before ripping the metal out.

Nearly passing out, John forced his powers and himself as he quickly made a portal for her to jump through. A cold chill brought John to his knee as the portal closed. He had lost a lot of blood. Focusing all his effort into his guts, John strained to heal his grievous wounds. "Come on. Close, you motherfucker!" John shouted as he pressed his hand against the sealing hole.

The second-to-last prisoner had been teleported away, and while his brief reprieve had been welcomed, it was shortly ended. Bending the wind to his will, Zähd sliced through the shipping crates John had hidden in just as he managed to close his wounds. Frantically, John dodged the brutal gust of wind as the metal structure around him caved to its will. Searching for the last prisoner, John, thinking he had evaded Zähd, rounded a corner to the full force of Zähd's foot. Very few times had John ever felt such strength in one punch or kick, but as Zähd's heel met his face, it proved to be the strongest. Breaking the sound barrier upon contact, John tore through three shipping crates before digging into concrete in front of the portal. Blood poured from his head and body as he tried to make sense of what had just happened. When he reached out, his hand slipped on the blood pooling on the concrete around him. Despite feeling his limits being pushed, John refused to use his trump card now. Looking down at his mangled prosthetic leg, John propped himself up so he could remove it. Drawing on his powers more, John pushed the limits of his ability to heal himself. Crawling forward, he shakily grabbed hold of the rubble around him, bringing himself up on one knee.

Grabbing the last male prisoner by the hair, Zähd directed him past John. "I have to give it to you, John Salvatore, you are quite the impressive fighter! Another three hundred years and you might have a solid chance at beating me!" Zähd congratulated John while he continued to try and stand. "Shame, though. Were my mission not so important, I would stay and finally put an end to your bloodline. But I'll let you live today," he continued, stopping at the sword at his feet. "Well, would you look what fell out of your hands?" Zähd's eyes lit up as he reached down with his transplanted four-fingered hand.

Gunfire rang out as a round smacked Zähd in the hand. Giving John enough time to sign his personal mudras, John reached out and pulled the sword back to him. Thankful for King's intervention, John held the sword close as he rolled away to recover. Looking to the mystery intruder, Zähd was met with King, who was about to fire at him again.

"I don't give a goddamn how tough you are. Eat shit!" King cried out as he emptied a fifty-round magazine into Zähd.

"King! No, run away!" John shouted as he struggled to push himself further.

Activating his curse powers, Zähd withstood every steel-cored round that pierced his body. Switching to his Masterkey, King fired every shell into the still-advancing behemoth. While the tenacity was admired, the interruption was disrespectful to Zähd as he snatched King up by the throat. Reaching for his sidearm, King fought on as Zähd ripped it from his hands in disgust.

"For a man with no legs, you sure fight like you're willing to die for this!" Impressed by the man's fortitude, Zähd held him high in the air.

"Let him go!" John cried out as he pushed his powers even further, causing his lower leg and finger to regrow as skinless, bone-armored extremities.

"So you *can* still fight? I'm impressed, but, *John Salvatore*, I want you to know that this changes nothing." Zähd watched as John's eyepatch fell to the ground.

The eye was nearly shut, but the blue glow peeking out was unmistakable. Zähd finally put the pieces together. "So you have *the* sight, I see. That won't change a thing, either. You can't stop what's to come, though this does make things more interesting now!" Zähd smiled while John covered his eye with his hand. "Regardless of what you've seen or what you think you know, your appearance here today has changed nothing, and once my mission here is done, I will finish what I started so many years ago by hunting down your family and killing you once and for all." Zähd's cold contempt chilled them to the bone.

"Not if I have anything to say about it!" John yelled, raising his sword to him.

"Funny . . . your ancestors told me the same thing—right before I killed them. Your family can change their last name, travel continents away, but I'll find you every time. Your bloodline will end with you, Salvatore." Zähd raised his sword.

"You may have bested my ancestors, but you won't best me!" John cried out, taking a step forward.

"Ah, ah, ah, not another step!" Zähd threatened him by putting his sword's edge to King's throat. "Talk all you want, fight all you want, but I will kill you one day. This is just the beginning, John

Salvatore—the beginning of the end," Zähd warned him before throwing King into the portal.

The two reached out for one another as King slipped through the rift. Reaching out for him, John felt his body thrown away by a heavy blunt force. Not watching his opponent, John slammed once more into one of the few remaining intact crates. Looking down to one of Zähd's claymores impaled in his chest, John struggled to remove it. Pinned by the force of his impact alone, John strained to remove the oversized stake in his chest. Reaching further into his powers, John bent the steel to his will as he inched it out. Dislodged from the crates, he fell to his hands and knees as his curse powers healed his wounds.

"Nooo!" John cried out while watching Zähd pass through the portal with the last prisoner in hand.

Weakened, he dropped his outstretched hand as the portal slammed shut. Breathing heavily, he dragged himself closer toward where the portal once was. With his wound healing, John struggled to lift himself up, beaten down by his fight. Hearing police sirens in the distance, followed by the van crashing through the gate, John struggled to remain conscious as he stopped crawling forward.

"Boss! Boss, come on, man. The police are almost here!" Michael yelled out as he ran over and checked John's vitals.

Dragging John to the van, Michael noticed that King's wheelchair had been thrown aside. "Where's King? Where's he at, John?"

"He took him. Zähd took him." John struggled to get the words out. Reaching to his sheath, John made sure his sword was still with him before grabbing the detonator from his rig. "I've set explosives around the warehouse. Leave no trace we were here." John managed to get the words out before passing out.

Laying John on the floor of the van, Michael jumped into the back as the sirens drew closer. "Drive, Gabby!"

Crawling into the passenger seat, Michael counted down in his head as they drove away. Reaching a safe distance, Michael wasted no time detonating the explosives behind them. The rupturing shock wave rocked the van's frame as they sped away. Slamming his hands against the dash, Michael was infuriated by the turn of events. Frantically wiping sweat and John's blood from his face, he forced himself to focus on what he could do at the moment. Looking back at John, he rushed back to tend to his wounds.

Stabilizing his condition, Michael was met with a shock as John awoke, coughing up blood. Anger boiled inside of him. He lacked the strength and preparation to stop Zähd, and it ate him up inside. Looking back, John knew he hadn't given his all. He was rusty and out of touch, but most importantly, he feared the power Zähd possessed. With his anger fading as Michael helped him sit upright, failure and regret took its place. He had failed his best friend and allowed him to be captured once again. The van's metal cried out as John slammed his fist into the floor. John hadn't held onto his promise to Abraham. He didn't give it his all.

"Find him. We crippled his supply of bodies, but he's going to need more! He's going to do this again. Find that pattern. Find the clues. I don't care how. He almost has what he needs now, and he has King, too!" John exclaimed before slipping on his own blood while trying to stand.

"Hey, wait. Take it easy, John! We'll find him. I promise you! Okay? We'll find him!" Michael meant the promise he made, looking to Gabriella for support.

Looking down, John had forgotten that his prosthetic had been destroyed. He remembered the horrible days he and King had

endured back in Vietnam. He knew what people could do to prisoners of war, and he could only imagine what Zähd had planned
for him. Feeling inside his pockets, John searched for the picture
of his nephew. Sighing in relief, John glanced down at the gleam-
ing smile of the young boy. He knew in his mind what was required
of him. If John was to save his friend, save the world, and save
his nephew from sharing the curse of his family, he would have to
use *all* of his powers. Forsaking his distaste for his powers, John
motioned for Michael to return to the front of the van. Meditating
briefly, John found the strength to sit up on his own.

I won't let you suffer the life I have, Dominic. I promise.

Channeling his energy once more, John peered out into the
distance, searching for answers. As he searched for clues to stopping Zähd, Natural Energy poured into him. The more he sat and
meditated, the more Natural Energy seeped into and closed what
wounds hadn't yet been healed. John could feel his ancestral power
growing within him. Following the thread of future events he was
searching for, John reached out with his mind and began pulling
himself toward them.

Flashing in his line of sight, the images he had seen from his
last vision hadn't changed. Nothing he had done in his battle with
Zähd had changed the course of events. Fighting the urge to cry,
John looked even further. He needed more answers. He needed
the secret to defeating Zähd. With each image that flashed in front
of his eye, all he could see was his nephew continuing the cycle.
Hate built up within his chest as the urge to cry grew too strong.
He refused to allow his nephew to suffer the same fate as him. The
cycle had to be broken, the fighting had to end, and it would end
with him. Pulling away from the distant future, John slowly broke
his connection with his visions. Wiping the tears from his face, he

refused to accept the truth before him. He was ready to give everything to change the future, to save his nephew from his life. No
quarter could be given now. Time was running short to save his
best friend and nephew. Stopping Zähd was all that mattered now.

CHAPTER 10
FROM BLUE EYES TO SUMMER SKIES

F inally turning sixteen near the end of his sophomore year, Dominic was determined to be allowed to drive his uncle's old 1960 Ironhead Sportster. It would take him the rest of the semester and the first half of his summer break before he would convince his father that he was responsible enough for the bike. Having the bike in his name brought Dominic closer to the memory of his uncle. The bike had sat in the garage for years, one of the many mementos Steven could never part with. The wear and tear on the leather seat, told a story, one Dominic could only dream of as he ran his fingers across it. From the scratches to the bullet holes and patch jobs throughout, the old beast still ran well. Sitting back on the bike, Dominic respected the power within it as he cranked the engine over for the first time.

With the bike now in his possession, Dominic would ride it everywhere. From the beaches of Maryland to his favorite childhood diner, there wasn't anywhere he and his friends wouldn't travel to. With the boys now mobile, their training would go with them. From sparring matches at night on secluded beaches to forested areas they'd find off the highway or country roads, Dominic would take the guys to new areas to test his friends and their ability to adapt to their surroundings. No matter where they traveled, no matter the distance, they always traveled together. They were brothers to one another, and nothing would break their bond.

During one late July afternoon, the boys had planned to meet at the diner, ready to eat after a long day of working out. Arriving late to the diner, Dominic returned a wave to Justin after removing his helmet. Fixing his helmet hair, Dominic swung out his kick-stand before dismounting. With his bike resting properly, Dominic turned and locked eyes with the table his friends were sitting at. Not seeing the young woman in front of him as he crossed the parking lot, Dominic bumped into her with full force.

"Oof!" Dominic exclaimed as the young redhead bounced off him. "Oh my god! I'm so sorry!" he quickly apologized.

Noticing that he had knocked her purse out of her hand, Dominic quickly dropped down to help gather her things. "I didn't see you there." Looking up, Dominic froze when he saw the most beautiful baby-blue eyes he had ever seen. His heart fluttered as his lips quivered and he tried to come up with more to say.

When she realized who was in front of her and looked into his bright olive eyes, the shy teen's ivory cheeks flustered and red-dened. "No need!" she replied in a high-pitched voice while trying to look away. "I should've been paying more attention to my sur-roundings!" she continued before rushing down to her fallen purse.

Glancing to his friends, who had noticed and began pointing at him, Dominic quickly returned his attention to her. "Here, let me get that for you!" Dominic offered his help as he grabbed her hairbrush for her. "My name's Dominic. It's nice to meet you." His heart raced when he looked into the girl's eyes. She left him nearly speechless.

"My name's Seras. Seras Lion.[2] It's nice to meet you, too, Dominic," Seras replied, trying to hide that she was biting her lip.

Reaching out at the same time, Dominic and Seras felt their hands touch. Brushing her soft skin, Dominic noticed that his surprise was outmatched by Seras's reaction. Quickly pulling her hand away, Seras watched as Dominic reached down and grabbed a pen for her. Offering the pen, Dominic tried to break the tension.

"So are you from around here, *Seras Lion*?" Dominic curiously asked while standing back up.

"I actually go to Roosevelt High School, same as you. We actually share third period together," Seras revealed, adjusting her hair to reveal a conch piercing in her ear before looking back up at him.

Getting a closer look at her baby-blue eyes, Dominic quickly blushed and looked away. "Oh really? That's crazy. I had no idea . . ." Dominic chuckled lightheartedly while scratching the back of his head. "So what brings you out this way?" Dominic asked while looking over to his friends as they laughed and pointed.

"The food. I don't eat it often, but it's where my dad used to bring me when I was a kid. Plus, the classic burger just can't be beat," Seras explained with a smile before looking over to Dominic's friends.

"Oh . . ." Dominic's voice fell short, and he felt a little awkward for asking.

"Oh, no, no! My dad's not dead!" Seras chuckled, embarrassed her words sounded worse than intended. "My dad is very busy with work! Both him and my mom are doctors and constantly work. I come here by myself, though. It's kinda been a special place to me," she continued as she swayed back and forth while holding her purse in both hands. "Those your friends?" she asked.

---

2 Seras Lion is pronounced "Ser-us *Lee-on*."

"Oh, them?" Dominic chuckled. "Yeah, those are my friends," he admitted bashfully.

"To be honest?" She paused. "I kinda already knew that. I see you guys hanging around the annex between classes all the time." Seras smirked as she played with one of her curls.

"Ha, that's fair! We're a pretty noticeable crowd when we get rowdy in the halls!" Dominic chuckled.

"Yeah, so what're you guys doing today?" she asked while she followed Dominic toward the diner.

"Oh, nothing." Dominic stopped as he bumped into a second person.

"Are you fucking blind, dude?!" Jackson yelled out, not realizing who had bumped into him.

"I guess so!" Dominic blurted out, surprised that he had run into another person.

Looking at one another, the two boys quickly swelled with pride. It had been almost two months since Dominic had to listen to Jackson's empty threats and bullying. Both of the young men's blood boiled, and they were ready to attack one another at any moment. Pushing himself away from Dominic, Jackson looked him up and down in disgust, then looked to Seras. Offended by the ugly stare, she gave him one back before noticing the floozy teen in heels running to his rescue.

"What's wrong, sweetie? Are they harassing you, baby?" she snobbishly cried out, trying to get in front of him.

"Nothing, baby. I got this!" Jackson boasted, moving her aside.

Seras looked to his girlfriend with one eyebrow raised, waiting for her to say something. Dominic, not moving from his spot, gave a slight hand gesture to his friends, telling them to hold on.

"I have no beef with you, Jackson. We haven't seen each other in almost two months. You and I—"

"Shut up, Salvatore! You're lucky I'm taking my girl on a date right now or I'd beat your ass right here in front of God, ya friends, ya ugly ass girl—"

"She had nothing to do with this. You do not involve her." Dominic's tone commanded respect. His posture was calm, but he was ready to strike.

"Oh yeah? And who are you to say what I can and can't say about some ugly little bitch, hmm?" Jackson spoke softly in Dominic's face.

Leaning forward with a smile, Dominic whispered into his ear, "How about me breaking your arm and jaw for disrespecting her? How's that sound?"

Maintaining his bravado, Jackson tried his best to ignore the cold chill that snaked down his spine. "You're lucky, Salvatore. I'm really trying to have a good day with my girl. I'll let you have that one, but next time I see you out in public, you're mine, ya hear?" he threatened Dominic before walking away with his girlfriend in tow.

"Piece of shit," Dominic cursed under his breath. "I'm sorry he spoke so poorly to you." he apologized after turning back to face Seras.

"Oh, no need. I've never had anybody stand up for me like that before. That was really sweet of you!" Seras smiled before blushing again.

"Well, I wasn't about to just let him talk about you like that. That was uncalled for!" He shook his head in dissatisfaction.

As he looked over to his friends signaling for him to join them, an idea came to mind. "So, hey, would you like to come eat with us? I'd really like to get to know more about you!" Dominic blushed while trying to hold back his big grin.

"Umm, sure!" Seras excitedly accepted while biting her lower lip. "Sounds like fun!" she added before walking closely behind him and toward his friends.

"Hey, guys! This is Seras! I just bumped into her *and* came to find out we all go to the same school together!" Dominic announced while introducing Seras.

"We know!" Justin chuckled.

"Yeah, we share third period with her, Dom!" Richard added before catching up with Justin's laughter.

Shocked, he threw his arms back. "Am I the only one who didn't know?!" he shouted.

"I'm guessing so," Seras exclaimed as she popped out from behind him, causing the boys to laugh in unison.

Glaring down at Seras, Dominic tried to hold back his smile. "Yeah, yeah, whatever. So do you guys know what you're ordering?" Dominic asked as he led the group up to the counter. Nodding to the cashier first, he turned back to his friends.

In unison, the group peered up to the menu above them. Distracted by Jackson and his arrogance, no one had taken the time to decide what they wanted to eat. Waiting for his friends to decide, Dominic stepped aside as Seras stepped up to the counter.

"The classic, please," she proudly answered.

Looking back to the cashier, Dominic chuckled. "Two of the classic burgers and two of the vanilla malts," Dominic confidently ordered.

Grabbing their cups, Dominic handed one to Seras as the boys finished making their orders. Strolling to the drink machine together, the two talked about their third period. Chuckling and laughing at one another as their conversation carried on, they began to lose track of time. With their food in hand, unintentionally they sat together as the group looked on from afar. It felt like kismet as the two clicked over their shared love of music, movies, and martial arts. The revelation of Seras's brown belt in Brazilian Jujitsu lit Dominic up inside. It was clear that Dominic wanted to talk more about the arts, but as quickly as his desires came to the surface, he just as quickly remembered the secret he had to keep. Together, the two formed a bond as their hands inched toward one another.

After they had finished their food, the group gathered around at one table as they sat and shared stories. Before anyone realized how much time had passed, the diner had already closed. Saying their goodbyes to one another, the group parted while Dominic walked Seras back to her car. Reaching her mossy green Outback, they stood in horror at the sight of her car keyed up.

"What the fuck?!" she exclaimed, her cheeks furiously red.

Kneeling, Dominic ran his fingers over the scars. "I'll help you get this fixed, Seras. That asshole shouldn't have brought you into this," Dominic calmly expressed, his hands balled into fists as he stood back up.

"And he's going to regret bringing me in. Him and his bitch!" she responded, stomping around to the driver's side door.

Pausing in place, and despite her anger, she found comfort in his words. Gripping her keys, she pursed her lips while she examined her vandalized car. Walking over to her, he felt her pain. He would feel the same if anyone did this to his bike. Pulling her in, he comforted her before giving her a hug.

"Thank you. You have no idea what this means to me," she said into his chest.

"Anytime, hon. You going to be okay going home?" Dominic asked her, pulling back to look her in the eyes.

"Yeah, I'll call my dad and tell him when I get home. I can't believe that bitch keyed my car!" Seras protested while stomping her foot on the ground.

"I'm going to head home. Before I go, could I have your number? I'd like to know you made it home safe," he asked, pulling away.

"You sure can." She smiled before grabbing her phone.

Trading numbers, the young teens left the diner. The streetlights flew by for Dominic as he rode home, his thoughts focused on Seras. She was encapsulating. He had only met a woman so beautiful once before in his life. Her eyes left him with an unshakable memory he couldn't place. Still, he couldn't help but feel amazed that he had met someone he connected with on such a personal level.

What a day it had been for her. She had always admired him from afar, but today, she finally had the courage to talk to him. He was so handsome and silly to her, and even though her baby had been violated, she couldn't help but smile about having spent so much time with Dominic. Her heart sang as she thought of him looking into her eyes. She had dreamed of this day for so many years. The boy with the bright green eyes, the one whom she had noticed so long ago at the diner and whom she had shared a school with for many years, now had her number, and he wanted to make sure she made it home safely. What a night to be alive.

CHAPTER 11
MEETING THE FAMILY

The months flew by, and before Dominic and Seras knew it, autumn had come. The leaves were magnificently in season, and Dominic was finally comfortable driving with a passenger on his bike. Having picked out a helmet and jacket to match, Dominic drove out to pick Seras up from her house.

Rolling into her driveway, Dominic brought himself to a stop as Seras ran up to him. Unbuckling his helmet, Dominic allowed his now shoulder-length hair fall. Happy to have finally seen him for the first time in days, Seras brushed his hair back before kissing him on the lips. Excited to see her as well, Dominic kissed her back and wrapped her up in his arms while holding his bike up. It had been nearly a week since they last saw each other.

Noticing how Dominic had gotten his second set of lobe piercings, Seras played with his ears. "I like these! Are you going to stretch these like your others?" she asked, playing with his jewelry.

"I am," Dominic replied. "So guess what?" He pulled away after kissing her again.

"What?" she asked excitedly, clasping her hands together.

"Well, I have two surprises for ya today," Dominic started, slowly opening his saddlebag. "The first are these," Dominic continued, revealing a black women's leather jacket and black riding helmet.

Surprised by the gifts, Seras understood the meaning behind them and jumped with glee. "Really? You'll let me ride with you now?" Seras nearly tackled Dominic to the ground, hugging and shaking him.

"Yes! We're going riding today, and later, you're going to get to finally meet my dad," Dominic revealed.

Shocked by the news, Seras pulled back momentarily, wondering if he was being serious. "Am I really?" She paused. "Like, I finally get to meet him?"

"Sure do!"

"Good! I was beginning to wonder if I was ever going to . . ."

"I know I've asked in the past for us to not talk about my dad or sort of my family life, but that all gets cleared up today."

"Well . . . I'm glad that you finally feel comfortable bringing me into this part of your life. It's been hard, but I've come to understand your reasoning behind it." She paused, holding his hand to rub it. "So is today also going to be the day you tell me about how you do martial arts?"

Recoiling in shock, Dominic had to know how she figured it out. "How the hell did you figure that out?"

Covering her face to laugh, Seras reveled in the reveal. "Because I overhear the guys sometimes when I go to wait for you after class, and all they talk about is training this and training that. Plus, all the times I've been asked by Justin and Cole before, 'Hey, will you let Dom know he's missed at his *after school club*,' it didn't take much to put two and two together."

"Them damn heathens! Well, actually yes, but I see the cat's out of the bag on that one! I do private martial arts at home. My dad taught me, and I've been teaching Justin, Richie, and Cole for years now."

"Oh really? What do you do? What's your rank?"

"Well, I'm considered a Mataas Na Guro in Filipino Kali." Dominic bowed his head to her shock.

"That's incredible. That's like, what, a third-degree black belt?"

"Kinda. It basically means I'm a master instructor. I took to Kali easier than anything else, and it and I just flow together like the water. Other than that, I'm a double black belt in Karate, and I just received my third black belt for Krav Maga over the weekend."

"That's why you were gone all week?" she shouted as she slugged him in the arm. "I would've killed to come see that!"

"Ouch!" Dominic chuckled as he rubbed his arm. "Yeah, my dad took me out of town for the final exam to earn it. It was hard-earned." Dominic looked away, twisting his neck to pop it.

"I can imagine! I see why you're so calm under pressure all the time. Nothing bothers you!"

"I wouldn't say that. There's plenty that bothers me. I'm just not bothered by some shit-talker who won't actually throw a punch. At least his brother was a doer and not a talker."

"What happened that day? You never talk about it."

"It was the first day I met Cole. I was fourteen, and it was on winter break. Me and Justin were walking back from the mall when I saw a group of guys harassing a kid. I didn't know who he was at the time, but I just couldn't walk away."

"Oh, my baby!"

"Yeah, heh. But I stepped in and we intervened. The bullies didn't take too kindly to it, and that's when the fighting broke out. A few hits and kicks later, Justin, Cole, and I had mopped the floor with the guys. We shook hands and parted ways."

"How does Jackson's brother fit into this?"

"That's the thing! So by luck, and without my knowledge, Jackson's brother was the leader of the group. After we were walking away, he tried to run up and stab us—"

"Oh my god! Baby!" she exclaimed as she slapped him on the arm.

"I know, but luckily I heard him and turned to counter. He got my arm, but when I had him on the ground . . ." Dominic paused as he felt a tremor in his right hand. "I . . . I broke his arm before throwing the knife away."

"Jesus! That's insane! You could've seriously died! If you didn't have half the training you did, you would've died that night!" she shouted as she grabbed his jacket.

"I know. I'm just grateful for how things ended. They . . . They really could've been a lot worse." Dominic looked off as he brought her in.

"I am, too, but please don't be doing things like that anymore! I don't know what I'd do without you."

"Hey, next time I'm in that situation, I won't be alone! I'll have a badass woman by my side who's a brown belt in Brazilian Jujitsu!"

Rocking her head back as she laughed, she buried her face in his chest. "That's a lot coming from a *three-time master* in martial arts."

"Hey, my dad's a master in seven and teaching himself his eighth one now!"

"Jesus Christ! That's not natural!" She paused to look at him. "How does he have time to parent?!"

"He parents while we train. It works out really well nowadays. But it was definitely a lot harder when I was younger."

"That's crazy! Like, I've never heard of anyone living like that before in my life, and you know what? It actually sounds pretty cool! I wish my parents were more into martial arts like me, but they both just work the craziest hours."

"I really hate that. I can imagine how hard it would be to not have a parent physically there, pushing you on some days." He paused as he moved back over to his bike. "So what do you say? Ready to come over and meet my dad? I can show you my training grounds. We can go a few rounds in the ring, if you'd like," he teased, throwing playful punches at her.

"You may have more belts under you, but don't think I don't already know how to take you down, *Dominic Salvatore!*" she reminded him with a look. The two both enjoyed the idea of sparring with one another.

Dominic gave Seras plenty of time to get used to sitting on the back of the bike as he demonstrated how she would hold onto him. Bringing the beast of a motor to life, Dominic revved his engine ever so slightly as he turned around and rolled out of her driveway. The sense of freedom was exhilarating to Seras as she held to Dominic tightly. Sticking to side roads until he became used to Seras behind him, Dominic's smile was so bright, happy to finally bring his partner into his life.

Together, they rode the back roads around D.C. as the autumn sun set. The sense of freedom was unbelievable for the two. Looking off to the orange sun burst sky, Seras closed her eyes before resting her head against his back. Rolling into his driveway, both were confused by his friends being at his house without him.

"What the fuck?" The words rolled out of his mouth as he looked to the empty vehicles in his driveway.

"Did you not know they were coming over?" Seras asked as he turned off the bike.

"No, that's the weird thing. I didn't think we were meeting

today." Dominic slid his keys into his pocket as Steven stepped out from inside the house. "You know anything about this?" Dominic asked him, pointing to the vehicles.

"They're out back. You'll need to see them later." Steven's fore-boding tone caught Dominic off guard.

"Steven Sensei?!" Seras shouted out as she took her helmet off.

"Lion? Are you the girl my son's been dating?" Steven bellowed out in laughter as he watched the shock roll over his son's face.

Hearing the words, Dominic was left speechless as his eyes wid-ened to Seras running up and greeting his father. "Um, can some-body explain this to me?"

"I don't know how I never saw it before, given that you and your dad almost look the same, but yeah, your dad is my Brazilian Jujitsu teacher!" Seras explained as she looked back and forth be-tween the two of them.

"And I'll be honest, work has kept me seriously busy and I was too focused on helping you achieve your belt last week to ever think about the fact that your girlfriend could've been one of my stu-dents," Steven added as he reeled in his laughter.

Dominic was left speechless as he silently rolled his bike further into the drive. All of his plans had been shattered in the first five minutes of coming home. Despite it all, Dominic found the whole event hilarious. Looking to his friends' vehicles, he knew that some-thing was wrong, but it would have to be address later. Grabbing his keys, Dominic walked over and reached out for Seras's hand.

"Well, Dad, this is my girlfriend, Seras Lion! She's an amazing woman and she already figured out that I had private training at home." Dominic reveled in the moment as he introduced her to his father.

"Does she now?" Upset that another person knew of Dominic's

training, but not surprised it was Seras who figured it out, Steven felt compelled to accept it. "So I'm guessing you're going to want to bring her into it as well?" he added, unimpressed.

"I mean, I'm not asking, but I could see myself asking in the future!" Dominic chuckled momentarily before stopping himself.

Steven rubbed his eyes as he sighed to his son. "Let's get through tonight first, okay?" he asked, motioning for them to move toward the door.

"Hell yeah. Sounds good to me!" he shouted as the three of them moved inside.

Steven held the conversation for most of the time, curious to understand how two of his students had met. Carrying the conversation for them, Seras regaled to Steven while Dominic was distracted, repeatedly looking out the back windows. The tree line was still, and the house was empty except for them, but Dominic knew his friends were nearby. His father's words left Dominic with his guts torn. Something was wrong, and he knew it. Still, he participated in the conversation as much as he could without being distracted.

Seeing his son's distress, Steven directed the two into the kitchen. Dominic and Seras sat adjacent to one another as his father moved toward the fridge. Pulling out the leftovers from lunch, Steven confused Dominic with the words as he whipped his head to the sink. The pile of dishes told it all. His friends had been at his house all day. Still, he was hungry, and his father always made the best food.

Digging into the wonderful assortment of cooked meats, fruits, and fresh vegetables, the three sat and laughed as they shared a meal. Sharing stories and jokes, the three grew to know and understand each other a little better that day. After Seras heard Steven's third joke, a burning question grew in her mind. A question she had to ask.

"So, Sensei—"

"Please, you're a guest in my home. You may call me Mr. Salvatore."

"Heh, so, Mr. Salvatore, I have a question."

"Shoot."

"Why train Dominic at home, away from everyone else?"

The room fell silent as Dominic's fork clanged against the floor. Dominic's heart raced at the words. Never had he questioned a day of his training or the methods his father employed, but he had always understood the desire to keep it private. Swallowing his food, Dominic shook, terrified of his father's response. Looking over, Dominic found himself even more confused about his father's calm demeanor.

"Honestly?" he asked, setting his fork down.

"Yeah, it just doesn't seem to make any sense. Your son is a martial arts prodigy with multiple black belts and he's not even eighteen. There's a huge desire to keep it quiet and a secret despite the fact that you took on three more students that your *own son* now teaches. There are so many questions to this all, and the biggest one I have is, why? Your son would be famous in the martial arts world if you brought him into the light, so why don't you?"

Listening, Steven nodded to her words. She wasn't wrong about any of it. Mulling over what she had said, he took another bite of his food before setting his fork down once more. Wiping his mouth, Steven prepared his words.

"Out in the world, there are dark and evil forces gathering their numbers to start a war to end all wars. I've trained him in private to prepare him for it." Steven held a stone-cold stare as he uttered the words he never thought he would.

Lost and confused, the two teens looked at one another in disbelief before looking back to Steven. Holding his serious face for as long as he could, Steven slowly allowed his grin to crack through. Bursting into laughter, he slapped the table. Realizing he had played them for fools, the two apprehensively joined in with his laughter.

"Did you think I was serious?" he asked before laughing again. "No, honey, I've trained him at home out of a personal choice. I'm trying to build something different and new through his training, and I've wanted to keep it tightly under wraps, but every time my *son* makes a new best friend, he tries to bring them into it all." He paused, taking a sip of his water. "I love the industry I'm in, but I'm trying to do something different with it. Bring it back to reality and make it more grounded and real."

"So that's why? His training has been a pet project for you?"

"Kinda. It's also been a family thing. But that's a more private matter. Does that answer your question?" he asked from behind his glass.

Dominic sat silently as he watched his father spin his ball of yarn. He couldn't tell where the truth ended and the lies began, and hearing both stories left him with confusion and fear. Steven was perfect in his execution. He made both stories sound so believable that either could've been the truth and no one would've known the difference. Looking to his father, Dominic searched for any answers, any clue to the truth. Steven felt confident in his misdirection, even though he could feel his son's turmoil building up inside. Winking at him while chewing his food, Steven hoped to ease the tension he had built.

Accepting the explanation that his father was joking the entire time, Dominic tried to write off the words. Still, Steven hadn't ever mentioned building his own style of martial arts through his training. With the other reason too crazy for Dominic to even consider being real, the reason behind his training remained as mysterious as it had before. Looking back down to his food, Dominic listened as the two continued their conversation.

All throughout their meal, Dominic grew increasingly concerned about the fact that his friends hadn't come inside yet. He felt bad for making them wait, but their absence left him wondering how badly they wanted to talk to him at the ring. As hard as he tried, Dominic could not decipher their plans.

Seeing the continued turmoil in his son, Steven could tell that Dominic was still wondering about his friends. He understood the situation and realized that he would have to send Dominic out there soon. Returning to his conversation with Seras, Steven knew that she was a good woman for Dominic. It only made sense that two of his best students, trained separately and apart, would come together like they had. Seras's desire to not become a doctor like her parents shocked him.

"What about you, Dom?" Seras asked, capturing his attention. "What're you wanting to do after high school?" Seras continued, rubbing his left hand.

"Uh, heh, I don't know, honestly. Me and Justin recently started playing music together, with him on the guitar and me singing. I might pursue that, but I hadn't fully given any thought to what my plans were." Dominic, surprised by the question, scratched his head nervously.

"Well, what about doing something in bio-engineering?" His father chimed in. "You're killing it in your science classes, and you did start taking that engineering class last year," Steven mentioned between bites of food.

"I definitely could do something like that. Honestly, I have so much I've been doing right now that I haven't even thought about the fact that I only have one year left in school after this year. It's been pretty crazy so far!" Dominic replied thoughtfully, pulled from the thoughts of his friends.

"That it has been! Just this year alone, so much has happened!" Seras added.

"You're preaching to the choir, hon! But hey, Dom, the boys have been out there waiting on you all day. Head on out there and talk to them. Then you all can come back in for the night, okay?"

"I will. Is it okay for Seras to—"

"Go on and take her, too. She's going to need to understand how you guys do things here if she's going to be coming around more often," Steven said before signaling for her to go with him.

Following Dominic out the back door, she couldn't help but look for answers. "So what's so important about you having to meet the guys outside? Furthermore, where are we going?"

"So I may have shirked my responsibilities, and the guys are probably mad about the fact that I haven't been training them," Dominic apprehensively admitted. "But we are walking to the training grounds we've built back in the woods. Me and my dad built the framework years ago, but all of us have improved it since. It's our little getaway from everyday life."

Seras gasped, shocked by the news. "Dominic! You have a responsibility as their master to teach them!" she exclaimed.

"I've wanted to tell you for a minute, but bringing this up is a difficult thing when I'm supposed to keep it a secret," Dominic began. "Trust me, I've wanted to tell you since you first told me you knew *Brazilian*. You were the first girl I ever met that knew martial arts like me. It's been eating me up inside ever since." Dominic stopped at the tree line's edge.

"It has?" she asked, looking up to him.

"Yeah, but thankfully that all changes today!" He sighed with a smile before pulling the tree limbs away.

Stepping into the clearing, Seras was blown away by the craftsmanship of all that stood before her. From the obstacle course that stretched around the back half of the clearing, around the main building and to her right, to the generator lights they had set up around a gravel circle, it was an incredible feat of construction and determination, and she couldn't help but admire it. Seeing the guys walking out of the side door of the modified barn, she turned to Dominic, who was looking at them as well.

"I need to meet them in the Circle."

"The Circle?" she asked, following him up to the gravel circle.

"It's our sparring grounds. It used to just be used for training, but once we started having issues and disagreements with one another, we expanded the gravel ring and made it our designated spot to fight out disagreements," Dominic explained as Justin began playing music.

"So you actually fight each other in the Circle?" Seras asked, trying to understand their strange rules.

"Well, all of our training is full-contact. So it's not like when we're in the Circle it's any different in terms of whether or not we hit each other. It's more about the emotion behind it. It's speaking without using words. Sure, we'll probably shit-talk one another if we're mad and ask why we were called into the Circle, but every time we go in mad at one another, we don't come out until that issue's resolved," he continued to explain as he nodded to his friends.

"Does it ever get too dangerous?" she asked, looking to the boys.

"No, not really. Richie did knock Justin out cold that one time. Boy's got the meanest left hook I've ever seen! But that's the worst of it. I teach them to subdue and stop their opponent from fighting. They all know how to execute that without killing each other. That's not their goal. I haven't been here for them like I should have."

"Because you've been spending so much time with me?" she asked with her head low.

"Yes, but don't think for a second you're the problem! You aren't. It was my job to balance everything, and I didn't. That's why you're here today to help bring balance to my life and to bring you into it even more," he expressed to her while looking into her eyes.

Hearing Pantera playing through the loudspeakers, Dominic knew he was about to go through a rough fight. All three were in their training uniforms, patiently waiting for Dominic and Seras to approach them. Unbuttoning his shirt, Dominic handed it over to Seras before untucking his tank top. Dominic could see the hurt on his friends' faces, and he felt their pain.

"Hi, Seras! How was lunch?" Justin hollered out.

"It was good. I really liked the corn!"

"I helped make the corn. It's my mom's secret recipe," Richard noted, raising his hand.

"Well, that corn was delicious!"

"So he told you?" Cole asked while taking a drag from his joint.

"No!" Seras stomped her foot. "I figured the majority of it out on my own." she continued.

"I fucking told you, Justin! Now pay up!" Cole exclaimed excitedly, extending his hand.

"Oh, shove it up your ass, Smokey!" Justin protested before pulling out five dollars and slapping it into his hand.

Dominic tried his best not to laugh at their exchange. "I thought you weren't going to smoke before a match, Cole?" Dominic questioned, looking over at him.

"Well, I wasn't, but you were dragging ass, and I got tired of waiting," he responded, shrugging before offering it to Richard, then Seras after he refused the offer.

"So how does this work, guys? You tell the other to get in the ring there and you duke it out?" Seras asked, taking a hit.

"Something like that. But we can go over all that later 'cause it's getting late and this has been a long time coming," Justin started. "Now, we don't have an issue at all with you two spending time together or even being together, but, Seras, Dominic made a promise and a commitment to train us and be our teacher at one point. He hasn't been following through with that promise all month. We're meeting here today to resolve that," he continued.

"He's told me this, and if he needs to be here to train you guys, I don't have an issue coming and watching you guys train! Hell, I'd probably want to join you sometimes. Show you guys some Brazilian Jujitsu!" Seras teased, punching Dominic in the arm.

"Man, I'm down for that! I'd pay good money to see you go against that big motherfucker!" Cole commented, signaling for her to pass to Dominic.

"Careful what you say, Cole. I might just train her in our arts to whoop *your* ass." Dominic winked at him, taking the joint.

"I'm game!" Seras exclaimed.

"Well, that'll have to be another night," Dominic began as he walked toward the center of the Circle. "You're all here tonight because I haven't kept my promise. I'm sorry for that, guys. I am . . ." He paused to roll his shoulders around. "But I'm more sorry that

I'm going to have to whoop all your asses in front of Seras tonight." Dominic smirked, raising his hands to them.

"Seras, you might want to stand over there," Richard warned her before following the other two into the ring.

"We're not gonna go straight to hand-to-hand on this, Dom," Justin began, throwing a training sword to him. "We haven't fought with swords in months. I've come for a rematch!"

"If it's a rematch you want," Dominic began as he caught the sword, "then a rematch I accept. Don't disappoint me, boys. I expect your best!" he finished, raising his sword to them.

Moving forward in a triangle formation, the three worked to surround Dominic. With their swords at the ready, they executed their plan. As the music changed, they all ran at him, attacking Dominic from multiple angles. Dancing around his friends, he remained light on his feet as he tackled them one after another.

Seras's jaw dropped as she witnessed the most finesse sword- and footwork she had ever seen. Never had she seen such grace and fluidity in a group of fighters. They all struck at one another with conviction, yet a single blade never touched their skin. Like rushing water carving the landscape, their movements were natural and deadly. With poise, Dominic moved their swords aside with his own before striking out at Justin. First a swing then a kick. Dominic managed to shove Justin away while fighting off Richard and Cole. The feats from Dominic left Cole and Richard furious as they found themselves evenly matched. Throwing the first punch with an open palm, Dominic moved Richard aside as Justin ran back in.

Justin barreled in head first as he came in with his own punches. Such an offensive move took Dominic back as he backpedaled to the ring's edge. With an opportunity before him, Cole rushed to Justin's aid as the two pushed to remove Dominic from the ring.

The pressure from his friends was real as Dominic stretched the lengths of his training and flexibility. Rolling away before he could fall out of bounds, Dominic was immediately met by a surprise attack from Richard: his left hand. With his right arm the first line of defense, Dominic raised it up as the punch came flying in. Barely blocking the punch in time, Dominic slid across the pebbles as his bones rattled from the hit. Such a powerful impact left him breathless.

The month of neglecting his training hadn't hit Dominic quite yet, but still, he could feel the difference in how much his friends had grown together without him. Their teamwork, shining through the use of their footwork and swordsmanship showed in their movements. Together they fought to show Dominic how much they had missed his training. Meanwhile Dominic fought for forgiveness.

With the need for a second sword, Dominic moved to disarm one of his opponents. Employing one of his signature moves, he was shocked as he found *himself* nearly disarmed. The sword's handle fumbled about in his hands as his body fought to remember its training. Regaining his composure, he attempted a different technique. Once again, he found his attacks nullified. Again and again, he cycled through his known techniques to disarm one of his friends, though it had become clear that time apart had gifted them new skills. Stepping back as the fighting paused, Dominic realized he would have to come up with something new if he was going to beat them.

The distress in his eyes was clear. Working together, Justin and Cole pushed to disarm him while Richard distracted Dominic. Back and forth the two struck at him, both refusing to give their friend any space. Pushing his limits, Dominic pivoted his feet about as he kept himself at arm's length. Without making a scene, he moved the pebbles beneath his feet, making a small mound out of the rocks. With Justin and Cole charging toward his trap, Dominic was ready. Scooping the tip of his sword into the mound, he launched the pebbles into Justin and Cole as they struck at him.

Distracted by Dominic's unorthodox tactic, Richard alone pushed on, doubling down on his assault. Feeling the immense power of his strikes in his arms, Dominic had to hold off his assault. Locking swords, the two teens held their ground as they tried to overpower each other. With sweat pouring from them both, together they held their position to quickly recover some of their energy.

"I won't lie, Richie, I'm impressed! You've become a lot faster here recently!" Dominic complimented him while catching his breath.

"Well, I learned from the best!" Richard replied before parrying his attack and pushing him away.

Surprised by the parry, Dominic stumbled to find an even footing. "Aw, thanks!" He paused as he looked up to see Richard running toward him. "But you still have a few things to learn!" Dominic exclaimed, knocking the sword from Richard's hand before he pushed him aside. "Remember, I am still your teacher!" He teased with a wink.

"Well, can ya teach me this?!" Justin exclaimed before jumping and throwing a punch at Dominic.

Stepping aside, Dominic felt a familiar sense around him. Like a tiger gazing at it's prey from the tall brush, Cole snuck around Dominic as the other boy's distracted him. Feeling Cole's eyes piercing the back of his head, he quickly moved forward to avoid the double slashing attacks from his sides. With a sword in

each hand now, Dominic finally found himself on an even playing field. Blocking both Cole's and Justin's attacks with near ease,
Dominic moved to take control of the fight. Moving his opponents
to where he wanted them, he wore down their stamina as he took
the offensive.

Showing off his true talent as a swordsman, Dominic twirled
his swords around as his hands remembered their place. His confidence had returned and as he stretched his back out, Dominic
started to feel at home again. Dominic's hubris had grown and Cole
and Justin knew it. They needed a plan if they were going to succeed. Joining his friends as they took a moment to compose themselves, Richard brushed the dust off his uniform and readied his
fists. The fire had been reignited in Dominic's heart as he looked to
his best friends. The healing of their bonds had begun. With smiles
all around to continue on, the four charged back at one another.

Never in her life had Seras seen such intense fighting, and she
was blown away by the sight. In all the time she had gotten to know
Dominic, his fighting prowess had remained a hidden gem until
that night. Though she could never imagine her boyfriend having
such skill, there he stood, covered in sweat and holding off three
fighters at once. Anxiously, she sat on the edge of the bench outside
of the ring, waiting for the next move to be made.

Taking center stage, Cole and Justin worked to hold Dominic's
attention. Holding back as the others fought, Richard moved
around the ring with the others and waited for an opening to take
Dominic down. Having a second sword gave Dominic the edge he
needed as he pushed his friends to their limits. Perilously, the two
boys worked to maintain their defenses as they awaited Richard's
next move. Pushing Cole and Justin as hard as he could, Dominic
forgot about his third opponent as he chipped away at their stamina.

Feeling his feet leave the ground, Dominic was caught off guard as Richard lifted him up and slammed him back down. The force he used turned Dominic into a shovel as he dug a ditch in the gravel. The shock hit Seras nearly as hard as Richard hit Dominic while she watched the action unfold. Despite their current situation, even the other boys were surprised by Richard's show of force while Dominic bounced his head off the ground. Groaning out as he struggled to stand, Dominic checked his piercings as he crawled to his feet.

Spitting the dust from his mouth, he wiped the blood from his lip. "So that's how we're doing this? Okay!" Dominic turned and face the three of them.

Dominic targeted Cole and Justin first. Left hook, right hook. He pushed them to the ring's edge. Witnessing the assault, Richard sprang into action as he took advantage of Dominic's blind spot. Aiming for his shoulder, Richard missed as his first hit smacked Dominic in the cheek. Committed to the action, Richard had no room to change direction as his second hit bashed against his friend's head. Pulling away as one punch after another rattled his brain, Dominic dropped his swords before forcing some distance between him and Richard. With half the fighters now without swords, Justin and Cole threw their's to the ground before returning to the fight. Gathering in their formation, the three boys worked to surround Dominic as they remained at the ready for his next attack. Returning to the basics of his training, Dominic prepared for the real fight to begin.

Trading one hit after another, the three of them unloaded their anger and irritation on Dominic. No words were needed as they grappled with one another. They were happy for their friend for finding a partner, but they missed their brother. Despite being out

numbered, Dominic danced with his friends as one hand movement flowed with another. Though the more their bout carried on,
the more it taxed their bodies. Putting some space between themselves, Dominic caught his breath as the pain finally settled into
his bones. He was battered and bruised, but so were his friends.
Calming the shaking in his hands, Dominic channeled his breathing to give him a second wind.

"Come on, guys, I know you have more in you. Show me what
you got!" Dominic exclaimed, ready for their next move.

Looking to one another, the three nodded, confirming that they
still had the strength in them to fight. Running at Dominic together, they attacked him with all their might. One after another,
the three of them laid into him. Dominic gave his absolute best
as he countered and struck back at them. Hit by hit, kick by kick,
Dominic began to wear down the more exhausted fighters.

Starting with Justin, Dominic exploited his known weaknesses.
Viciously he broke through Justin's personal bubble as he turned
the pressure up. One fast jab after another left Justin stunned as
he struggled to avoid being hit. He hated having to fight so closely
to Dominic, and he was exploiting that. Sweeping Justin's leg out
from underneath him, Dominic fought off the other two as Justin
crawled away to get back on his feet. However, Dominic refused
to allow Justin to escape. Forcing himself through the others,
Dominic push Justin to the edge of the ring as Cole and Richard
ran to his defense. Desperate to hold the line, Justin fought off
Dominic before having his feet taken out from under him. With
their friend thrown from the ring, they paused as Dominic's gaze
turned to Richard.

Tackling Richard to the ground, the two wrestled about as
Dominic worked to pin him down. Gravel and sweat flew about as

the two larger teens battled it out. Out of all his friends, Richard matched Dominic in pure strength. The two were equal in their own rights. Pulling Richard into an arm-bar, Dominic didn't notice as Cole jumped across the ring, landing his foot on Dominic's cheek. Releasing Richard, Dominic rolled away from the two as he reached the ring's edge and as he brushed the dirt from his face, he grew tired of the constant head pummeling.

Still feeling the effects of the kick, Dominic buckled over from the fatigue of skipping his training for so long. Despite his weariness, he took solace that his friends were fatigued as well. With an exhaling breath, Dominic shook his head about before barreling toward them.

Everyone grew sloppy but still they fought on. Grabbing Dominic's leg as he failed to kick Cole, Richard flung him away before rushing after him. The airtime was shocking as Dominic's feet touched back down on the earth. Though as the rest of his body caught up to him, the exhausted teen struggled to stay conscious as he felt himself getting light-headed. Falling to his rear, Dominic quickly rolled away as Richard began to punch down at him.

It had been a long time since Dominic had ever really felt cornered in a fight but as he struggled to find a place to stand up, there was Richard hammering away at him. Crawling to his feet brought no source of relief though as Cole flew in with another kick. Grabbing Cole from the air as he ran after Dominic, Richard picked up his pace to catch up to him. Meanwhile Dominic struggled to figure out a path to victory as the three duked it out.

The bruises that ached the three of them was taxing as they broke off one another. Bending over, Dominic looked to the two as his chest heaved up and down. They were just as exhausted as he was and they couldn't hide it any longer. Sweat nearly blinded

Dominic as he pushed the loose hair out of his face. Resting his hands on his hips, Dominic focused on his breathing as he watched the two of them do the same. The music had long since stopped and the hum of the light generators had replaced the empty void. With labored breath, Dominic's ears rang out to the tune of his exhaustion. However, as the three looked to one another, they knew only one could be left standing.

Making the first move, Richard and Cole ran at Dominic at the same time. With little space between them, Dominic prepared for the onslaught. Holding up his arms, he withstood each kick and punch they threw. Though it certainly didn't feel good, Dominic held off his friend's weakened attacks. Seeing that he was reaching the edge of the Circle, desperate times called for desperate measures. With Cole and Richard about to swing at the same time, Dominic ducked down, moved in, grabbed Cole and Richard, and lifted them into the air.

A gasp rang out as Justin and Seras both found themselves blown away by what they witnessed. Cole and Richard also found themselves shocked by what happened as they turned to one another before they were slammed to the ground. Stumbling forward to the center of the ring, Dominic leaned over and caught his breath. He was beyond exhausted, and his body was sore. Waiting to see if either would stand up, Dominic dropped to one knee. Wiping the sweat and spit from his face, Dominic heaved his chest up and down. Looking back up, he saw only Cole still standing.

Shaking his head, Dominic was impressed by his determination. "You don't know how to quit, do you?" he remarked with a smile.

"I learned it from you," Cole replied, spitting away from them and raising his fists.

"Damn right you did," Dominic commented, standing back up and raising his fists in turn.

Moving toward one another, the two best friends fought out the last of their aggression. Tired, they placed what energy they had left into each of their throws. Knocking each other around, the two had never felt closer as they knelt over, drained of their energy. Looking to each other, they knew they had one more punch in them before they could fight no more. Their chests heaving, the boys gathered the last of their energy into one final punch. As Dominic's fist collided with Cole's cheek, the two fell away from one another. Managing to land on one foot, Dominic dug it into the ground as he tried to stay in the ring. Bouncing off the ground, Cole skidded out the ring.

"Draw!" Steven yelled out, walking up to the group.

"The hell do you mean a draw? I'm still somewhat standing!" Dominic announced from his position.

Pointing to his back foot, Steven showed Dominic that he was wrong. "Your foot is out of bounds. So this is a draw."

Dominic's head dropped when he noticed that his foot had fallen out at the last second. "Well, shit!" he stated. "You okay, Cole? Richie?" he asked, struggling to stand back up.

"Oh, okay. Forget Justin then," Justin sarcastically remarked, helping Richard up from the ground.

"I know you're fine. I knocked you out of the ring first," Dominic teased before walking over to Cole. "Hey, take my hand," he continued, reaching out to Cole.

"Damn, I hate it when you hit me like that," Cole complained, shaking his head lightly.

"I know, man. That's why I tried to hit you where it'd hurt the least," Dominic told him while knocking the dust and dirt off him. "But other than that haymaker, you good, bro?"

"Yeah, I need a good soak in the tub and a blunt, but I'm straight, man," Cole attested, shaking his hand with a smile.

"Hey, Richie, that left hook is really something else, man!" Dominic commented while helping Cole over to the bench where Seras was.

"Thank you. Justin doesn't like it, either." Richard chuckled as he faked out Justin by raising his fist.

"Alright, that's enough, boys." Steven calmed the group down as they huddled around him. "So, guys, has Dominic adequately reprimanded himself?"

The three looked to one another and shook their heads. Cole spoke for the group. "It's not that we were really mad, Dom. We were just upset that you weren't spending time with us. We're cool with you spending time with Seras. We just want to still be trained by you at the same time."

"Well, like I said, I'd be down for coming to practice with you guys, if that's okay with all of you," Seras remarked to the group.

Looking to each other, then to Dominic, they all agreed to the notion. "We'd be happy to have you here, Seras!" Dominic smiled before pulling her into a hug.

Despite how sore they all were, the five of them hugged out as the boys winced at their injuries. They were happy and whole again. Joking and playing around with one another, Dominic playfully took jabs at Justin, purposely missing each of them. Moving back toward the main building, the group laughed and joked throughout the night. For a lot of them, it was a night of growth, but for them all, it was a night of bonding.

CHAPTER 12
ACT IV: SUFFERING

Year: 2008
Location: REDACTED

For four years, John, Gabriella, and Michael followed every shred of information on Zähd. From one end of the Earth to the other, they stayed one step behind him. At every turn, John would have him in his grasp, and he would slip away. Through the help of terrorist organizations, espionage, and subterfuge, Zähd eluded the three of them with ease, and with every escape, he drove John through the mucky pits of hate.

With their lives permanently changed by the revelation of the paranormal, Gabriella and Michael were helplessly compelled to dive into the new world that had been revealed to them. Together, with John's help, they dug through forgotten history to understand the ancient warrior and how he worked. Their search led them to the ends of the Earth and back into Hell. Their journey strengthened their bond as they survived one perilous journey after another, and even through the insanities of visiting Hell itself, Gabriella and Michael never wavered in their conviction to John's cause. Through teamwork and perseverance, the three of them formed a formidable team as they chased after Zähd. Unfortunately, no amount of digging for answers ever brought them closer to a location where he worked from, nor could they ever catch up to him.

As time dragged on, John's resolve slowly withered with each failure. He grew impatient with the lack of results. Turning to his sight for aid, John continuously looked into the future for answers. Again and again, he would see the same images in his mind. They taunted him, burning every detail into his psyche. Needing to take more drastic measures, John returned to Hell once more.

It was the sixth time John had returned to Hell that month. Again, he scoured the fourth and fifth layers for answers. The once calm and reserved man had become frantic in his search. Rage controlled his interrogations of the demonic hierarchy he would ambush out on patrols, but with each dead end, he slowly began to crack. With all leads exhausted, John made one more trip to Hell, hoping an old friend could lend some support to his mission.

The doorbell chimed as John walked into Abraham's shop. John avoided eye contact with the customers Abraham was assisting. Looking to many of the same old items on the shelf, John found himself picking up an old set of three scrolls. Wiping the dust from their faces, he ran his fingers across the wax seals on them. Stamped with an early Edo-period seal, the ancient Japanese text was somewhat visible from the corners. Peering around the store shelf corner, John looked to the leaving customers, then to Abraham walking behind them. Hearing the doors lock, John looked around once more to make sure no one was in the room.

"You came just in time!" Abraham started. "I didn't know how useful this information would've been to you if you had come any later, so come on, follow me," he continued, rounding the corner to the same aisle as John.

"What's going on?" John queried, following him with the scrolls still in hand.

"Now, I'm not even going to start with scolding you over all the chaos you've been causing! All these *sightings* of a curse-wielder ambushing patrols have left the whole place on high alert! But none of that matters right now. I can't say how reliable this information is, but one of my contacts told me he just spotted Zähd. Now, before you get all excited, this was a few days ago," Abraham announced while opening the door at the back of the room.

"We talking Earth days or Hell days?" John quickly interjected.

"Hell days, so this just happened for you," Abraham replied.

"Okay, so why are you telling me if you're so skeptical about it?" John questioned him while they walked out of the main room and toward the back of his shop.

"Because the minute he told me, he was picked up off the streets," Abraham explained, looking into each room as they walked down the hallway.

"Picked up by who?" John asked while keeping pace with him.

"Who do you think? He's being shipped down below! They're throwing him in the hole and forgetting about him. I had one guy track his transfer and they're heading straight to the sixth layer. Souls don't go past the fifth unless they're high value or need to be removed from the general populace," Abraham began. "This guy's nothing to them. Any other time, there wouldn't be a need to take your average soul and throw them down there, so if he's been taken down, then there's a good chance his information was solid." he finished before opening his office door.

"So what did he say? How'd he find out about him?" John asked.

"All he got to tell me was that he found Zähd, and before he could tell me more, that's when they got him. If I had to guess, he found some way to break through the border security and snuck down the layers." Abraham held the door open for John before closing it behind him.

"Dammit!" John exclaimed.

"Yeah, I know, but look, if you leave now, you may be able to reach him before they throw him in a cell. Hell, break him out, even. Even those assholes down there have to do their paperwork before they toss someone away." Abraham walked around to the closed window in his office.

"Yeah, but that's two layers down. I only have the strength to reach the fifth with my powers," John argued.

"So teleport there, get as close as you can, and sneak the rest of the way. I know the lower you go, the easier it is for you to be sensed out, but it's worth the risk, and besides, there aren't many hypersensitive beings in layer five," Abraham argued.

"It is, but, Abe, if they find me, things could end very badly. It'd be even worse if they somehow caught me. I need to be able to get down there without being caught. It's difficult enough nowadays teleporting here." John was conflicted. His goal was so close yet so far away.

"That's your own fault! I mean, I'm not complaining. You're doing what you need to do, but no one on Earth gives off energy like you do, so using your powers that much is going to get their attention. I know this is a hard choice, but you know it's the only one. It's fight-or-flight time, my friend," Abraham reminded him sternly.

"I know, I know," John, frowning and sullen, agreed.

"Look, I may be able to find some way to give you a distraction down there, but it'll all be up to you." Abraham paused, noticing the scrolls in his hand. "Are you wanting those scrolls?" he asked, pointing toward them.

"I was looking at them. Could only read a little bit of it, but its text is fragmented without opening them," John explained, presenting the scrolls.

"They're some old powerful magic. They were stolen from a temple back during the Edo period. Some old sage made them to control the weather." Abraham waved his hand about before turning back to the window.

"They work?" John asked, looking up to him.

"I'm guessing so. I was told they were a one-time use after you open them, so I wasn't going to waste something valuable, ya know? Take them. You're going to need them," Abraham expressed softly while looking through the blinds in the window. "You've spent the better part of a decade looking for Zähd. You've come close to stopping him before, John. Are you going to stop now? Or are you going to *Sha'are Mavet*?" he asked, looking through the blinds.

"You already know that answer," John replied swiftly.

"Then you better get going. You're running out of time," Abraham continued while raising his blinds.

"Thank you, Abe, for everything." John thanked his dear friend while standing up.

"John, I have one question before you go. You've been looking into the future again, haven't you?" Abraham asked, looking away from him.

"Yeah . . . I have," he reluctantly answered.

"I've warned you before, John! Let it come to you. Don't seek it out!" Abraham lectured him while turning around.

"I needed it! I was out of options." John protested.

"No one needs that! It drives people crazy when they use it," Abraham argued before looking back out the window.

"No, it doesn't," John defensively protested.

"It does. You might not think it does, but it does. Using it too much changes you. You get this look about you like all you can see is what it shows you. You get these blinders on your head and you don't even know it. I warned you the last time. Don't use this anymore! After the last time, it gave you a vision you should've left alone like I warned you!" Abraham protested, hurt and angered that John had broken their promise.

"It's brought me to this point." John tried to explain.

"Yeah, but you don't know at what cost. That power shouldn't exist in the first place. That's not something for mortals to be toiling with!" Abraham yelled, furthering his point.

"Neither is half the shit we use Natural Energy for, but here we are!" John added.

"All of that is nothing compared to the powers within you! Especially you, John!" Abraham paused to exhale. "Look, please stop using it. It's going to get you killed. I don't know what you've seen, but please, for your own sanity, stop." Abraham pleaded with him.

John hesitated. He knew the dangers, but he also saw the need for them. "I'll try. I know it can be dangerous. I haven't forgotten your warnings Abraham, but I need to save the world. You said it yourself: go all the way."

Realizing there was no changing his mind, Abraham sighed before walking to his safe in the corner of the room. "You're right, I did, and I guess that's my fault for installing that drive in you." He paused to open the safe. "But if you're going to be doing some dumb and crazy shit, you might as well have some weapons to do it proper-like."

"You're acting like this isn't enough?" John chuckled, grabbing his family sword by the pommel.

"Oh, that's plenty, but it's one sword. But you rarely carry anything on you that's deadly enough to really cut these demons down," Abraham began as he sat items aside. "Sure, your tantō and Bowie have spilled enough blood, but you're going to need something more. You can't always rely on that one sword. You get into the wrong fight and it falls out of your hands, that could be worse than anything Zähd could be cooking up. Ah, here we go!" Abraham continued, pulling out a set of old, weathered kodachis.[3]

Looking to the set of blades, John watched as black dust slowly churned around them while they were pulled from their sheaths. "What're these?"

"They belonged to a friend long ago. He killed an entire horde of oni demons attacking his village with these two swords. The blood soaked into the steel, making them quite deadly to the supernatural, and it prevents any sort of resurrecting. They've been sought out by every collector in Hell since then, and now I'm giving them to you. They can't cause as much damage as your blade, but they will keep a demon down," Abraham explained before returning the blades to their sheaths and handing them to John.

"Wow, thank you, Abraham. I never knew such a blade existed," John stated, surprised by the gesture.

"Yeah, it kinda falls in the same category as your sword. It's only known about by those in the know. But take them and go. You've wasted enough time here!" Abraham ordered, opening the window to his office. "I'll make some calls and see if I can't get some trouble

---

3 Kodachi: a slightly smaller version of a katana.

started up for you near the checkpoint to layer six." Abraham was apprehensive about looking John in the eye, worried for his well-being.

"Hey, I'll be safe—"

"No, you won't, John. Don't lie to me. Just go. Stop Zähd, and please try to not get yourself killed." Abraham reluctantly looked to him, showing him the pain he held within.

"All the way, Abe. I'll push it all the way." John reaffirmed to him before tying the swords to his belt and jumping out the window.

Watching John run off, Abraham, exasperated, sighed before pulling his hands down his face. Abraham knew how dangerous John's path was, still even as he turned back toward his desk, he knew his old friend needed help one more time. Reaching over and closing his window, Abraham sighed heavily, making preparations for things to get a lot worse in Hell. The rhythmic tapping of his wooden leg against the floor filled the empty noise in his office. Looking to his phone, Abraham snatched it up from it's resting position.

John covered his face as he exited the alleyway. With a patrol down the street, he turned a corner while sifting through the crowd until he reached an empty alley. He needed answers; John had to stop Zähd at any cost. The images of his nephew carrying on the struggle of their family's curse echoed in his mind anytime Zähd's face came to him. Releasing his sword, John opened a portal to the farthest point he could reach below him before jumping through.

Exiting through the portal, John quickly sealed it behind him before the sound of it could alert anyone in the surrounding area. Landing in the bog that surrounded the center of the layer's top,

John intensely searched for any demons that might have heard him entering the layer. The area was barren of life; only disembodied howls and cries echoed out. A sense of rage permeated in the air, seeping into the skin like a morning dew. John rose from the bushes around him, weary as he continued through the marsh. Walking toward the center of the layer's edge, he could feel the gravitational change as he looked down.

Just as the layers above and below it, the center of the fifth layer was hollowed out, top to bottom. Tunneling around, inward, and down through the crust were large, dreary, mist-covered cities. Twisting his head, John popped his neck as the old, uncomfortable chilling sensation crept up his spine. The fifth layer, like the others, called upon the sin in one's soul. John could only ignore the call for so long. From the mist in the air to the mud he walked on, everything that grew in this sorrowful land drove at the anger in his heart. Grabbing his shaking hand, John knew he couldn't stay long. The longer he stared in any one direction, the more images of his nephew and Zähd would appear before him.

Looking down to the center of the layer, John could faintly see it's end and the fiery gates that barred entry to the next layer. The rushing of wind that pulled toward the center of the opening was his only chance at survival if he was to make it through the layer in time. Stepping away from the edge, John struggled with the anger boiling under his skin. He actively avoided the fifth layer when he could. For the deeper he traversed through the lower levels the stronger they pulled at his sins. Turning back around, John activated his powers to manipulate the wind around him. The wind bent to his will around his fingers, and as John ran off at full speed toward the edge, it propelled himself into the wind tunnel.

Using his powers to quickly traverse the dark and confusing

swamps around him, John steeled his focus. The further he traveled through the layer, the more he struggled with his anger. Mile after mile, the anger stacked up inside of him, causing his arm to shake harder and harder the further he descended. Despite the almost uncontrollable and instinctive desire to break out in an incomprehensible rage, John focused on his nephew's innocent smile. The memory of their last day at the park remained his only anchor to reality.

The swamps that surrounded the cities held a stench like none other. Such a primordial smell was only recognizable by his body's DNA. Recoiling in disgust as it fed on his internal anger and hatred, John fought off the insanity. Though no matter how hard he tried, he could not fight off the barbed hands of the swamp as it took hold of him. It was truly maddening.

Grateful for his training and ability to manipulate the elements around him, John called upon the wind more and propelled himself forward through the air. With every city he passed, the pounding in his head grew. Making haste as he pushed himself even further, he held his powers at their first stage as he flew past the second-to-last city. He was getting closer but with the wind tunnel around him dissipating as the air thinned out, John relied more on his powers as he pushed himself. The deeper John descended through the layer, the more it took a toll on his body. Fatigue turned to exhaustion while he fought the convulsions in his body. The end of the swamp was near, and the cold chills had begun to set in. Despite his troubles, he remained headstrong and determined to find answers.

Like he was trying to swim through a sea of spiderwebs, the fog weighed on John, pulling him down, closer to the water's surface. It took all his strength to pull away as lost souls reached out from the treacherous black waters. Like sirens, they cried out from their inescapable torment. With land in sight, John fought through their deafening wails as they continued to grab at him.

Reaching the edge of the swamp, John found the slightest reprieve to his psyche before he tackled the final city between him and the sixth layer. Worn down from the screaming, both his body and his willpower had been tested.

Don't you give up on me, John. I know you got more in you than that! If you can lose a leg and still fight harder than us, then I know you can do this!

The echoes of his best friend's words rang through his delirium, helping him find the strength to keep pushing on. Though it became clear that he had spent too long in the layer as his sweat grew and ears rang.

Through the thick fog John made out the orange glow of the fiery gates beyond the city. *Ignis Portas Inpenetrablies.* The infamous bulwark, a powerful deterrence worked also as a seal to contain the worst Hell had to offer. Barring the entrance to the sixth layer, John knew he would have to employ stealth if he was to ever break through its defenses. The stories John had heard of the gates gave it no justice as he flew toward it like a fly to a human. Crossing the sea of fog that clouded the city around him, John kept to the shadows to avoid detection. He hated having to travel through the fog with every drop seeping into his skin. Catching a shadow from his side, John quickly ducked into the shadows of a nearby building. The squealing screeches gave away the popobawas position as they called out to one another. Happy to avoid them, John glided down closer to the ground as he neared the gate.

Wet from all the fog, his damp clothes sagged as he touched down on the ground. The numbing cold it brought only worsened as the harsh winds blew around him. Death seemed almost preferable

to an eternity of *this* Hell. Without warning, John fell to his hands
and knees as he was hit with a near inescapable sensation of anger.
His vision waned as he struggled to remain conscious. Something
needed to be done. John pulled a zippo from his pocket and quickly
struck it. Pulling the fire from the wick and into his hand, John bil-
lowed the flame as he combined the air around him in an attempt
to dry his clothes. A temporary relief it would provide, but he remained hopeful that it would be enough to carry him through the
gates. John looked over in disbelief at the roaming rolls that carried off into the fog above him. The cylindrical landscape left something to gaze at as the tall murky grass blew in the wind.

With blurred vision and shallow breath, John relentlessly
pushed on. Leaning against the wall of a building, he wiped the
sweat from his eye as he gazed upon the final gate between him and
his goal. He had reached the city's limits and with it, the layer's end.
Though the layer's end brought relief to John's sight, the fight was
just about to begin. Slipping into the hip-high grass before him,
he held to the shadows as he inched closer to his goals. The metal
construct before him wrapped around the rocky edge of the layer,
stretching so far above him the fog obscured it's end. Sigils of energy and fire illuminated the many focal points around it's barrier,
helping to maintain it's shape and form. Looking up from the shadows of the skyscrapers, John failed to see the end of the grand display of power. Despite everything, it was truly a marvelous sight to
see. No guards patrolled the grounds as he surveyed their security.
Though the strange sight was unusual, the open invitation to try
and attack the front of the gates was quickly dismissed. Like birds
flocking back to their nests, the Popobawas scanned the grounds
around the base before returning home. It was clear that trying
to fly through would be foolhardy. Where the forces of Hell failed

in their protection of the gate's grounds, they rivaled in the air as manned catapults guarded the skies. Moving into billowing grass, John caught a glance of a group of heavily armed guards, patrolling all along the catwalks of the base. They patrolled with suspicion, given by the contorted scowl on their orcish faces.

Shit. Have they already made me?

John hugged the darkness as the guards looked down in his direction. Holding his breath, he nuzzled himself under a protruding rock as the wind shifted the grass around him. His heart raced as he stared down the guards, anxiously awaiting the moment he was spotted. He couldn't get caught now, at least not before he reached the Sixth layer. He was nearly facing the guards as he hid in the faintest of shadows but as the wind continued to blow, the guard's suspicion began to breakaway. Finding nothing in sight, the patrol slowly broke off to continue their search. With a sigh of relief, he waited and watched the guards until they disappeared. John's eye shot up to the impenetrable gates, he knew it would take a swift and violent strike to attempt to break through the defenses if he was ever spotted.

Checking his surroundings before moving on, John spotted one soul looking to him from a window. There was nothing around or in sight, but as his eye focused on the strange soul, he felt strangely at peace. On alert but refusing to move, the two locked eyes with one another. Then with a slight nod to John, the man stepped out of sight before the sound of a cannon firing broke the silence around them. Jarred from the percussion, John searched for the source of the loud explosion. Barreling through the air, multiple fiery cannonballs flew between the skyscrapers, directly at the base.

Cheers cried out as the cannonballs tore through the face of the base. Reacting in turn, immediately, the sounds of alarms bellowed out from inside the base as a mob of angered souls poured out of the fog to attack the base. Scrambling to organize, the security poured out from the holes made to fight off the rioting souls. Abraham had come through for him, and in a big way. With the moment right, John quietly snaked through the tall grass until he breached the perimeter. Hearing the squeaks of door hinges, John hugged the walls while a door near him flung open. Demons, armed with batons, ran out and past him, toward the raging battle nearby. Watching the combat unfold, John found the opportunity to slip past all the action. With his back against the wall, John crawled around the door as he slipped into the base.

Carefully, he moved from one hallway to another, avoiding any confrontation. Despite having no knowledge of the building and no clear idea of where to go, John continued on through the base. Explosions rocked the building around him as the fighting persisted outside. The old familiar thundering of bombs brought John back to his youth and the rat tunnels of Vietnam. Though the dirt had been traded for steel, the combination of dark labyrinth hallways, explosions and hostiles everywhere completed the sensation for him. With his mind on high alert, John carried on, tanto in hand.

After an exhaustive search, he finally found his way to the other side of the base. John slowly cracked open the exit door, careful not to grab the attention of any possible guards. Catching a glance of a group of them, John quickly closed the door again before any of them noticed. With his back against the wall, John grew tired of the sneaking around. He had reached the other side of the gate, and the time to strike had arrived. Reminded of the set of swords Abraham had gifted him, John ran his hands over their pommels. The blades were eager for battle. With curiosity and excitement, John unsheathed the blades.

With a few quick breaths to pump himself up, John turned and kicked the door open with all his might. Hearing the door slam open, the guards turned to see John, arms at the ready. Steadying his breath, John clicked his feet against the metal scaffolding as he ran toward the guards. Everyone yelled out as they all ran at once, their blades crossing as another explosion rocked the base. John found a fair challenge in the group as he struck them each down one after another. Dancing around the tight space, John slaughtered the unprepared demons as they fell one by one.

Tossing a body over the railing as he struck down the last guard, John alerted another nearby patrol as he finished off the first one. While mapping out how the guards would reach him, John looked out to the fiery stone prisons lining the top and the tunnel of the sixth layer below. The gap between layers left quite the fall between him and his destination, but with his goal so close and in sight, the risk was worth it. Seeing the guards coming in his peripheral vision, John said nothing as he spun the blades around in his hands. Blood sprayed about as John quickly dispatched each of the guards one after another. The kodachis worked wonderfully despite them not carrying the *umph* that his family's sword did, though together, they worked masterfully in dispatching any foe. Tricking the guards, John tossed many of the demons over the ledge as he quickly finished off the last of them. With the coast clear, John found his moment to jump. Sheathing his swords, he gave one final exhale before leaping over the railing and falling to the layer below.

A prison within a prison, the sixth layer of Hell was the worst place for any damned soul. Built to house the worst offenders of Hell, as well as anyone deemed unfit for normal punishment, the ancient and grand masonry spanned the majority of the top of the sixth layer. Medieval in design, the stone- and ironwork was a foreboding, fearsome sight, even for John. Wrapping around the perimeter and concentrated at specific points, an inextinguishable fire greeted any would-be visitors to the prison. Not only did the great stronghold keep away any unwelcome guests, but they guaranteed that escape was no option.

Scanning the main base's layout, John mapped his entry point as he continued to fall. The open courtyard lay barren except for the tortured souls strung up for punishment and the occasional patrolling pack of guards. The torture devices were visible from the sky above, and the dread and sorrow were such palpable sensations that any man would fret at the sight. From the spiked pyres across the grounds, where souls remained impaled and set ablaze, to the macabre architecture and the dreary lands around it, everything piled together in creating a disparaging mindset for its prisoners.

John had only seen the outside of the prison once before, but even still, he felt a sense of dread as he fell through the air. If he was captured, he would surely return to this place in chains. With little time left before he would need to choose a landing spot, John took notice of the center of the layer's tunnel. All along the walls of the tunnel, upward-protruding serrated spikes acted as a net, catching anyone unlucky enough to fall through. The impenetrable prison of the sixth layer maintained its reputation as John drew closer. Finding an abandoned ledge to land on, John watched the guards carefully as he adjusted his trajectory and moved in for the landing.

With the slightest assist from his powers, John used the wind around him to soften his landing, making no sound as his feet hit the stone walkway. With a door before him, John slipped inside before anyone could see him. Turning to quietly close the door behind him, he heard the sound of feet stopping in place and echoing throughout the silence around him. The hairs stood on the back of John's neck as he peered over his shoulder. Like a predator ready to pounce, he stared into the eyes of the terrified guard.

The two made no moves as they stared at one another, for the first move would be crucial to their survival. Seeing the second-guessing going through the guard's mind, John turned and lunged at him as he tried to shout out for help. Tackling the guard to the ground, he covered the guard's mouth as he brought his knife up to the guard's eye level. Dragging the guard into a nearby room, John held him against the wall by his face.

"Now listen very carefully. Do you want to live?" John whispered to him. His crimson eye glowed violently in the dark room.

The demon nodded in confirmation.

"Good, then you're going to tell me where you bring your new inmates to before they're sent off to their cells," John told the demon before slowly removing his hand from the creature's mouth.

"Main office. They have to go through processing," the terrified demon explained.

"And where's the main office?" John questioned further.

"It's connected to this one. It's located at the entrance of the tunnel. The majority of the cells line the tunnel heading down, so the head office overlooks it all. You can find processing on the third floor," the demon continued to divulge.

"And how do I reach the third floor from here?" John politely asked.

"The hallway you came into, follow it down, hang a left, then follow it until you come to a stop. Take the right, then immediately left. That'll be the entrance to the main building from here. Find the flight of stairs and go down three levels. Then you're there.

Half the whole floor is for processing incoming inmates," the demon continued.

Surprised by how forthcoming he was being, John continued on. "What about the other guards? Should I expect resistance along the way or in the main building?"

"Not really along the way. I'm the only guard that patrols this sector for the remainder of this cycle. Now, the main office will most likely have a lot of guards there. There's usually four or five guards in processing at all times."

"Hmm, I see. One last question: how can I trust what you've told me? You've been quite forthcoming with me. How do I know you're not leading me into a trap?" John questioned, pushing the blade against his throat.

"Oh, no, no! I wouldn't do that to you! You're one of them curse-wielders, aren't you? I may be a guard here, but I'm not an idiot. I know the reputation you guys carry! My life's in your hands. I want to live!" the demon pleaded.

"So you can continue to torment and torture souls?" John's tone quickly changed, scaring the demon.

"No! I swear I don't do any of that! I do the best I can to avoid torture duty! I'm just doing what I'm told to do. I'm not like most of the demons here, I swear. Please don't kill me!" the demon pleaded while trying not to move too much.

Glaring down at the frightened orc, John found the interaction too strange. "A prison guard demon that doesn't like to torture the souls he guards." He paused to chuckle. "I have seen it all." John shook his head before pulling the blade away and standing back. "Hell's not quite frozen over, but damn if today's not your lucky day," John stated while the frightened demon slowly rose to his feet. "I'm going to let you live. Now, how long that'll last will depend on the quality of your information. If it all turns out good, then you can continue on with your existence, but if this all goes tits up and I find out you told someone I was here, I'll make sure you go through every torture device in that courtyard out there." John threatened, pointing at the wall beside him.

"It's all good, I swear!" he continued pleading, insisting on his information.

"It better." John pointed at him before walking toward the door they had come from. "One more thing. When I walk out of this room here, what're you going to do? Continue to do as you're told, or are you going to take this second chance to make better decisions?" John carefully asked the demon.

The demon paused to gather his thoughts. "If given the chance, I'd want to make better decisions. Yeah, I'm stuck in Hell, and yeah, it's all I've known, but if given the chance, I want to make better decisions. Take a different path in life," he expressed, praying he had the opportunity to do exactly that.

With a slow, drawn-out exhale, John nodded. "Then, when the opportunity comes to you, take it and run. Don't look back. Run from this place and find those souls out there fighting to make Hell a more bearable place for all the damned souls. Live a pious life giving back to the damned souls you've participated in holding in bondage. This is a new beginning for you. Take it and make it worth something," he finished, looking to the door out of the corner of his eye. With nothing left to say, John opened the door and closed it behind him. Believing he had made the right decision, he pushed forward with his mission.

Following the path the demon had laid out for him, John remained cautious of any threats, despite how forthcoming the demon had been. The demon was honest in his information as John crept through the empty halls. Though the sounds of tormented souls and erupting fire could be heard in the distance, not a sound filled the hallways around him. Picking up his pace, John carried on his search for the main office. It didn't take long for him to find the stairwell and as he slipped through it's door he leapt over the railing. Catching the right rail, John made no sound as he jumped to the exit door. Careful to rise up to the viewing window, John leaned around the glass pane, searching for any guards. The coast was clear. John's heart raced as he felt more and more of the pain from all the suffering around him. Firing off like a bullet from a gun, John pushed himself despite the taxation on his body. One corner after another, he flew until he was met with a heavy steel door, carrying a weathered sign.

"Fuck," John whispered, walking forward to read the ancient writings. "*TaaCho . . . ettan . . .*" He struggled to read the eons-old language. "Damn these difficult bastards. Is this it, or is this a fucking kitchen?" John struggled as his finger ran over the sign.

Wary about the possible warning across the door, John readied his two kodachis. A massive amount of energy pulsated from the room before him and as he calmed his breathing he knew there was no turning back now. Kicking the door in, John squashed one guard immediately as the flying twisted steel pinned him against the opposite wall. The swift violence left the room shell shocked as John used the confusion to dismember another guard. Yelling out to his squad mates, a third guard fell to John's destructive hands. Despite his speed, the surprise was over. Throwing his sword across the room, John only helped in sounding the alarm as the last guard reached for a lever.

Shit!

With the alarm sounding off, John retrieved his Kodachi from the stone wall. Many of the souls had dispersed in the confusion but as John checked his surroundings, he found that he was not alone. Bound in chains and surrounded by six armored guards, John stared off with the unfazed demons in the corner of the room. With nothing to say, he charged at the guard on his right. The two crossed swords with ease as they matched each other's swordsmanship. John was surprised by the skill of the demon before him. Slamming his pommel into the nose of the guard after a brief clash, he quickly spun to avoid another's attack.

With all of them striking at each other at once, John threw one sword through one guard's chest as he parried the attack from another. There was only seconds to spare as the final attack came around but with him too close to move away in time, John hedged his bets as he grabbed the demon's sword from the air. Squeezing the blade, he ignored the pain as he continued to fight off the other guard. Precarious as the situation had become, John pulled one guard in, using him as a shield as another bashed against his friend's armor. The three danced as one guard attempted to escape John's iron clasp and the other fought to kill the intruder. Leading the attacking guard into a wall, John released his body shield before skewering both guards through their mouths.

John retrieved his sword from the mouths of the demons as another stepped up to the plate. The stampeding loudmouth knew nothing of surprise as John pivoted to his next opponent. With a quick parry, he raised his good leg and kicked the demon across the room. Despite lifting the demon off the ground, John was left surprised as the armor held it's shape. John was stunned. Even at his first stage of power he knew the capabilities of his strength and the power behind his kicks. As curiosity grew, John readied himself as he sat on the cusp of pushing his powers to the next level.

"That's some special armor you boys got there! Who gave y'all that for one little prisoner?" John teased, searching for information.

"You can drop the act, *Salvatore*. We know who you are!" one guard shouted out.

"Yeah, Commander Zähd knew you'd come looking for this prisoner and he supplied us with them so we could kill you!" another rang out.

"Oh, is that so?" John scoffed as he lowered his blades slightly, "Then how about we see about that?" he finished as he began pouring Natural Energy into his swords.

"You think those little toothpicks are going to hurt us?" The first guard boasted as they closed in.

"Ask your friends."

"You should learn when to give up, old man!" the third guard taunted as he moved forward, flail and buckler in hand.

Switching his stance to southpaw, John led the three as they stepped around the dead bodies. The armor was old, and while the magic in them was powerful, John knew it wasn't powerful enough. With an exhale of breath, John relaxed the grip on his swords. Making the first move, the guard spun his flail about before sending it forward. Focused on the guard in front of him, John leaned away as the flail nearly kissed his cheek. Seeing the break in the older man's defense the three struck out in unison. One attack after another, John avoided while trying to not trip over the bodies he had already made. Striking out to break up the barrage, John was taken aback as his attack got parried by the buckler shield, but as the shock set in for him, it was followed up with a far worse feeling. As the spiked flail ripped through his side, the blunt force trauma wasn't even the worst part as his feet left the ground and he began hurling through the air.

With blood pouring from his head and guts, John focused his energy into healing his wounds as he crawled from a hole in the wall. He hated to admit that the attack hurt, but it did. Stumbling to his feet, John grabbed a nearby chunk of rubble from the ground. With the stone in one hand and one of his kodachis in the other, he began to redirect the flow of his energy into the stone, hardening it's composition. His wounds were mostly healed but as he looked to three waiting guards, John knew he would have to fight harder than he had been. Tossing the stone in his hand, he glared back at the guards as he walked forward.

"Alrighty, boys. If we're playing that game, then we're playing *that* game!" John shouted before he tossed the stone to the guard on his right.

He was short on time and with the alarm blaring all around them it was only a matter of time before more guards would arrive. Making some space between himself and his opponents, John manipulated the stone and wind around him, creating a pillar of rock and rubble he could throw. It was time to end the fight. Hurling the pillar across the room, he managed to almost take out two of the guards as the mass of stones crushed one of their bodies. Those that were still left alive began questioning whether or not they could win the fight. With one of his friends pinned under the pillar, the final guard struggled to fight off the old man. Locking their swords together, John fought to overpower the final obstacle between him and the information he needed.

The two violently fought for control over one another. Back and forth they'd push each other around the room, neither one giving the other a break. Pulling himself out from underneath the rubble, the second guard struggled to move after having one of his legs badly broken from the last attack. With a weapon procured, he hurried back into the fight, only to be taken down immediately by John's hands. There was no mercy to be had for the demons around him, John needed the answers the soul had.

Falling away from the fight, the final guard scrambled for the prisoner as he curled up underneath some rubble. In the confusion of the fight, the guard hadn't yet noticed his helmet had fallen off but with bloodied and shaking hands, he held a knife to the prisoner's throat. John stopped in his tracks as he watched the demon's hand shake. He was too close to what he needed to fumble up now.

"Stand back!" The demon shouted. "Stand back or I'll end him!"

"Okay, I'll step back." John paused as he raised his hands.

"Drop your weapons too!" He demanded.

"Okay, okay, I'll drop them." John complied as he slowly moved his energy toward his fingers. "So, tell me? You boys had a little more than just some powerful armor. You actually knew how to fight, and more than a normal guard would—"

"Yeah, what's it to ya?" The demon said.

"Well humor me, who trained you?" John continued as a small spark of electricity ran over his fingers.

"Hah!" the demon laughed out. "Who do you think? Zähd did, of course. We're some of the few that survived his training. We were trained specifically to kill you!"

"Oh really now?" John smirked as he poured more Natural Energy into his fingers. "Tell me, did he train you for this?"

In a flash of light, John dropped the final demon. Scarred and confused by the thunderous clap that followed the flash, the prisoner slowly opened his eyes. Looking behind him he stood in awe at the smoldering hole between the demon's eyes. The prisoner couldn't comprehend what had just happened. Turning his sight back to John, he watched as lightning arced from his hand.

"I guess not." John smiled as he released his powers.

"So you're *the* John Salvatore?" The prisoner spoke up.

"That'd be me. So I heard you and I have a mutual friend."

"We do, and mutual goals as well. Word is you're looking for Zähd."

"Aye, I am. Word also has it that you have some information on his whereabouts," John replied as he helped the prisoner from his chains.

"That I do. I tried to relay the message to Abe before they caught up to me, but we both see how well that worked out," he stated, raising his hands to the room.

"So where'd you see him?" John asked.

"I saw Zähd leaving for Earth last week. I know that's not the best of news, but here's the thing. Before he left, I saw him leaving from the *eighth layer*." The man paused to collect his thoughts. "As well, I also know where he was leaving for. Dubai. I managed to overhear some chatter while the portal was being prepped. Those assholes were talking about all the shipments he's been making back and forth and the guy's planning something big, and *nobody* is trying to stop him," he continued to explain.

"Any clue as to what? Did you learn anything else?" John asked as he kept an eye out for more guards.

"No, unfortunately. I watched Zähd walk through the portal, all dressed up and carrying his swords. He didn't even say a word besides 'Dubai' to the guys in charge of the checkpoint down there. I tried to find out more, but next thing I knew, I was on the run. Made it all the way back up to the central city on layer four before they caught me," the man finished, dropping his head low.

John sighed but accepted that he managed to at least learn

something. Patting the man on his shoulder he adjusted his gear. "So what do you say we get out of here?" John offered.

"Oh, I can't leave man. They already have me in their system. I could run, but they'd find me eventually, and when they did, they'd just make my punishment even worse. I've accepted that the *freedom* I once had up there is long gone. I knew the risks when I accepted Abraham's job but don't worry about me. You're needed elsewhere. The world needs you!" The man's once-smiling face disappeared as a look of sullen acceptance took over.

John could see the defeat in his body language. "Thank you. . . Someday, I hope I can free you from all this."

"That'd be impressive, John Salvatore. It really would." The man forced out a smile.

Hearing the running footsteps of the guards down the hallway, John quickly focused his energy while releasing his family sword. With a nod to the poor soul, John opened a portal back to Earth. He had a location and he was hot on the trail. John refused to stop now. Returning to the abandoned gas station that he had made his home base, he prepared to face his nemesis.

The arid night left John in despair as he arrived to an empty base of operations. Judging by the state of affairs, he could tell Zähd had just left. After a lengthy interrogation to just find the base, all John was left with was dismay as he kicked a empty box away. He was too late again. Punching the side of the office wall, he refused to give up. There had to be something. Searching the building from top to bottom, John felt his spirit wane as he wrapped up his search. No clues had been found to where Zähd had gone to.

One office room remained, and his hope of finding a clue sank until the smell of iron gripped his nose. He knew that smell, there was blood in the air, and accompanying it was rotting flesh. Pulling his 1911 from his shoulder holster, John gently pressed himself against the door as he cracked it open.

Turned-over furniture and trash littered the room as he continued to open the door. Scanning around the room, John's eye locked onto a folded letter and a small, wrapped package sitting on a desk. He remained apprehensive as he drew closer. Taking in a whiff of the air, John confirmed his suspicions of the smell. Only so many things could fit within a small box and John's heart sank to his gut as he imagined what could be in the package. Looking to the folded piece of paper partially tucked underneath, John pulled the note out.

John, wish you were here! Let the games begin.

-Z

Fewer words had ever cut so deeply for John. He could almost hear Zähd speaking them to him as he looked back to the box. John felt nothing but dread as he cupped the palm-sized present Zähd had left for him. His mind dreadfully raced as he pulled on the string of the ribbon, fearing what was inside.

Cut at the knuckles and beginning to decompose, two of King's fingers rolled around on the blood-stained cotton fluff. Peeking inside the box, John immediately slammed it back shut. John's chest and eyes swelled as he was flooded with emotions. Looking back again to the severed fingers, John failed to hold back his tears as he fell to a knee. Anger and pain swirled within him as he struggled to pull himself together.

John's rage boiled within him as he wiped the tears from his face. It broke his heart to see the dismembered fingers of his best friend. Collecting the note as he stood, John turned and walked out of the room. He refused to allow the chase to carry on. He wasn't going to let Zähd hurt his friend any longer. He refused to allow Zähd's plans to come to fruition, but most importantly, he wasn't going to allow his nephew to carry on the burden of their family's curse. Activating his powers, John pulled on the energy around him and summoned a ball of fire into his hand. Seething with anger, he chucked the ball aside as he exited the building, setting it ablaze.

A bubbling rage not even Hell could create swelled inside of him. Once again, he was too late. His chest heaved as John tried to remain rational in his decision-making, but the further he traveled on his journey, the harder it became to see the right path. The idea of his nephew carrying on the curse haunted John. Not even closing his eye gave him any relief. The taunting glimpses of the future continued to flash before him. Left with no leads, John, angry and devastated, prepared a portal. His conviction had been solidified, his resolve established, and his quest for vengeance borne from his malice for Zähd.

Teleporting back to his base, John sullenly stared off as Gabriella and Michael looked on, waiting for his news. Immediately, they noticed that something was wrong. Michael jumped from his seat as he chased after John. Never had he seen their leader so downtrodden. Down at his desk he sat, softly sitting the box before them. Pulling the string to his desk lamp, John struggled to find the words to say. Slowly but surely, Michael began to piece together what might have transpired.

"What happened in Dubai, John?" Michael's voice fell flat as he looked to the box.

"I was too late. They had already packed up and left," John groaned as he sat back in his seat. "All except for that box and *this* note," he finished as he revealed the slip of paper.

Smelling the growing stench as she walked up to the desk, Gabriella grew suspicious. "What's in the box, John?"

"A reminder," John struggled to say as Michael lifted the lid.

An audible gasp emerged from them both as they realized who the fingers belonged to. Closing the lid, Michael looked away as Gabriella turned to tend to her erupting tears. Setting the box back down, Michael stepped away from the desk as he rubbed his face to the news. Both of them were devastated, and it showed in their faces. Looking back to the note on the desk, Michael needed to know more.

"Well, what did the note say?"

"*John, wish you were here! Let the games begin.*' Signed 'Z,'" John replied as he looked to the pile of papers on his desk.

"We're gonna kill this motherfucker, I swear it!" Gabriella shouted as she slammed her hand against a wall.

"No, *we* won't," John annunciated, looking up from his spot.

"What do you mean 'we won't'? We're a team, John. We're in this together," Michael retorted.

Seeing the darkness before him and the enemy he had to face, John knew that it was only a matter of time before it was their fingers he was finding. Or even worse. "After today, *we* are no longer a team," John began. "Zähd's holding nothing back to get at me. There's no line he won't cross, and I can't have him coming after you two."

"We'll be fine, John!" Gabriella protested.

"No, you won't." John looked to her. Pain and anger swirled in his eye like a violent typhoon. "If you stayed working with me, it would only be a matter of time before Zähd would knock down that door and torture either one of you for information about me. He would use you to get to me!" he paused as he struggled to pull himself together. "Now, I offered you a way out years ago before things got this bad, and now that offer is my wish. I want you two . . . I want you two to live a long life, to love and enjoy your time on Earth. I don't want you to have to live the life I have."

He paused to compose himself. "Everything I've done up to this point has been to save the world from whatever kind of attack Zähd has planned. But more importantly, all I've done has been to save my nephew from having to go down the same path that I did if I should fail. I love that boy with all my heart and soul and would move the stars themselves to let that child live a normal life." John's arms shook as his fists tightened. "You two have taken every single bit of this life in stride, no matter how insane of a mission we would go on. No matter how life-threatening things would get, neither of you would falter in your commitment, and I can never begin to repay that. I love you guys, and that's why I can't have you here anymore."

"And we'll follow you all the way to the end John, no matter what!" Gabriella stood behind her words as she grabbed John's shaking hand.

"But you can't, Gabby. Neither of you would be able to safely follow me into Hell. A short trip or mission is one thing, but this? There's no way I'd be able to protect you two while fighting Zähd at the same time. There's just no way." John's words drifted off as he pulled away from her.

"So after all that, you're just going to make us leave? Like, '*Thanks* for sticking around all those years, guys, and helping me track down this ancient warrior from Hell that's trying to take over the world, but now that things are getting a little heavier, I'm going to have to ask you to leave'?" Michael questioned him as he grew upset. "John, you may have offered us a way out, but when you're *asked* to help save the world from ending, you kinda grow a commitment to it! We're in this till the end, no matter what!" Michael pointed out as he pressed his finger onto the desk.

John softly smiled as he listened to Michael's words. He couldn't have asked for better friends to have by his side. Looking to the two of them, John contemplated giving them one more assignment, the final way they could help him while also keeping them safe. Pulling a key from his pocket, he worked the old lock on one of his desk drawers.

"I hate to admit it, but you're right Michael." John paused as he gave him a half smile. "But regardless, I'm disbanding the group after we're done talking here today." "But I'm not sending you out empty-handed. I have one final assignment for the two of you. My final request for you." He looked to them with love in his eyes, wanting them to understand.

Silence fell across the room as John pulled out two manila folders. Separating them, John cleared his throat before speaking.

"*These* are your last assignments. They're dated and not to be opened before these dates. Once the time has come, open them and carry out my last mission for me." John struggled to look his friends in their eyes. "All that you'll need will be inside of these, but make no mistake: this will be the most difficult mission I've ever given you. But with the amount of knowledge you two possess and combining your incredible ability to uncover the hidden truths about the supernatural world around us will make for an invaluable skill to you in the future." John paused as he handed them their folders. "I encourage you two to work together, to never lose sight of the incredible team you are! When you two work together, you produce your best work. Thank you both for your companionship. I will always cherish it." John's chest swelled as he held back his tears.

"John . . ." Gabriella tried to hold back her tears as they began to fall.

"Gabby, sweetie, please don't cry," John comforted her as he stood up from his desk.

"You're going to get yourself killed, you know that?" She paused as John pulled her in for a hug. "If you go out there, alone, you're going to get yourself killed!" she shouted with tears running down her face as she pounded on his chest.

"And you would be, too, if you stayed. At least with this, you have the chance to continue helping me whether I come back or not!" John expressed as he directed her attention to the folder.

"Zähd's been around for over eight hundred years," Michael commented.

"So what makes you think you can do it alone?" Gabby added as John pulled away.

"Someone has to stop him! I'm the only one with the power to do it, so it has to be me! This is my burden to bear, and I will not have any more people dying on my watch," John asserted as the words left his mouth. "I promise you, I'll stop Zähd one way or another. I'll give it my all, all the way to Sha'are Mavet!" John meant every word. He'd succeed even if it cost him his life.

Realizing there was no changing his mind, the two accepted their friend's decision. It was the most difficult thing he had ever asked from them, but with heavy hearts, Michael and Gabriella returned to their stations. John looked back to the note and box on his desk, worried for King's safety. Watching his friends pack up their things tore John's heart to pieces, even if it was to keep them safe. After stepping out the back door, John climbed the ladder to the roof of the building, searching for a place to sit and breathe. Turning to the sun, he sat on a wooden box and massaged his left knee.

John sighed heavily as he thought of the road ahead of him. When he looked down, a picture of Dominic caught his eye from his shirt pocket. The small portrait carried many crinkles and scrapes across its surface; just like John, it had endured the journey with him. Reflecting on everything he had done since his mission began, since his first vision of the world his nephew was destined to inherit, John wanted nothing more than to change it. To take that pain away from Dominic was all he could ever ask for. John's family had done more than enough to help save the world for eons, and he would end that—with himself. All he wished was to break the chains his family had been bound with.

Feeling the cold, arid wind cutting through his bones, John rubbed the scars on his arms to keep warm. The scar tissue he had acquired throughout the years covered him. He had not been kind to his body in his younger years, and now he felt it. Despite the many healing benefits of his powers, they never regrew that which he truly lost. Hearing footsteps on the ladder, John looked off to the disappearing sun.

"We're almost packed. Mike's just loading up the truck now." Gabriella tiptoed around her words.

"Okay. Thank you for coming and telling me," John replied as he watched the sun disappear.

"I'm going to miss this place when we're gone," Gabriella commented as she sat down next to John.

"This place is falling apart," John replied as he leaned over toward her.

"Hey! It's in a lot better shape than when we first arrived. We all put a lot of work into this place, trying to make it a home!" she responded, punching him in the arm.

"Ow!" John laughed as he rubbed his arm. "Yeah, I guess we have."

Silently, the two sat as the howling winds filled the void and Gabriella kicked her feet back and forth. "Are we ever going to get to work together again?"

"I don't know, hon. I really don't." John paused before clearing his throat. "If we're lucky, no, because I would have stopped Zähd from invading Earth and prevented the future from becoming reality."

"You're talking about your nephew, aren't you?" she asked as she pointed to the picture still in his hands.

"Yeah, I am." The words broke his heart as he said them. "But if we're *really* lucky and I manage to return, then it's possible. But that's if we're *really* lucky . . ."

"We're not *that* lucky, are we?"

"She asks the man trying to save the world," John replied as he looked up to her.

The two shamefully chortled together as Michael stepped out onto the concrete below them. "We're all packed up. Meet y'all inside?"

"Yeah, we'll head down there," John replied.

"John?" Gabriella spoke up as the two of them stood. "Promise me you'll come back?"

"I can't, Gabby, and I'm sorry. I won't give you a false hope that I'll return." John hated the words as they left him. "I'm completely okay with sacrificing my life if it means I can stop Zähd, if it means my nephew can grow up and live a normal life." John looked deeply into Gabriella's eyes as he spoke his words. He hoped that she would understand someday.

With nothing left to say, John led the two as they got off the roof. The once-packed room of books, notes, and all the information they had gathered throughout the years was now little more than an empty shell of something great. Only John's corner remained partially decorated. The hollow pit that had started to form within John sank deeper as he walked to Michael.

"I put all of your personal effects over on your workstation. I found those scrolls you were going crazy over last month. They were stuffed under like four boxes of books!" Michael lightheartedly spoke as he tugged on the straps in the bed of his truck.

"Hah, how the hell did they end up under there?"

"Who knows? But I'm glad they were found."

"Me too." John trailed off as he looked away.

"Hey," Michael called out. "Kick his ass! You hear me?"

"I hear ya."

"No, I mean it! You find him, save King before he loses anything else, and kick his demonic ass back to Hell!"

"That's the plan."

"You've shown me a lot John, working with you for all this time. You opened my mind to the larger world around us and to so many different things. I personally don't think I would be who I am today if it weren't for everything you've done for me, and for that, I will never waste what you've given me. But don't you waste that opportunity when it comes to you. When the moment to strike comes, attack with all you got!" Michael finished as the two of them clasped hands.

With a heavy heart, John gave them one final hug before sending them off. Watching two of his only friends leave, John felt the remains of his heart crumble. He promised them that he wouldn't fail, and he intended to keep his promise. John looked around his empty home. The memories flashed like echoes around him. Sitting down at his desk, the hollow pit within him widened further with a heavy sigh. It had been a long time since he had felt such loneliness, but in that moment, he did.

* * *

Two years later

From the Middle East up through Eastern Europe, John followed Zähd's trail. Their game of cat and mouse left John tunneling with misery and rage. With each failure, he was left another taunting note and finger. A torturing reminder of his inability to stop Zähd. It wouldn't be until the fall of 2010 that Zähd would put an end to their game.

The fall night came soon as John crept up to a warehouse dock off the coast of Chefchaouen, Morocco. As the game progressed, more and more Zähd raised the veil of his secrecy, as shown by the heavily guarded cargo around the shipping dock. Sneaking past security, John scaled the side of the building and entered from a second-story window. From the look of the place, John guessed he had arrived early.

His heart raced as he felt his brand pulsating to the presence of another. Not only had Zähd been growing his forces, but he himself had grown in power. The realization caused John to stop in his tracks, for if he could feel Zähd's presence, Zähd could definitely feel his. Though his cover was soon to be blown, John pressed forward.

Entering into an executive office, his eye fixated on an open notebook lying on the floor. Such an obvious ploy did not fool John as he looked to the bay window overlooking the main floor. But with determination, John avoided detection from the window as he grabbed the book. Opening the worn red leather journal, John saw how the pieces of Zähd's plan came together.

"He's going to take a curse-wielder and possess them with a demon." John couldn't believe the words that came from his mouth.

The journal contained lists of people to kidnap, ingredients to perform mass rituals with, and old magical texts to gather, all for the singular goal of creating an abhorrent supernatural creature with more power than any demon or run-of-the-mill curse-wielder. John tore the room apart. With caution to the wind, he searched and prayed for any other conclusion. Retrieving his past notes from previous missions, he compared them all. They all confirmed his fears. Taking a knee, he lowered the book as he tried to clear his mind of distractions.

Without time to mull over the information he just received, a thunderous clap rang out, followed by the sound of whooshing air as a portal opened up on the main floor below him. Running to the bay window, John witnessed Zähd motioning for his men to start transporting their crates and vehicles through. The anger within him rush to the surface, and John's face grew red just before his sight caught something else. Looking off to the right, John watched as King, fingerless and beaten, was rolled out in his wheelchair. Not able to contain the rage inside him any longer, John activated his powers and punched the glass out in front of him.

"Zähd!" John's hate-fueled yell echoed out across the entire dock as tears ran down his face.

Everyone including Zähd stopped in their tracks and looked to the enraged old man. Zähd smiled gleefully as he watched John jump down to the ground. With his bare hands, he killed any guard who ran after him. Grabbing King's wheelchair and bringing him in closer, Zähd signaled for his crew to continue with what they were doing.

"Well, if it isn't my old *pal*, John Salvatore!" Zähd teased as he rested his hands on King's shoulders.

"I'm not your pal, and get your fucking hands off my friend!" John yelled as he raised his family sword to Zähd.

"Ah, ah, ah! Stop right there, John," Zähd commanded as he pressed one of his sharpened claws against King's neck.

"King, you okay?" John yelled out as he stood his ground.

"I could use a hand or *two* . . ." The weakened King tried to remain positive for his friend, despite how weak his body had become.

"I'm going to get you out of here King, okay? You're going to be fine!" John tried to comfort him while the rage swelled inside of him.

"So sweet. Even after being apart for so long, you two still try to help each other out," Zähd sarcastically remarked.

"Shut up!" John barked.

"Ah, ah, remember, I hold your friend's life in the balance," Zähd warned him, pressing his claw even farther against King's neck. "So did you read my journal? I left it for you." Zähd smiled as he narrowed his eyes, enjoying the torment he was inflicting on John.

"Why? Why leave it?" John shouted while tightening his open fist.

"Because you can't stop it, and it's fun to watch you try," Zähd revealed.

"I'll stop you! You won't get away with this, and I won't let you succeed in creating that abomination!" John protested angrily.

"But I will, and I think you know that. I have been given a very important task, and I will succeed in it. Nothing will change that, and neither will you, John. This, all of this, is just the beginning." Zähd smiled as he looked around the room. "The chase is over, John. I gave you the chance to catch up and save your friend here, but you've run out of time. I'm needed elsewhere and must tie up my loose ends before it's time for the *big reveal*." Zähd continued, using hand gestures to accentuate his words.

"Not if I stop you right now!" John shouted as he adjusted his footing before leaping across the room.

"See, I thought you'd say that," Zähd commented before pursing his lips.

Bringing his sword around, John swung as he propelled himself forward. Shaking his head, Zähd reached behind the wheelchair and revealed a large knife. Seeing the blade, John hurled himself further as the milliseconds passed. Looking up to John, Zähd frowned. In that moment, time moved so slowly for the three of them, each certain of the outcome.

"You have only yourself to blame," Zähd said as he drove the blade through the back of the chair and out King's chest.

Mortified by the pain spreading across King's face, John dropped his defenses just long enough for Zähd to jump up and swat him away. Flying across the room, his body skipped across the shipping crates as he knocked into them. Falling to the ground, John, battered and bloody, used his sword to help himself to his feet. With the last of the vehicles through the portal, Zähd looked to the dying man before him.

"I'm sorry you had to be in the middle of this. I hope you understand this is purely business and I never held any animosity toward you." Zähd apologized while patting King's shoulder.

"Oh, believe me, the feeling's not mutual." King struggled to get the words out as his lungs filled with blood.

"Well, at least there's an afterlife waiting for you." Zähd commented before pulling the knife out from his back and walking away.

"Get back here! Get—ugh" John shouted as he stumbled around.

"Get. Back. Here!" John screamed as he pushed his curse powers beyond the first level and leaped across the room.

Reaching out, John barely missed Zähd as the portal closed before him. Grabbing the floor as he landed, John spun around and violently punched through the concrete. His rage poured out of him as he pounded the ground with his fists. His hatred turned to suffering as he watched King's hand fall limp.

"King! King, man! Antoine King, you son of a bitch, come on, man, open your eyes!" John pleaded and yelled as he held his friend's lifeless body. "King! Please, King, answer me!" John couldn't hold back his tears as he laid King's body on the ground. "Come on, man, you gotta still be with me!" John begged as King's blood soaked his hands and clothes.

Using Natural Energy, John worked his magic as he tried to repair the damage to King's heart. Such delicate work made nearly impossible by Zähd's brutal wound but as the sweat pooled on his forehead he managed to repair the damage. King had lost too much blood, but with his wounds sealed, John refused to give up. Using his control of lightning, he repeatedly tried to restart King's heart. Again and again, he begged and pleaded for King to open his eyes. When John realized that King was gone, his heart ached as he wailed out in anguish. Falling back onto his butt, John sat, broken from the loss of his friend, and in that sorrow, the pit within him hit rock bottom.

Wiping the last tear away, John walked back over to his prosthetic leg and reattached it before returning his powers to their base level. Signing his own mudras, John reached out and called his sword back to him. The emptiness he felt weighed heavier than King as he walked over and hoisted him onto his shoulder. With nothing to return to, John summoned the electrical currents around him and formed a lightning bolt that struck some wooden boxes behind him. The following explosion set the warehouse ablaze in a matter of minutes as John walked away with vengeance in his eyes.

After burying King and settling his affairs, John returned to his base one final time. His hands had been stained in blood a hundred times over, but washing off his best friend's had been the most difficult. All the times he had peered into the future taunted him as he changed his clothes. John had felt enough pain, and he was prepared to go to war one last time. He grabbed every powerful item he possessed. He armed himself with everything from the six scrolls filled with powerful ancient magic to the last of his explosive trinkets from the Soviet base and the multiple grimoires he had collected over the years, the pages all but disintegrated. Knowing that his prowess with magic would only help with part of the fight, John also armed himself with the twin kodachis, two Bowie knives, his personal tantō, and, lastly, his family sword. With almost everything he needed, John prepared to meditate in order to gather energy for the coming battle.

During his meditation, John felt overwhelmed by an old sensation he hadn't experienced in years. For the first time in a long while, *he* was receiving a vision. Blue light glowed out from behind his eyepatch as images came to his mind. Opening his eyes, John peered out through time. Seeing the same images that began his quest, John was left confused as he continued to see the same series of events he had fought so hard to prevent. As his vision continued, he was met with images of battles won and lost, images of pain and loss, of hate and suffering, but also of love, sacrifice, and happiness.

With tears streaming down his face, John straightened his

posture, needing to see the vision's end. His facial expressions changed with each passing image. The cycle of pain and loss and of love, hope, misery, and despair continued on, despite all that he had done to prevent them, leaving John empty. Witnessing Dominic's life unfold, John understood the measures he would have to take if he were to prevent the future from happening. Drained of emotion, he stared at the final images in his mind as they faded away and reality returned.

Regaining his senses, John felt a change within him. The hours he had sat meditating had paid off as he felt a strength within he had never before. Natural Energy swirled throughout his veins, churning like snakes under the skin. His hands tingled as he rubbed them together and as the electrical friction sparked it created static electricity between his palms. Never in his life had John absorbed so much energy through meditation. The sensation it produced fooled John as he felt his missing pinky finger, and in a flash of light, it almost appeared as if it were still there. Looking to his stump, for a moment, he could see his leg again. His seventy-year-old body felt rejuvenated for the first time in years.

Feeling the power within him, John reached out across the room and pulled at a replacement leg. Switching out his prosthetic, he rose from the floor, feeling prepared. He would avenge King, he would stop Zähd from creating an abomination and he would save Dominic from *his* life. Walking to the door, he stopped as he turned to a picture pinned to the wall. Gabriella had left a photo of the four of them from early on their journey. With a wide smile, she grinned in the foreground in front of John, King, and Michael as they looked on in confusion. Slipping the picture into the same pocket as Dominic's photo, John walked away from his home.

As he closed the door behind him, with no effort and without activating his powers, he set the door handle ablaze. Looking back in confusion, John realized he had absorbed far more energy than he initially thought. Electricity ran along the surface of his skin as he watched flames engulf the building. Activating his powers to the first level, he was surprised that they felt like the strength of the fourth. The incredible surge of power flowing through him gave life to an idea. Releasing his sword, John opened a portal and reached out further into Hell than he ever had before. As he felt out through the void he found the *Ignis Portas*. It was close enough.

Landing on a rooftop facing the gate, John looked to the re-paired base he had snuck through one year prior. With no time to waste, he leaped from rooftop to rooftop until he reached the door to the base. John threw stealth to the wind as he ran through the familiar halls. The gate was still intact and it gave John the perfect defense to protect his rear. Looking down to the layer below, he glared beyond its surface, through the tunnel and to the seventh layer below. He could almost see Zähd looking back up at him as John felt his presence out of everyone's in Hell. The two of them stood out in the moment, and they both knew it.

Looking up into the ceiling, Zähd grinned as he realized that John had arrived. His presence whistled across the static of all the energy around him, like a distant call of an old memory. The sound of war drums echoed in his ears as he felt out to John's presence. Smiling gleefully, he returned to commanding the demonic scien-tists and lackeys around him, preparing for John's arrival.

John reached into one of the satchels on his leg, retrieving a burnt grimoire. The first grimoire he had ever seen. His father would have approved of the use of his gift. With his hands over the cover and the assistance of some Natural Energy, John restored some of the book and it's pages. Power poured from his tongue as he read the ancient text. Conjuring a great round, translucent golden shield before him. There was no mistake to forces below that, that an attack was imminent. Hearing the sirens from the base, followed by the flashing lights of the prison below, John leaped from the scaffolding.

The wind whistled around him, for it was the only sound to fill the air just before storm. The scene reminded John of his first firefight in Vietnam. Terrifying, but exciting. Fiery stones crumbled against John's shield as he continued his decent. Following the stones with volleys of lightning and plasma, the *legendary* defenses of Hell were for once being put to the test. Outstretching one hand while holding the book in the other, John embraced the blasts of energy from the cannons below. The spell he wielded held incredible power, but with the pages of the book beginning to burn once more, knew his time with it was running out. Through all his pain and conviction, John still admired the effort they gave as he absorbed their attacks with his shield.

The speed of their attacks increased the farther he fell, each attempting to break his defense, but as the shield grew heavier, John knew it was time to attack. He could see the Sixth Layer's fiery tunnel beyond the barrage and as John roared out, he returned all of their attacks back out them. Extending his hands, he pushed against the shield as a massive beam of energy expelled from it's face. Nothing survived as the bean touched down. It's erasing light obliterated everything it touched. John leveled the face of the prison as he finished off his continuous attack. He had cleared a path for himself as he fell through the center. Looking down to the smoldering remains in his hand, John released his shield as the ashes flew away.

With his kodachis drawn, John adjusted his pitch as he sped

down the sixth layer. From all around, one guard after another lashed out at him as he flew by. He gave no quarter as he forced his way down. Nothing would stand between him and his goal and with the wake of John's destruction tumbling behind him he aimed to take everything and *everyone* with him.

Reaching the edge of the sixth layer, John opened another grimoire, summoning a destructive blast of sound as he slammed his hands together. The thunderous clap and shock wave from the attack shattered and splintered the rock foundation and stonework around him. While it crumbled apart, John watched as massive sections of the prison began falling from the layer's gravity. Following the destruction down, he glided between the sections of falling rubble as it rained down atop the military bases below.

The seventh layer of Hell housed most of Hell's armies and John stared on with conviction as he neared it's impending horde. Military bases covered every face and side of the five-hundred-mile-long barren layer. Choosing to face the forces on the outside of the layer rather than attempting to face the bulk within the interior tunnel, John moved himself toward the layer's exterior edge. Looking back, he watched as chunk after chunk of rock and mortar tore the main base apart.

Right at the ground's edge, John landed just to look back as the last of the falling rubble added insult to injury for the forces of Hell. Engulfed in flames, the base crumbled away from the devastating attack. As explosions rang out across the land, the ground shook to John's will. He could hear the cries of Hell's army echo out in dismay. There was no regret to be had. He wouldn't be stopped. Walking to the edge, John looked down at all the military installations that lay between him and the eighth layer. He could feel Zähd like a heartbeat, his presence pulsing like a fiery pain inside of him.

Retrieving his third grimoire, John once again reversed the burn damage to the pages before opening it. He read from the old Swedish text, speaking its masterful spells. By his own power, John conjured a massive storm cloud that covered the entire side of the layer. Feeling sweat form on his temple, he knew he was beginning to push his limits. Though just like before, the book burned away as he toiled with the pure energy surging in the clouds. His hands tingled to the power. Never had he felt more connected to the elements around him as he focused on controlling the clouds. Looking down toward his prosthetic, John twisted his leg around until a hidden tantō blade revealed itself. Standing over the edge, he planted the sword's diamond tip into the brimstone crust, ready to attack.

For a moment, John felt at peace, looking off at the thundering clouds. "All the way . . ." Taking a deep breath, he exhaled heavily. "To Sha'are Mavet!" he yelled as he propelled himself over the edge.

Unsheathing his kodachis, John fired bolts of lightning from his fingers as he blasted through building after building. Meeting the unsuspecting demons with such a violent force left them with no time to react as he sliced through and decapitated demons while he flew through the first base. Still there was nothing they could do as his trail of destruction began to grow once more. Fleeing demons tripped and fell as John devastated their forces while lightning laid havoc to the buildings. No one had ever tested the demons like John was in that moment, for even if it killed him, he would stop Zähd. Like a whirling vortex of lightning and rubble, John hammered down on their crumbling defenses as he descended the side of the layer. Nothing could withstand his physical strength as he tore the base asunder.

John left no survivors in his path, and body parts piled in his wake as he tore through the first installation. Reaching behind himself, John directed the rear of the storm to follow him as he continued falling. The more he compacted the clouds above him, the more violent the storm grew. Touching the ground only made the damage worse with every step building on the wave of falling debris behind him. Witnessing a rainstorm beginning to form from the clouds, John reached out and forced a monsoon to pour out over the base.

He hadn't even reached halfway down the side of the layer and John had already dealt a serious blow to his enemies. But as the momentum continued, so did he. Rearing his fist back, John wasted no breath as he punched a hole through the exterior wall of the next base. He flooded the lowest levels as he swept away enemies with the water while currents of electricity churned like snakes in the clouds. They wished to be released and he was happy to oblige. John reached out and with a hundred billion volts of electricity in his hand, he slammed it down, through the violent currents of waves. In a blinding flash of light, hundreds of thousands of demons disintegrated as the electrons traveled throughout the waves that carried them. Creating a chain of explosions as the storms raged on, there was nothing that could stop him as he fought his way down.

Seeing the damage to his bladed leg, John quickly reached down and pulled his prosthetic off. The space might have been great between him and the third base, but even from a distance, it was massive. Reaching within himself before landing on the ground, John activated the second stage of his powers and regrew his leg and finger. They were skinless, muscled, and armored with hardened bone, and as his left foot touched the ground, John catapulted himself. Breaking through the sound barrier turned what was once a far distance into a brief passing.

The percussion and plume of ringed clouds were the only indication to the demons that an attack was imminent. Destroying the base walls just like the others, John used his hands and feet to tear and kick demons apart. In a matter of minutes, he found himself surrounded as the horde piled around him. Feeling the jagged cold steel of a pike impale him from behind, John found himself hoisted up as others began to do the same. One after another, swords and pikes pierced his body, raising him high in the air. John was speechless. Due to the amount of Natural Energy he had consumed, he felt no pain from the blades as they ripped through his flesh. Looking back as a sound caught his attention, John felt a smile grow on his face. His laugh began as a light chuckle and grew into a full-on cackle as he watched the destruction come crashing toward the demons.

"Fuck you all!" John shouted as the rubble came crashing down. While still impaled, he spun himself around until he created a tornado with the demons and their blades. Pulling the rubble in around them, John turned his tornado into a blender as the demons failed to escape the powerful winds. With the falling rubble around him, John flung the debris around, tearing the base asunder. As many demons fled from the swirling twister of blood and death, many found themselves crushed under the falling debris from John's previous conquests. There was nowhere safe to hide. Using a significant portion of his absorbed Natural Energy, John forced all the rubble and debris in the air to the ground, flattening the surrounding area. Gliding back to the ground, he continued with his warpath, unwavering in his destruction. In just under fifteen minutes, he had eradicated over one and a half million demons.

Seeing the last base between him and Zähd, John reached down for two of the scrolls by his side. Flinging them open, he transferred his energy into them before releasing two massive bolts of lightning into the clouds. The roaring thunder rolled around in the clouds as John continued running down toward the base. Retrieving the last of his four scrolls, John pushed himself as he poured his energy into them.

Through the scrolls John summoned a tornado around him. Reaching up to the clouds, he carried his move one step further as he reached out at the currents. Streaks of purple lightning arced across his hands and arms as he bellowed out a strained scream. John pushed his curse powers even further, bringing himself to the fourth stage. Sprouting his giant bat-like wings from his shoulder blades, John used their massive wingspan to hurl him downward. He had to hurt the demons around him if he were to have an uninterrupted chance at stopping Zähd. Feeling his skin pulled back from the G-forces, John roared out across the land as he reached the base's walls.

Bringing his fists forward, John expelled the lightning from them, creating a massive blast of energy. The lightning melted the steel, stone, and anything directly in its path. What wasn't melted by his constant stream of electricity, the tornado around him ripped apart as he flew through the base. John held his roaring war cry as he witnessed the destruction flow from his hands. To him, it all had to be destroyed if he were to stop Zähd. Reaching the center of the base, John extended his tornado as he spun around, eradicating anything around him.

Feeling the drain of his reserves and the power of the scrolls waning, John carried on. Using the last of the scrolls' power, he grabbed the tornado and flung it away toward a part of the base he hadn't hit yet. With the layer's edge in sight, John gazed upon the army of demons waiting for him. Stopping at the crust's edge, John looked down at the demon army with excitement and hatred.

Reaching behind his back, John pulled out his final grimoire. "I was going to save this for Zähd, but allow me to show you all what a true *Salvatore can do!*"

Healing the brittle pages of the book, John placed his hand onto it as a blue light peeked out from behind his eyepatch. Pouring in almost every ounce of reserved energy left in him, John beckoned the storm clouds from behind him. Certain of his attack, he stared on as the demon horde fired a volley of attacks at him. Raising his hand from the book and into the air, John willed the lightning from the clouds and sent it hurling toward the army. Writhing like a snake, the deep purple lightning absorbed their attacks before jumping from body to body and decimating their forces.

Controlling the lightning snake with his hand, John smote millions of demons in a matter of minutes as their defenses crumbled. They held no candle to the power he had as they, fell to his will. Whipping the snake around, John sent it flying into the checkpoint that guarded the entrance of the eighth layer. Creating such an explosive blast upon impact, John knew that Zähd had heard him arriving. Flying down and through the debris in the air, John prepared to fight him.

"Zähd! I've come for your head!" John yelled out as he drew closer to the ground.

Unsheathing his family sword and the tantō, John embraced the demons that flooded out from the rubble. Striking down demon after demon, he walked away from the destruction and closer to the center of the layer. The closer he drew, the more he could feel Zähd's presence as he slaughtered his way through the scrambling forces. Refusing to be stopped by Hell's best, John carved a path through the hordes that tried to surround him.

Hearing the ensuing chaos outside, Zähd held the men under his care in check, making sure they continued with their objectives. "Alrighty, just 'cause we have one man outside wrecking the place doesn't mean you're free to stop what you're doing! Everyone, get back to your posts. This is our last test subject, and we will not fail in our mission." Zähd announced to his team while looking to the lifeless body of an Asian man marked with the Vampire Curse.

An assistant panted as they ran up and stood at attention behind Zähd. "Sir!"

"Yes, Private?" Zähd acknowledged him before turning around.

"John Salvatore has breached our defenses. He's making his way toward the layer's center now!" the private announced while maintaining his position.

"Good, send more troops. We need to hold him off for just a moment longer. Is *he* ready to go again?" Zähd asked, alluding to the figure.

"Yes, sir. He's been quite patient with us through this difficult process," the private replied.

"Good, and yes, he has. Inform him that we're ready and send the troops out. We need to hold Salvatore off just a little bit longer," Zähd commanded, looking back at his last test subject.

Hearing the wheels of a gurney rolling toward him, Zähd turned to the disheveled husk of a demon. Curled up on the bed with IV tubing connected to his extremities, the weakened, malignant creature clung to life. Carefully, Zähd's subordinates lifted and transferred the demon from the gurney to the bed next to their test subject. Covered in scars, battered from abuse, and missing limbs and fingers, the demon boiled in rage as he lay in his shell of body. His cracking gray skin flaked away as they laid him down, a reminder to everyone in the room that they were running low on time.

"I'm far more confident in this subject than the last," Zähd confided in the demon as he rested his transplanted hand gently on the demon's shoulder.

"Good, he promised me a new body in all these crazy experiments." The demon's rough and low voice showed his determination to see their trial through.

"And a new body you will have." Zähd reminded him with a confident smile.

"Good. Who's causing all that commotion outside?" the demon replied, wincing as the straps and clamps were applied to his body.

"A curse-wielder,"

"This deep down?"

"A curse-wielder, of royal blood."

With a raise of his brow, the surprised demon settled himself into his position. "Let's get this underway."

"With pleasure, Victor." Zähd smiled before signaling for his team to begin.

The ground shook below John's feet as he continued his fight toward Zähd. Time was running out. Quickly he dropped the enemies around him in one spinning strike before he pushed his powers to grow his wings again. Rarely did he even feel the need to use them since he mastered his control of the wind, but desperate times called for desperate measures. Launching himself into the air, John released his exploding trinkets along the path to thin out the horde. The center of the layer drew near and with it so did Zähd's and another unknown presence revealed itself to him. Infuriated, John pushed his powers even further to gain the speed he needed.

John avoided every attack and projectile thrown at him. His

heart raced as the sounds of Dominic's laughter rang through his ears. He refused to fail him. With the edge of the opening within reach, John pulled away as a fiery explosion of energy erupted from the layer's center. With no time to waste, John dove down into the fiery blast of energy, withstanding it's incredible force as he followed his instincts to find Zähd.

John followed the source before he barreled through the exterior wall of the layer's tunnel. Zähd was so close he could almost touch him. Looking to the floor beneath his feet, John dropped to his knees, then brought his fists down with him. With a thunderous roar, he pounded against the stone. Cracking and shattering the floors around him, John caved in the floor beneath his feet.

Looking over his shoulder, Zähd motioned for everyone to stay calm. "Well hello there. It's nice of you to drop by." Zähd smiled as he looked back to Victor.

"Zähd! Your plans end here!" John demanded, raising his family sword.

"Really? From my point of view, they're well underway," Zähd replied calmly, turning to face him. "But I still need another five minutes, so that's what I'll give you, John. Five minutes of my time," he continued, slowly unsheathing his claymores. "If you can stop me in five minutes, you may just succeed," Zähd finished, raising his swords for battle. "It's been a *long* time since I've had a proper fight against one of your kind. Don't fail me, John *Salvatore!*" Zähd yelled out as he activated his curse powers.

Still at his maximum power, John met the lightning-fast speed of Zähd's attacks. Immediately feeling the power in his swings, John refused to stay on the defensive. Grabbing his tantō and quickly parrying Zähd's sword, he threw the hulking warrior across the room and into the stone walls around them. Weathered from the fight to get to him, John was surprised by the effort it took to toss him. Cracking his neck, Zähd pushed himself out of his hole and brushed the rubble from his chest. The first move did not fail to impress as his berserker blood pumped through his veins. Zähd doubled his speed as he pushed his powers further and propelled himself across the room. With only milliseconds to react as Zähd swung at his neck, John dodged his lightning-fast movements.

With one hand, John summoned the ground from behind him, using the surprise attack to send Zähd flying away. Jumping back to gain some ground, he manipulated the Natural Energy around him and attempted to seal Zähd in a stone prison. John reached out and gripped the air with his hands while he struggled to maintain the behemoth. Punching a hole through the dense rock, Zähd smiled as he pushed his curse even more, reaching the fifth stage of his powers. Immediately the fight excited Zähd, since their first bout left him craving for more. Ready to return the showmanship, Zähd manipulated the energy around him, and created a ball of electricity in his hand. The squealing sphere of energy rolled in and around his hand as he focused on controlling it's form. One of the truest feats of a curse-wielder, Zähd demonstrated with finesse. Changing its form, he focused the energy into a beam of lightning and fired it at John. Were it not for his own powers, John would have surely perished as the blinding light struck the stone walls behind him. Teleporting away, he watched from across the room as Zähd finished his display of power.

In all his days never had John witnessed electrical manipulation to such a degree. Thinking back to the hole he had found in the base when he began his search, John finally understood what really left that wound. With the pile of melting stone and magma where he once stood, acted as a signal of what to expect from their fight. Using his family sword to teleport once more, John evaded a second attack from Zähd as he placed some space between the two of them.

With a thrust of his sword, John went in for the kill. Dodging the attack, Zähd burst from his prison and swung behind him, knocking his opponent away. Even though he was only hit with Zähd's hand, the wounds it left were nothing to scoff at. Stumbling to his feet, John winced as he tried to heal himself; his brand, aching from the stress. Signing two separate mudras with his hands, he imbued his hands with lightning and his feet with fire. Quickly killing the subordinates around him, John stared Zähd down.

"Hurry, John. You're running out of time!" Zähd teased him as he pushed his powers even further.

He was right and John knew it. With no time to mull over the situation, John leapt into action. Bouncing between his fiery kicks, the lightning flowing from his arms and his family sword, John maintained the offensive as the two fought around the room. Zähd was surprised by the ferocious attacks he had launched at him. While the two crossed blades, Zähd found himself employing *all* of his skills as John held him on his toes. Likewise, John had faced many swordsmen in his time, but Zähd stood out among them all as he showed what eight hundred years of fighting experience looked like. Cracking John across the face with his pommel, Zähd launched him across the room and toward Victor. Though as he caught his footing, he found his opportunity to stop the procedure.

Meeting John just before he could strike at Victor's vulnerable body, Zähd and John locked their swords together. Neither one would give to the other. Violently they struggled to gain control of the fight while they slid up and down the bed, their swords intertwined. Grabbing for his tantō, John and Zähd fought back and forth, moving around Victor and the body he was trying to possess. The two were matched as they fought it out. Still, the seconds were counting down.

The ground shook around them as time ran down. The ritual was almost complete, and with it, Zähd would have the weapon he needed to take Earth. He had enjoyed their bout, but with it about to end, he hated to admit that it had been too long since he had a proper fight. With seconds left, Zähd kicked John away and across the room.

"No!" John roared out as he clawed at the stone to stop himself.

The sounds of fighting awoke his conscious mind. It had been too long since he could take a full breath of air, but as Victor opened his eyes to John, he immediately began to use his new powers. With minimal effort, he rose from his bed and swatted the old man away. Pausing to his own strength, Victor had never felt so much power before. Like tentacles under his skin, the curse powers and his own tried to merge. The sensation enticed him, for the first time Victor had his hands on *true* power. Looking to Zähd, Victor remained confused about his situation as deep red symbols formed from his neck to his feet.

"The ritual is complete. Don't destroy those markings on your body, Victor. Do you hear me?" Zähd commanded as he handed him a katana.

Following through with his part of the agreement that gave him this new body, Victor pulled the sword from its sheath. "Can do."

Disoriented, John moved the rubble from around him. Seeing everyone run from the room, John looked around before making eye contact with Victor. His head ached and as the blood leaked from the top of his skull, his eye patch fell from his face, revealing the power he *really* held. Surprise struck Zähd more than anyone.

He hadn't see such an eye in nearly eight hundred years. Stepping forward, Zähd reveled in knowing their fight had only just begun.

"So! That's how you've been keeping up with me. Hah hah! I've been wondering, young Salvatore. You've been holding back on me!" Zähd boasted as he stepped forward.

"Let's end him quickly, Zähd. I don't wish to waste time with this fool," Victor snidely remarked.

"Hush, Victor. You have much to learn about royal curse-wielders," Zähd commanded as he stared John down, excited to fight him once more. "Come on, John! *Really* show me what you can do!" Zähd bellowed out maniacally.

Looking down to his family blade and the blood resting in the vial at the blade's base, John regretfully knew he would have to use his eye's power. There was only so much blood left and John wondered if it would be enough. Throughout most of his life, the blood wasn't meant to be touched. A rare commodity, his father once called it. But Zähd qualified as someone the sword could feed off of, if only John could touch him with it. Closing his left eye, he pulled on the power of the blood within his sword and channeled it into him. The blood of the fallen and the energy within it, started to slowly be siphoned by the sword into it's wielder's hands. Like a second wind, John felt his injuries heal and his body became rejuvenated. With his curse powers at their maximum, John felt the immense pressure weigh on him. Looking back to Zähd and Victor, his eyes glowed brightly in their red and blue hues.

With the slightest adjustment of his foot, John shot across the room and viciously kicked Victor in the head before slamming his fists down on Zähd's skull. Like liquid fire burning through his veins, the unnatural dosage of power the sword provided rivaled all. Nothing compared to it. Tears ran down John's cheeks as he fought for Dominic's future. Knocking the two powerhouses away, he immediately turned to Victor and leaped across the room to grab his feet. Victor had to be removed first. Tossing the abomination about, he slammed him against the ground, walls, and ceiling. For even if Zähd killed him, John would not allow Victor to live. Ripping the demon's arm off and throwing him at Zähd before he could attack, John was met with a constant stream of the future.

A change occurred, but it wasn't enough. Angered and enraged, John screamed out in anguish as he ran at the two men. Still learning his new powers, Victor quickly forced his curse to regrow his lost limb before meeting John's ghastly lightning strikes. Zähd was right, Victor hadn't seen the true potential of the royal-blood, but as he panicked to heal himself, an understanding was found. Finding that he had finally seen the true strength of John, Zähd ripped his shirt off before grabbing one of his claymores. The fires of war were stoked within the old men's chests. Blood had been spilt from both parties and the time for formalities had come to an end. It was time for things to get dirty.

Zähd bellowed out from deep within his gut, a sound so beastly no ears had ever heard. The turn of events pleased his ancestral blood, and a worthy fighter stood before him. Zähd ushered in the fight with a bolt of lightning, fired from his hand. Quickly John teleported away, avoiding the attack. From portal to portal, he leapt through and attacked at their blind spots. Outnumbered and nearly overpowered, John kept a close eye on the slowly evaporating blood while he continued to confuse and elude his foes. Enraged, John's screams echoed through the room as he came through one portal sending out a cone of fire and electricity from his hands.

Target hit. Catching Victor in his crosshairs, John turned to Zähd while the abomination writhed around on the floor in pain. Despite the successful hit, it came with a cost. Feeling Zähd's sword pierce his chest, John faced his attacker as he lifted him off his feet. He felt no pain as he reared his fist back and swatted Zähd away. Across the room and through the wall it sent him and as Zähd caught himself with his other sword, he admired the broken jaw he had received. He hadn't been hit quite like that in a long time. Pulling the sword from his chest, John payed no mind as his body easily healed the grievous wound. John scoffed as he looked to Victor in pain, and as he raised his sword to him, he was stopped by Zähd's electrical beam.

Though he felt no pain as the blast of energy surged through him and melted a hole through the upper part of his chest, John was still taken off guard by it's deadly force. Jumping away to grab his falling sword arm, John was left in disbelief as he looked down to the melted stump of a shoulder. With no choice but to push his curse further, John held his severed arm up to his shoulder as he willed his powers to repair the two. Retaliation was imminent. John ripped his tattered gear off and tossed them to the floor as Zähd extinguished the fire from Victor's body. Looking down to his sword again, John grew desperate as the blood slowly drained out.

With the signing of his mudras, John manipulated the stone around him, creating pillars from the wall and slammed them into Zähd and Victor. Launching them through a wall and out into the layer's center, John carried his attack through as he followed them. Though it nearly caught them off guard, the two men managed to withstand the attack even as the ground left their feet. Using their powers, they quickly sprouted wings from their backs

and fired their collective energy into the room in the form of lightning blasts. With the sight to avoid the attack, John avoided them
through a portal.

The fight had grown out of hand for Zähd but with no backup in
sight, he knew this would be his mess to clean up. Together, he and
Victor looked down at the destruction they had caused, searching
for John's body. But with no body in sight, Zähd's suspicion grew.
Opening up a portal behind them, John struck out at their heads.
Zähd barely heard the portal open in time as he grabbed Victor and
threw them both down. The old man's speed was incredible as he
appeared behind them. Confused, Victor looked back to John. He
hadn't even heard him arrive, but there he was staring him down.
The three flew around the open space, fighting just to hit one another. Frantically the two fought to avoid John while they struggled tp create a plan. Taking the brunt of John's fire and lightning,
Zähd created a distraction for Victor. With no time to spare, he flew
out and around to grab John by the back of his shirt. Grabbing him
from behind, Victor spun and hurled John back down into the hole
they had come from.

John's body whistled as he flew through the air. He was completely taken off guard and with no time to react, his body slammed
into the ground. Such an impact shook the whole layer as the entire area around John crumbled to the blast. Twisted and mangled
under the rubble, John felt his powers wane. He barely managed
to hold onto his sword as he made impact but as his body began to
heal his wounds, he looked down toward it's vial. There was just
enough for three more attacks. Using some of his power to peer
into the future once more, John was almost pleased that his attacks
had made some difference, but with more room to improve and
the strength to still stand and fight, he carried on. Moving the last

of the power stored in his left eye into his hands, John gritted his teeth as he prepared to end their fight.

His body and brand ached as he mustered himself together but with shaking hands, John raised them up toward Zähd and Victor. His roar grew louder and louder as he began lifting the stones around him while lightning arced and surged all across his arms. Igniting small fires in the palms of his hands, he pulled the stones in around him until the two mixed into lava and with one motion of the arms, launched the lightning and magma into the air. John cried out in pain as he expelled his strength and energy at his foes. The attack came too soon for the recovering duo and as it caught them off guard, Zähd stood in front of Victor. The mass of liquid fiery stone and lightning was too much for the legendary fighter to contain as both were swept away from the attack. As their burnt bodies flew from the destruction, John leapt across the distance, grabbed the two men by their ankles and flung them back down into the crater below. With one hand, he returned to Victor the same treatment he had received. Slamming into the stone, the layer rumbled to their destruction.

Victor looked back up to John in disbelief. The power he once had paled in comparison to the man before him, but as his brand worked to heal him, he believed he could survive the fight. Looking to Zähd as he dragged himself out from underneath the rubble around them, a massive shadow obscured their light. Sweating from head to toe, John harnessed as much of the broken rubble around him into a single stone. The three-hundred-foot-long slab of condensed rock towered above his head.

"This. Is. Where. You. Die!" John bellowed out as he launched the stone down.

As John released the rock from his hands, a clarity came over him. He realized he had pushed himself all the way. Assisting the stone with a gust of wind to carry it along, John strained himself as fire and lightning erupted from his hands. Every part of his body hurt but it was all worth it just to kill Zähd and Victor. Tears poured from his eyes as he focused the violent streams of energy together, his bones shaking as he exhausted himself. By the end of the attack, he felt weak as he struggled to stay in the air.

The layer had been permanently scarred by their fight and in large part to John but as the dust settled his eyes widened in disbelief. Encased in Zähd's vampiric wings, the two had survived. Zähd opened his wings as Victor looked on in wonder. Wounded and exhausted, Zähd could finally admit he had fought a true warrior. He was in serious trouble and his berserker blood chortled under his skin as he sought more violence, but as he locked eyes with Victor, something caught his eye. John's sword laying unattended.

Something felt off. Despite his anger for not killing them, something was wrong. John followed Zähd's eyes as the realization hit him. Looking down to his empty hands, John hadn't yet noticed that he no longer held his sword. Looking back to Zähd smiling up at him, the two knew what was about to happen. With a strained push of the air around him, John shot across the space, right for his sword. Zähd likewise, pushed Victor aside as he raced John on foot for the blade for it would be the one thing to decide the battle.

Kicking the sword away, John, too, was kicked away by Zähd in retaliation. Violently he slammed his head against the ground before catching his sword out of the corner of his eye. With a rock in hand, John smacked Zähd against the back of the head as he reached down for the prize. So close to victory, Zähd felt insult added to injury as John kneed him in the nose. The imminent threat had been removed. John heaved over and spat blood out as he lifted the blade from the ground. He was delirious from their fight but as he heard someone running up on him, John turned and locked swords with Zähd. Sloppily the two locked their blades together, neither one refusing to quit. Though with the strength to continue fighting, Zähd powered through and held John on the defensive.

John held onto his fading strength as he created portals when he could to avoid attacks. Dancing around the rubble, the two men knew their fight was reaching its end, but still, each refused to give in to the other. Reaching down to his tantō, John quickly remembered that he had torn off his gear—and with it, his swords and sheaths. The surprise was apparent to more than just John and as Victor saw an opportunity at hand, he flew in and kicked John off his feet.

The pain sank in for John and with his breath gone, he released his hold on his powers. Seizing the moment, Zähd and Victor both launched after John and his sword. With one eye still open, John watched as Zähd charged at him, sword at the ready, but with the absolute last modicum of his sword's power, John swung and opened one more portal behind him.

Though he might have fooled him many times before, Zähd was prepared for his portal-jumping. Launching himself further than Victor, he impaled John in the stomach. The sneak attack caught John off guard, and with it, he knew he had been bested. Losing his grip on his sword, John waved three quick mudras and sent his sword back to its sheath as Victor reached out for it. John fell through the portal behind him as his body grew cold and as the blood pooled in his mouth he flipped Zähd the finger. Locking eyes with his enemies from the portal's entrance, John fell, knowing he had at least temporarily held off Zähd's plans.

The area grew eerily silent as the portal slammed shut. The fighting had come to an end and Zähd remained victorious. Looking around, Victor found the chained-up sword.

"I wouldn't bother trying to pull that sword from its sheath. It won't move for you." Zähd spoke up as he listened to Victor pulling on the sword's handle.

Despite the warning, Victor was disappointed to find that Zähd was right. "Well, this is garbage." Slamming the sheathed sword against a piece of rubble, Victor demolished the stone while the sheath remained untouched. "What kind of nonsense is this?!"

"*Old* magic. Very old magic," Zähd commented as he examined the sheath. "But fret not, my newly minted apprentice. The opportunity will come when we can release this sword and gain control of its powers." Zähd smiled as he looked longingly at the sword as a whole. "Come, we need to report our success both in your transition and the *killing* of John Salvatore," Zähd remarked as he turned to walk away. "This is the beginning of something far greater than you realize, Victor, so take note and learn a thing or two." He finished as he stepped out into the open crater around him, sword in hand.

The fight had ended too soon for Zähd. Looking around, he almost hoped that John was still in the area and waiting to strike at him. As he turned to walk away, something reflective in the rubble caught his eye. Pulling out a picture of the young Dominic Salvatore, Zähd slowly realized *another* Salvatore yet lived. The news came as no surprise though. There *always* seemed to be another who slipped through the cracks, and as he chuckled under his breath, Zähd came to understand why John had fought so hard to stop him. As his chuckles turned into a cackling laughter, an idea came to mind.

CHAPTER 13
THE CALM . . .

The sounds of giggling and laughter from Dominic and Seras were muffled by the songs of Marvin Gaye. Tossing around in his bed, the young couple kissed and cuddled while poking and tickling one another. Seras played with his three sets of stretched ear lobe piercings. Between them and the three he had recently got in his lower lip, she had grown a liking for them herself, so much so, that she had gotten her nose and philtrum pierced.[4]

The new year had come for the seniors in high school, and their 2012 had started off right. Seras had adopted a love for body piercings and adapted to Dominic's training, finding it far more enjoyable than she initially expected. Feeling the raised scars on his arms, Seras traced them with her finger.

"Baby?" she softly whispered.

"Yeah, hun?"

Quickly growing flustered, she turned her head away as a huge smile grew across her face. "I . . . I love you."

Chuckling, Dominic gently pulled her face to his. "I love you too, baby."

---

4 Philtrum: the vertical indentation in the center of the upper lip.

Kissing softly, Dominic and Seras adjusted how they laid until he was atop her. With his fingers through her rosy curls, Dominic embraced his lover, thankful for the first moment they'd had together, alone in such a long time. Seras too shared his feelings as she embraced him. With her arms wrapped around him, she could feel many of the scars that had accumulated since she joined in his training; even the ones she had put on him. Bringing her hands up to his head, she ran her fingers through his hair while he continued to play with her curls. The two had grown so close in the almost two years they had been together.

Not hearing the music or knowing what was going on inside the room, Justin, sporting his growing beard, barged into Dominic's room. "Yo, man, did yo—" Justin quickly stopped and turned his head away after seeing Dominic's bare ass on display. "Woah! Woah! My bad, man!"

Aggravated, the couple sighed loudly. Rolling over and covering their bodies, Dominic and Seras sat back in his bed. "What, Justin? What's so important, man?" Dominic asked as he rubbed his forehead and adjusted himself.

"Well, I . . . Well, I had this video to show you, man. You know, the new terrorist everyone's been talking about on the news?" Justin carefully looked over his shoulder before turning around.

"Yeah, Zähd or whatever his name is?" Dominic replied, waiting for him to get to the point.

"Yeah, well, President Ramirez just gave a speech about the soldier cam footage that got released last December," Justin replied as he walked to the edge of the bed and sat down.

"Wasn't that the one where he got shot in the face and still survived?" Seras asked as she scooted closer to Dominic.

"Yeah, that one! Well, he didn't deny that it happened." Justin commented.

"Well, can you give me the gist of the video?" Dominic asked as he caught a glimpse of Richard and Cole standing at his doorway. Exhaling through his nose, he signaled for them both to come in. "I guess everyone can come on in."

"Is he showing you that speech President Ramirez made?" Richard asked as he and Cole entered the room.

"He was trying to." Seras replied to him.

"Did he barge in on you guys again?" Cole asked while putting his roach out in an ashtray.

"Yeah. . ." Dominic agreed while nodding.

"Well, I'm sorry. Put a sock on the door next time," Justin sarcastically replied.

"Next time I will," Dominic derided him. "But anyway, what did he say in his speech?"

"He was talking about how despite the video making it seem like he was some kind of unkillable monster, he does bleed, and if he can bleed, he can be stopped," Justin explained.

Dominic scoffed and shook his head in disbelief. "Yeah right. With what? A nuke?" Dominic sarcastically remarked. "We've all seen that video. The dude just looked pissed off when that soldier shot him!"

"Yeah, but if a nuke works . . ." Richard commented quietly.

"If they have to use a nuke to take that motherfucker out, then I'll eat my shorts!"

"That's a bet I'd like to make!" Justin shouted out as he threw his hand out.

"It's a bet you'll lose!" Dominic laughed as he shook his hand. "So, hey, did you get your things moved in, Cole?"

"Yeah, Justin and Richie both helped me carry my things in," he replied to Dominic.

"That's good. What do you guys say? Wanna go get a bite to eat?" Dominic replied.

"I thought you'd never ask. Where ya thinking about going?" Justin asked first.

"We haven't been to the diner in a minute. Wanna head there?" Dominic asked, looking to Seras.

Nodding, Seras agreed. "Yeah, sure, right after the guys leave the room."

"Alright, you heard the lady. We'll be out in a minute," Dominic informed his friends, motioning for them to leave the room.

Waiting in the kitchen, the three continued their conversation until Dominic and Seras finally emerged from his bedroom. After deciding who was driving and who was riding, the group set out. The January sun shined brightly through the light gray spotted clouds as the winter winds blew Dominic's hair aside. Between the beautiful sights on the highway and the roaring of his bike, the moment signaled a distant memory in his mind. For even though it had been nearly thirteen years since he had seen him, Dominic still thought of his uncle John to that day.

The young Salvatore drifted off in his thoughts while he pondered where John might have been in that moment. Despite his father's persistence to not bring it up, Dominic continued to struggle with his request, feeling as though John was still out there, somewhere. Grasping to remember every detail, he struggled to remember his uncle's smile, a detail that had all but faded from his memory. There were so many questions he had for him, too many his father wouldn't or couldn't answer. Distracted in his thoughts, Dominic was brought back to the present by Seras's soft grip around him.

"You were thinking about him again, weren't you?" She shouted over the roaring engine.

Nodding, Dominic couldn't muster the words to speak.

Wrapping herself around him, Seras did her best to comfort her boyfriend. "He would be proud of you, Dom. I know he would be!"

"Thank you, baby. That means a lot coming from you," Dominic replied before pushing his feelings aside and speeding ahead.

With Seras riding on the back of Dominic's bike and Richard and Cole riding in Justin's pine green '98 Durango, the group rode close together across town. Reaching the diner in record time, Dominic and his group arrived to Jackson and his friends eating there as well. Noticing each other, Dominic and Jackson both quickly grew angry.

"Baby . . ." Seras called to Dominic, concerned about what could happen.

"It's okay, baby. Just stay behind me," Dominic whispered as he looked to Justin and his friends.

"Hey, Salvatore, I thought I said next time I catch you out in public you were mine?" Jackson yelled out as he strutted toward Dominic, chest puffed out. "If you think having your little buddies here or that ugly ass bitch here—"

"And I thought I told you not to involve her. Or did you not hear me last I saw you?!" Dominic hollered out as Jackson got in Dominic's face.

"Yeah? The fuck you going to do about it, boy? Me and my boys here will beat your friends' asses. My girl will beat yo bitch's ass, and I'll whoop you up and down this block!" Jackson continued threatening him, spitting in Dominic's face as everyone stood around them.

Wiping the spit from his face, Dominic tossed aside his previous notions of being peaceful with Jackson. "That's a whole lot of talk from an itty-bitty mouth, son. Now, I already have a beef with you and *your* girl for keying my girlfriend's car up, but then you just had to go and keep piling the shit on, didn't ya?" Dominic's rage bubbled under his skin, and he felt that primordial desire to fight. "So how about you follow through on your threats, Jackson, or fuck off?" Dominic whispered as he leaned in close to him.

Hearing glass breaking, everyone quickly turned to Jackson's girlfriend, who was breaking Justin's windows.

"You goddamn bitch!" Justin yelled as he started to run after her.

Before anyone could react, Seras leaped past Justin and hit the woman straight in her face, setting off a chain reaction. Everyone piled in on one another. Punching and kicking the two sides fought each other off. Grabbing her by her hair, Seras pounded away on Jackson's girlfriend, who had now defaced both her and her friend's vehicles. Very quickly the fight grew out of hand as onlookers began to form around them all. Defending his partner, Dominic quickly overpowered Jackson before his friends tried to back him up.

"Beat her ass, Becky!" Jackson yelled out as he looked over to see her momentarily taking the advantage.

Their fight soon drew the attention of a crowd, who pointed and watched on from the sidelines. Pulling out their phones, many people began filming the fight while others began calling the police. It didn't take much for the trained fighters to easily overpower their attackers and before they knew it, Dominic and his friends had gained control of the fight. With blood shed, Jackson was infuriated as he shuffled back while helping his girlfriend up.

Hearing police sirens in the distance, Jackson knew he had to run away. "Let's get out of here, everybody! Cops are coming!"

"Uhh uhh, boo-boo! I'm not done with you, motherfucker!" Dominic shouted as he kept walking forward, popping his bloody knuckles.

"Dom! We need to go! C'mon, man. We gotta get out of here! We'll follow them!" Justin insisted as he grabbed Dominic by the arm.

Dominic's scowl grew as he agreed to the plan, growing angrier as he watched Jackson ride away while flipping him the bird. Turning around, Dominic quickly ordered his friends to go ahead of him as he hopped onto his bike and started it up. He tossed Seras her helmet. She didn't question him once as she hopped onto the bike with him. Hearing Justin's tires squeal as he peeled off, Dominic revved his engine before spinning around and following him.

CHAPTER 14

... BEFORE THE STORM

Following Jackson across town, the group finally managed to catch him stopped at a rundown underpass. Shanty houses, trash, and tents surrounded the abandoned underpass. Seeing Richard waiting for him at the entrance, Dominic learned of the events he had just missed. Hearing the skies rumbling above, Dominic parked his bike under cover to avoid getting it rained on. With Justin and Cole ahead of them, scouting out the rundown underpass, Dominic, Richard, and Seras proceeded in.

"If we're quiet and lucky, we'll have the element of surprise," Richard whispered as he covered Dominic and Seras.

"Oh, he's getting one surprising ass-beating when I find him!" Dominic whispered through his teeth as his rage rumbled in his chest.

Rounding a corner, Dominic came up to Justin and Cole, spying on Jackson and his gang. "Hey!" He whispered to get their attention. "What's been going on?"

"Dude's been trying to save face and justify getting wrecked earlier!" Cole commented as he stood up.

"Oh yeah. He's been talking mad shit," Justin added as he turned and stood up.

"Really now? Well, let's go see what he's been saying," Dominic remarked with a smirk as he began walking forward.

"Look, what I'm saying, man, is maybe it wasn't a good idea to pick a fight with him. I mean he broke your brother's arm years ago, and—"

"*Ohhh, Jackson!*" Dominic sang, interrupting one of Jackson's friends. "I heard you've been talking that good shit about me," he continued as he stepped into the light. "How about I hear some of those sweet words of yours?" Dominic taunted him with a smile as Seras and everyone else stepped out of the shadows.

"Fuck this shit, man! Dominic, we have no beef with you, man!" the same friend shouted as he and three others from Jackson's group ran away.

Pointing out each of the remaining five people across from him, Dominic teased Jackson by scolding him with clicks of his tongue. "That's no good, Jackson. You just lost your numbers advantage. I mean, it didn't help you earlier, but it's definitely not going to do you any justice now."

"Grrr, shut up, Salvatore! I'm beating your ass for hurting my brother!" Jackson shouted, trying to hold his ground.

"Your brother was a scumbag trying to rob and gang up on an innocent kid. You're not mad that I broke his arm. You're just mad 'cause I don't scare easily and I bruised your ego," Dominic stated as he laid out the facts. "But that's okay, son, 'cause you're gonna learn today!" Dominic confidently shouted as he charged Jackson.

Following behind him, everyone returned to fighting. Forced to stand his ground, Jackson did his best to avoid the barrage of quick strikes from Dominic. They were secluded and Dominic was able to stretch his fighting legs a lot more now. Relentlessly Dominic pushed Jackson, teasing the pain he would feel as he barely clipped his knuckles against Jackson's body. Realizing he was about to have his back against the wall, Jackson acted fast and knocked Dominic in the jaw.

Stunned, Dominic stepped back and smiled through the pain before jumping back into the fight. Creating some distance between him and Dominic, Jackson reached for a broken metal pipe from the ground. The move was met with one of his own as Dominic grabbed a nearby pipe to match him. It had been too long since Dominic had fought someone other than his friends or girlfriend but with Jackson standing before him armed, he grew more and more enthralled by their fight. With their pipes banging off of one another, Jackson did all he could to lead Dominic away from his friends.

Seras held the advantage as she fought against Becky. While she hadn't spent as much time training as Dominic or her friends, she kept up her guard against the flailing teen. Hearing encouragement from her friends, Seras wasted no time knocking Becky out and turning her strength onto another of Jackson's goons.

Seeing Seras coming in from his side, Justin moved out of the way as her fist flew into the cheek of his opponent. Taking over his fight, Justin stepped aside as Seras jumped onto the goon and tore into him with a barrage of punches. Seras intergraded into the group's movements with fluidity, her flexibility and ferocious kicks providing a much needed balance to the other boys. Catching eye contact with Richard, Justin and him nodded and devised a plan to take out their next opponent. Working in tandem, the two laid another of Jackson's friends out cold as they struck him from the front and back, knocking him to the ground.

Jackson's goons were outnumbered and they knew it. Forced to avoid one strike after another, the final fighter realized that these weren't ordinary teens; they were trained. Pummeled, beaten, and covered in sweat, he felt his strength waning. Catching a glimpse of Justin and Richard coming in from his side, the boy found himself left with only one option; running. Hightailing it away from the fight, he ran in the direction of Dominic and Jackson.

Reaching an opening in the underpass, Dominic and Jackson found themselves fighting on a decommissioned entryway to a nearby overpass. The old ramp was littered with spare supplies and tools from a nearby construction site. Hearing the rolling thunder above, the two violently fought one another. Gone were their egos; their fight had been about seeing who would bend to the other's will. The fight had grown so vicious that their pipes had become twisted and jagged.

"You. Will. Bend. To. Me. Salvatore!" Jackson announced as he slammed his pipe into Dominic's.

"Then fucking make me!" Dominic retorted before disarming Jackson and punching him to the ground.

Jackson's head bounced off a pallet of sandbags. The force caused the bags to rip open and pour sand onto the ground around him. Jackson shook his head while he attempted to stop the ringing in his skull. Looking up from his delirious state, he watched Dominic pace back and forth. He seemed distracted. As Jackson tried to sit up, his hands squished the sand beneath him and with it, came up with an idea. Grabbing some of the sand around him, Jackson quickly flung it up and at Dominic's face. Temporarily blinding Dominic, Jackson found the upper hand.

Tackling him to the ground, Jackson laid into Dominic, hitting him again and again. The boys wrestled back and forth for control, pummeling one another when they could. Feeling his anger grow with each passing minute, Dominic reached within himself and found the strength to overpower Jackson. The rain soaked them both as Dominic fought to pin Jackson down. Then, with Jackson's hands, slipping against his own, Dominic found the gap he needed as his fist met Jackson's face.

With one hand around his throat and the other pummeling away at his face, Dominic lost himself in the fight. The rage he once held in check slipped into the driver's seat. Jackson, fearing for his life, frantically searched for any way to end the punishment he was enduring. Feeling the rough stone pattern of a brick in his hand, Jackson quickly raised it into the air. A hit, but not a good one. Jackson panicked as he continued swatting at Dominic with the brick. Feeling Dominic's grip tighten around his throat, Jackson swung again, missing his target.

The brick had done nothing to bring Dominic back from his haze. His consciousness had slipped away as the rage took over. The sinister sensation had returned once again, and his olive eyes grew cold as he stared into Jackson's. In the moment, he had regretted picking a fight with Dominic. For Dominic, the world and everything around him had grown quiet except for the rain and Jackson gasping for air. Scared for his life, he swung once again for Dominic's face, this time finding his mark.

Feeling the brick smashed against his face, Dominic found himself brought back to reality just before his head smacked the concrete. As Dominic fell away, Jackson too crawled up the ramp and toward safety. The fight had become more than Jackson wanted. Rolling over on his back, Jackson coughed for air while Dominic's words about his brother rang through his head.

Dazed, Dominic's ears rang out as he lifted himself off the

concrete. Tasting the iron in his blood, he spat out the mouthful while bracing himself against the remains of the destroyed pallet. With his head and mouth bleeding, he stumbled after Jackson, determined to end their fight. Enough was enough for Dominic. Looking back, Jackson panicked more, throwing pipes, buckets, and anything he could grab to keep Dominic at bay. Desperately Jackson fought off the terrifying teen. Reaching the top of the ramp, Jackson was met with another obstacle; currently under construction, the ramp was not connected to the rest of the highway.

With the drop being too great to fall and having nowhere else to run, Jackson stood at the ramp's edge. "Why won't you quit, Salvatore?! What is your deal?" Jackson yelled out while throwing a pipe wrench at him.

"You and me, Jackson. You've wanted this fight for years now! Don't tell me you've had enough of it already?!" Dominic shouted as he swatted away the wrench. "You want this to end? Admit you're wrong for coming after me for breaking your asshole brother's arm!" Dominic shouted as he swung at Jackson.

"Fuck you. He can't use that arm the same anymore!" Jackson shouted as he fought back on the ledge with Dominic.

"What kind of brother robs from a child?!" Dominic shouted as he broke Jackson's nose.

Nearly falling to the ground, Jackson held his nose as the rain and blood fell from his face. "Okay. . . Yeah, it was ugly of him, but you didn't need to break his arm!" Jackson admitted while looking back up at Dominic.

"You see this scar on my arm? You see this? This is from him trying to kill me after I beat his ass! He's lucky I didn't do worse!" Dominic shouted as he raised his sleeve to reveal the scar on his arm. "Your brother was a liar and a piece of shit!" Dominic continued to shout before spitting blood from his mouth.

Jackson for the first time listened to what Dominic was saying. Panting heavily, he looked at the scar, then back at him. He had never known that his brother wounded him first. Catching a glance of Dominic's friends running up the ramp, he realized that he was in the wrong the whole time.

"So what is it going to be, Jackson? We going to continue this bullshit fight or are you going to come to your senses? 'Cause I don't want to spend my eighteenth birthday in jail," Dominic asked as he relaxed his stance, waiting for a response.

"I . . . I guess you were right all along, Dominic. I hate to admit that, but my brother never told me how he swung at you with a knife," Jackson remorsefully admitted.

"What about his actions toward Cole? Because that little kid he tried to rob was him. Right there," Dominic furiously asked while pointing to Cole. "Look him in the eyes and tell him that your brother was justified!"

Jackson's face dropped when he realized that Cole was the boy Dominic was talking about the whole time. For the first time, he saw the other side of the situation. Looking back and forth between the two of them, he finally accepted that he was wrong. Rising slowly to his feet, Jackson felt Dominic's hand grab his.

Shocked by the kind gesture, Jackson was left almost speechless. "I . . . I'm sorry," he said softly.

"Don't apologize to me. Apologize to them," Dominic stated, pointing to his friends.

Embarrassed and ashamed, Jackson turned to the group. "I'm sorry. I'm sorry for all I have done to you. I'm sorry for my actions. I hurt you all out of misplaced rage and hate. My brother lied to me, and I didn't see the truth. I didn't want to see the truth. I thought Dominic was lying to me about that kid, but I didn't realize he was telling me the truth all along." Jackson paused before looking to Seras. "And I'm sorry to you as well. Dominic was right. I shouldn't have dragged you into our fight years ago, nor should I have influenced my girlfriend to key your car. That was ugly of me. For that and for every time I called you outside of your name, I'm sorry." Jackson's head dropped as he felt the guilt all over him.

"Speaking of which, what of your girlfriend and friends? Will you still associate with them and join them in their actions?" Dominic asked, curious of his answer.

"She's not my girlfriend anymore, nor are those my friends. I need to rethink who I choose to be around. I need to find out who I really am, not this person I've become. I didn't always have this hate in my heart." Jackson shook his head, thinking about his actions up to that point. "Don't worry about that window, either, man. I'll pay to replace it, and I'll pay you back for keying your car. It's the least I can do to begin making up for all I've done," Jackson added while looking to Justin and Seras.

"Well, that's mighty nice of you, man! Won't lie, I wasn't expecting that from you," Justin replied as he stepped forward to shake hands with Jackson.

"I have to agree, Jackson. I wasn't expecting that," Seras added as she and Richard stepped forward to shake hands.

While shaking hands, Jackson couldn't help but see Cole looking him down. Cole debated how he wanted to feel. He wasn't sure if he could forgive him. Looking to Dominic, who was nodding, Cole apprehensively reached out with his hand.

"Cole, right? I'm sorry for what my brother did to you forever ago. That was wrong of him, and it was wrong of me to believe his lie without question." Cole could feel Jackson's guilt in his words and his grip.

Cole remained apprehensive until he caught Dominic's eye from behind Jackson. "Well, I guess I can't be too mad at you. You weren't the one who cornered me in a snowy alleyway."

"He wasn't, but what he has done he has paid for in blood. I forgive you, Jackson. Now, I have to know, do you forgive yourself?" Dominic said as he walked up from behind Jackson, setting his hand on his shoulder.

"Not yet, but I think I can bring myself to that point," he replied, cracking a smile from his frown.

"Well, that's good. Find that place within and forgive yourself. Then pay that kindness and goodwill forward," Dominic replied as he extended his hand. "You had the opportunity to change your life for the better today, and you made the right choice. Keep that trend going, okay?" Dominic added as Seras walked around to his side.

"I will, and I'm sorry for everything, man. I feel like a real asshole about all of this," Jackson apologized again as he shook Dominic's hand.

"Hey, we all make mistakes man. At least you got the opportunity to make the right decision," Dominic informed him while the rest of his friends stood behind him. "You going to make it home safe?" he added as he turned to see everyone.

"Yeah, I'll be fine, man," Jackson said softly as he held his head up and pursed his lips. "Bye, everyone. I'll have that money for you guys when I see you at school Monday, okay?"

"That's fine. Be safe getting home," Dominic replied as everyone started walking away.

Jackson stood in the rain until everyone had left. Beaten and bruised, he was exhausted and conflicted. Returning to where his *friends* had parked, he found that his leather jacket had been tossed aside. Knocking the dirt and mud off the leather sides, Jackson flung the jacket over his shoulder and began walking.

The night carried on for him as Jackson walked the streets of D.C. The rain had let up and became scattered throughout the city and as the hours grew long, he had time to reflect. All the lies his brother had told him about Dominic unravelled as he really took the time to think about them. There was so much he would need to do to make amends but surprisingly, he had found a way to begin forgiving himself.

Passing through the city, Jackson had found a new outlook on life. The town he had grown up in for so long seem so different to him now. Passing a hooded homeless man, Jackson put his last dollar in the man's can as he passed by. He had decided that he would give more back to those who needed it.

The night had come, and the streets had grown dark except for the streetlights on his path. Jackson neared his home and was ready to confront his brother for his wrongdoings. As Jackson rounded a corner, a strange sensation crept up his spine. Catching a glance at a suspiciously familiar hooded homeless man, he tried his best to ignore his suspicions as he walked past him again. Listening carefully as he walked past the man shaking his can, Jackson's ears took notice to the sound of the man's can falling and a second set of footsteps starting to follow behind him.

Uncertain of the person behind him, Jackson exhaled as he questioned if he were about to be caught in the middle of a mugging. Lowering his head he picked up the pace, but as he did, the footsteps matched his own. Nearly at a full sprint, Jackson pedaled away as he tried to shake his tale. He wanted to avoid any conflicts, but as the unwelcome guest continued to follow him, Jackson knew something had to be done. Making one unnecessary street turn after another, the tired teen grew angry. With his pursuer running behind him, Jackson quickly stopped, turned, and raised his fists.

"Who the hell are you and what the fuck do you want?!" Jackson yelled as the hooded figure stopped in his tracks.

"Information," the low, gravelly voice replied.

"Information? What kind of information?!" Jackson replied, confused and angered.

"Dominic Salvatore. I'm looking for him," the man replied, pulling out a still image from one of the videos taken of his fight with Dominic.

"Fuck off, asshole. I'm not telling you shit about him," Jackson shouted as he raised his middle finger and began walking away.

"I don't think you understand," the man replied as he grabbed Jackson's shoulder.

Quickly turning around and shoving the man's hand away, Jackson raised his fists once more. "Don't touch me, motherfucker. Do that again and I'll knock your ass out!"

"Tell me where I can find him, and I'll leave," the man replied as he stepped back.

"I already told you I'm not telling you shit. Go kick rocks asshole!" Jackson held his ground as he spat at the man's feet before walking away.

"That's a shame, but—" the man started as Jackson heard a knife being unsheathed.

"The fuck do you think you're do—" Jackson quickly turned to the man as he thrust the knife into his gut.

"You've already given me all I need to know!" the man replied as Jackson squirmed in pain.

Feeling his feet grow cold and the blood pour from his stomach,

Jackson frantically grabbed at the man's clothes. Pulling the hood off, Jackson was able to see the face of his killer as he fell to his knees. Confused to the evil look on the asian man's face, Jackson couldn't understand why he wanted Dominic. Standing over him, Victor looked down emotionlessly at him. Jackson squirmed as he began to crawl away, pushing against the gaping hole in his stomach.Wiping the blood from his blade, Victor reached down into Jackson's pocket and retrieved his wallet.

"Well, *Anthony Jackson*, if you had just told me where I could find Dominic, you could've walked away today." Victor declined to his response as he tossed the wallet to the ground. "But you didn't. But don't worry, Anthony. You've given me more information than I had anticipated," Victor finished as he held up Jackson's school ID.

With his last breath, Jackson struggled to get his words out. "It's Ja . . . Jackson, asshole."

"Even in your dying moment, you remain defiant. Impressive, to say the least," Victor commented as he began walking away and reaching into his pocket. "Hey, I found the other guy in the video. He wouldn't talk, but I found something interesting we can look into," Victor explained over the phone. "Ye . . ." Victor paused begrudgingly. "Yes . . . Master, I'll return at once." Victor gritted his teeth, angered, but with little choice, he continued walking away into the night.

To be continued . . .

ABOUT THE AUTHOR

At the early age of thirteen, one boy had a magnificent spark of creativity, forming an idea and story that would send him on a journey that he is still following to this day. That journey? To tell the most amazing and incredible action-packed story he had ever imagined. It would take him nearly fourteen years to properly cobble together his thoughts and to put the right words on the page, but through hell, high waters, and insurmountable desire to finish it through to the end, *Garrett M. Pearson* has now taken the first real steps in achieving the goals he had set out for himself oh-so long ago. From traveling across the country for a friend in the pursuit of love, to his various janitorial jobs to help pay his way through life, *Garrett* never gave up on his dream of becoming a self-published author. Now-a-days, he works as a professional body piercer of three years and counting, a stock investor and an entrepreneur, working diligently to fund his self-publishing goals and dreams. With a solid and expansive story to tell, *Garrett* begins his journey as an author with this debut novel, The Blood Heir Chronicles: Origins, the introductory book for the series that will follow it.